IF I HAVE TO BE A SOLDIER

Praise for the Book

'Nikhil Alva's *If I Have To Be A Soldier* is a vital reminder of the challenges facing Indians living on the margins of the nation's consciousness. A searing exploration of fragmented identities, this enthralling novel brings to life a fraught period of India's history: the Mizo insurgency of the late 1960s. Deeply ambivalent about his Mizo identity, Sammy—the novel's troubled protagonist—is a man struggling to escape himself and the cataclysms that have (mis)shaped him. As he endeavours to become a gallant officer of the Indian Army, he finds himself being mired in a past he had sworn to forget. And that, perhaps, is his biggest undoing. Keenly observed and poignantly limned, *If I Have To Be A Soldier* marks an impressive debut.'

– **Shashi Tharoor**, noted writer and Member of Parliament

IF I HAVE TO BE A SOLDIER

NIKHIL J. ALVA

HarperCollins *Publishers* India

First published in India by HarperCollins *Publishers* 2024
4th Floor, Tower A, Building No. 10, DLF Cyber City,
DLF Phase II, Gurugram, Haryana – 122002
www.harpercollins.co.in

2 4 6 8 10 9 7 5 3 1

P-ISBN: 978-93-5699-870-4
E-ISBN: 978-93-5699-701-1

Typeset in 11.5/15.7 Minion Pro at
Manipal Technologies Limited, Manipal

Printed and bound at
Gopsons Papers Pvt. Ltd., Noida

MIX
Paper from
responsible sources
FSC® C191020

This book is produced from independently certified FSC® paper to ensure responsible forest management.

For the great Mizo people,
may your suffering, your sacrifices, and your stories,
never be forgotten.

'Write down the revelation and make it plain on tablets, so that a herald may run with it. For the revelation awaits an appointed time; it speaks of the end and will not prove false. Though it linger, wait for it; it will certainly come and will not delay.'

Habakkuk 2:2

CONTENTS

REVELATION

At dawn, a shrill, anguished, full-throated wail pierced through the dense fog that hung over the village, rousing the villagers from their slumber. When minutes went by and it hadn't stopped, the villagers stepped out of their bamboo huts begrudgingly, into the cold, to see what the commotion was all about. Soon, the entire village had gathered – huddled in small groups, peering into the fog, searching for the source of the disturbance, unsure of what to do next.

Then someone shouted, 'It's the Witch! It's the Witch, wailing!'

The villagers let out a collective sigh of exasperation. They'd grown tired of the Witch's, or as she was locally known, the *Dawi Thiam Pitar's*, frequent shenanigans, and many of them cynically dismissed her early morning wailing as another one of her attention-seeking ploys. The cynics retreated into the warmth and comfort of their huts to try and eke out a few more minutes of sleep. The more adventurous clambered down the slippery, slush-covered path that led to the giant bamboo grove at the edge of the village.

It was where the Witch lived, alone, deep inside the grove, in a dilapidated shack she'd built for herself with corrugated sheets of rusted metal and discarded wooden crates she'd scavenged from the village.

When the villagers got to the periphery of the grove, the first rays of the early morning sun had broken through the giant bamboo stalks. The morning fog that had enveloped the village had begun to lift. It was only then that the villagers saw that the bamboo had flowered overnight. From each node, on every plant grew long, spiky, pale-yellow flowers, thin-stemmed and without petals. Backlit by the rays of the early morning sun, the flowering of the bamboo presented a stunning spectacle that enthralled the villagers.

But the elders were filled with a sense of foreboding. They remembered the last bamboo flowering forty-eight years ago, and the devastation it had wrought on the Mizo Hills. The bamboo flowers had transformed into fruit. The fruit, that had avocado-like seeds, had drawn swarms of rats from the jungles. The rats had chomped and gorged on the fruit and the seeds, day and night, making them stronger and much more fertile, multiplying their numbers exponentially. When the fruit and the seeds had been devoured, the rats had turned their attention to the crops in the fields and the food stocks that villagers had stored in their huts. Soon, entire villages were overrun by the rodents, forcing the villagers to flee, abandoning their houses and their crops. In the ensuing famine, hundreds of Mizo men, women and children had starved to death.

The Witch, then a girl of twelve, the oldest of eight siblings, had used her last ounce of energy to flee her village in the dead of the night, abandoning her family, leaving them to their wretched fate. When the girl had sought to return to her tribe, after the famine had passed, she was branded a 'witch' by the tribesmen and banished. After years of persecution and being chased away from village after village across the Mizo Hills, the Witch had finally sought refuge in the bamboo grove. It was where she'd lived, in seclusion, for as long as the villagers could remember.

But it wasn't to mourn her long-dead family that the Witch now wailed. She'd woken up that morning to an apocalyptical vision that had dissolved the barriers of space and time. The sudden flowering of the bamboo she took as validation, as a sign, that the terrible suffering and devastation she'd seen in her vision would soon come to pass. The Witch wailed for the villagers, raising her frail hands to the heavens, asking her God to spare them from the hellfire that she'd seen rain down on the Mizo Hills.

I AM A SOLDIER

CHAPTER 1

Eight years is a long time, long enough to turn a boy into a man. Growing up in Asakhua, Sammy had chafed under the yoke of an oppressive Christian moral fabric, where violence was frowned upon and a brave man always 'turned the other cheek'. The army had freed him of that irksome framework. At first, he was surprised by his capacity for violence. But, in time, he forgot the boy he once was and embraced the man he'd become: Captain Samuel Rego, an Indian Army officer, his uniform absolving him of some of the moral restrictions that society imposed on ordinary men. His excuses: survival, the defence of the motherland, and the destruction of the enemy – in no particular order.

His enemies kept changing though.

1962: The Chinese, who'd gobbled up over 38,000 square kilometres of Indian territory in Aksai Chin and had crushed the Indian Army in the short war that followed in the mountains to the north of where he was now stationed.

1965: The Pakistanis, whom the Indian Army had fought for six long months on the western frontier, forcing the UN to intervene and order a ceasefire.

1966: Guerrillas of the Mizo National Front (MNF), who had overrun vast swathes of the Mizo Hills in India's northeast.

Indira Gandhi, who had taken over as India's prime minister in January 1966, was looking for an opportunity to show the rebels in her Congress party, and anyone else who dared challenge her, that she was no pushover. She got that opportunity in March 1966, when the MNF, under the leadership of Indian Army veteran Pu Laldenga, declared the highlands inhabited by the Mizos an independent nation and launched an armed insurrection against the Indian state. The prime minister called in Lieutenant General Sam Manekshaw, who commanded the Indian Army's Eastern Corps, and gave him a carte blanche to crush the uprising. The general immediately moved the troops of 61 Mountain Brigade, under Brigadier R.Z. Kabraji, to the Mizo Hills.

That's how it was that a year later, in 1967, Captain Samuel Rego, of 7 Bihar, found himself returning to the land of his birth – a land he despised from the very depths of his soul.

A month after being assigned to Brigadier Kabraji's personal staff at the headquarters in Aizawl, Captain Samuel was sent by the brigadier's officer on special duty (OSD) and his commanding officer, Major Niladri

Mukherjee, to Lunglei to interrogate a Mizo National Army (MNA) guerrilla in custody of the local paramilitary force, the Frontier Rangers. The MNA was the armed wing of the MNF, tasked with the use of violence to achieve its goal of Mizo independence. It comprised eight infantry battalions, and its recruits, many of them ex-Indian Army soldiers, had been supplied with weapons and ammunition by Pakistan. Captain Samuel had been handpicked by the major for the assignment because he spoke the local language, which was what had got him the prized posting on the brigadier's staff in the first place.

Getting to Lunglei from Aizawl wasn't easy. An army officer couldn't just clamber into a Jeep and drive there. If he were stupid enough to try, he'd be a sitting duck for the guerrillas, who regularly ambushed vehicles on that vital road that ran all the way down to the border with Burma. The captain had to wait an entire day to join a scheduled resupply convoy headed out to Lunglei.

It was early June and the monsoons had just begun. The incessant, unrelenting rain had turned the narrow, untarred mountain roads that criss-crossed the Mizo Hills into strips of slush and loose rubble. A platoon from 8 Sikh had been assigned to protect the convoy of forty army trucks and Jeeps that left Aizawl at the crack of dawn, headed due south for Lunglei, over 200 kilometres away. The platoon had been divided up and placed at the head, middle and rear of the convoy by the convoy commander. The pilot and escort jeeps had light machine guns mounted on them, and the troops were all on high alert. The captain rode shotgun in one of the Jeeps in the middle of the convoy. Every few kilometres along the route, the convoy passed army foot patrols, checking for buried Improvised Explosive Devices (IEDs) that could blow a truck right off the road. The commander took no chances, and the convoy stopped like clockwork every hour to regroup and make sure every vehicle was accounted for, before setting off on the next segment of the journey.

About a hundred kilometres out of Aizawl, on the outskirts of Serchhip, the convoy ground to a sudden halt. A patrol had spotted heavily armed guerrillas on a ridge overlooking the road. The convoy commander wanted the ridge cleared and the road checked for buried IEDs before they proceeded further. It took the platoon from 8 Sikh over three hours to get the job done, so it was well past noon when the convoy began inching forward again.

With over a hundred kilometres still to go, Captain Samuel decided he'd have to take his chances and break from the convoy if he was going to have any hope of keeping his 3 p.m. appointment with the Frontier Rangers commandant, V.C. Aiyar. He asked the driver of his Willys CJ3B Jeep, painted in camouflage green and brown, to break formation. They accelerated past the line of slow-moving trucks and drew parallel with the convoy commander's Jeep. The captain pushed his torso as far out of the Jeep as he could and yelled over the cacophony of engines as the convoy crawled up the steep mountain road: 'Thank you, sir, I'll take off on my own now.' The convoy commander shrugged and waved him on as the driver accelerated to pull away from the group.

As the Jeep struggled along the steep, twisting mountain track, Captain Samuel thought about the last time he'd travelled along that road. It was the night of his seventeenth birthday, eight years ago. Forced to flee his home like a thief, accused of a crime he hadn't committed, his father had driven him along this very road, in his Hindustan Landmaster, to Aizawl, from where he'd boarded a bus to Calcutta. A few months after he'd fled, his parents had left the Mizo Hills and moved back to Mangalore, in the south of India. They'd written to him often, begging him to visit them. But the captain hadn't replied to any of their letters. In fact, he'd never allowed himself to think of them or to wallow in the nostalgia of his childhood. But that afternoon, as he raced towards Lunglei, to the hills and valleys he'd grown up in, he let himself remember – his parents, his home and the girl he'd never stopped loving.

CHAPTER 2

Just after 4 p.m., Captain Samuel's Jeep arrived at a fork, where a mud track led away from the road to Lunglei and wound its way up the hillside, disappearing into a dense patch of forest. The driver swung the Jeep on to the track, switching to a low 4x4 gear ratio to account for the loose rubble and the steep incline. Half an hour later, the Jeep pulled up at the gates of the Frontier Rangers' garrison.

Built in a trough at the foot of thickly forested, rolling hills, the garrison housed a few hundred troops in thirty large tin sheds, each about fifteen feet wide and forty feet long with sloping roofs. The sheds were arranged around two rectangular brick-and-mortar buildings that housed the administrative offices, stores and the officers' quarters. A ten feet high barbed wire fence ran around the periphery of the garrison, with watchtowers at four corners, each about twenty feet high, manned by heavily armed sentries.

The garrison was buzzing when Captain Samuel's jeep cleared the gates. The MNA had attacked a Frontier

Rangers' post in Demagiri and reinforcements were being rushed to the area. Soldiers were racing to load ammunition and weapons on to trucks that were already revved up and ready to go. The driver manoeuvred the Jeep cautiously through the chaos and pulled up outside the administrative building. Twelve hours spent breathing in exhaust fumes, bouncing and rolling over terrible roads, had left the captain with a splitting headache. He was glad to finally get out of the Jeep. He straightened his uniform, stretched his legs and lit himself a cigarette. He was already an hour and a half late for his meeting, so he figured a few minutes more wouldn't make a difference. When he was done smoking, he went looking for the commandant.

The administrative building wore a deserted look. A long, narrow corridor greeted him, with glass-paned windows spaced out with military precision every ten feet on one side and wooden doors leading to offices on the other, each with a wooden nameplate. The captain walked down the corridor, reading the nameplates, looking for the commandant's office.

About halfway down the corridor, a door with a nameplate read, 'Commandant V.C. Aiyar'. The door was shut. The captain knocked on it politely and waited. There was no response. He knocked again, this time a little louder.

'Fuck off!' a gruff voice barked from inside. The captain was thrown off guard. Should he wait or 'fuck off' as the voice had commanded? He decided he'd wait.

A few minutes later, the door was thrown open. In the doorway stood a well-built, dark-skinned man in uniform, of medium height and with cold, cruel eyes, a lit cigarette hanging from his thin lips. A name tag above the flap of his shirt pocket confirmed he was the commandant. The captain snapped to attention and saluted him smartly.

'Who the fuck are you?' the commandant snarled.

'Captain Samuel, sir,' the captain replied. 'I had an appointment with you?'

'Oh. You're the captain they sent me from Aizawl? Get in here,' the commandant said, waving him into the room.

The room was narrow and long, a conference room that had been converted into an office. Two heavily barred windows looked out on to a courtyard, one at each end. The commandant's recently polished solid oak table was placed near one of the windows. Behind the table was a wooden swivel chair for the commandant, with two mismatched metal chairs for visitors, facing him. The room had been white-washed recently and smelt of fresh, damp chalk and lime. On the wall behind the commandant's desk hung a huge army contour map of the Lunglei area. The other walls were bare, except for a few photographs of the commandant, at different points in his career, that hung randomly with no consideration for symmetry. Three forty-watt bulbs that hung from wires on the ceiling, spaced out at eight-foot intervals, lit up the room, dimly. A fireplace was built into one of the walls. Although stacked with small wooden logs, it hadn't been lit on that warm June evening.

The commandant ambled across to his desk and lowered himself into the swivel chair. He nodded towards one of the metal chairs, which the captain took as permission to sit. Even as the captain planted his arse on the cold, uncomfortable metal, the commandant swung his legs up on the table, crossing his right leg over his left, the soles of his shoes not more than a foot away from where the captain had placed his hands. The strong smell of Cherry Blossom shoe polish, one of his favourite smells as a child, hovered in the air. The captain took his hands off the table and settled back in his seat. The commandant looked pensively out of the window, puffing on his cigarette. They sat in silence until the commandant was done smoking. He stubbed out his cigarette, swung his legs off the table, and said: 'You were supposed to be here by three this afternoon?'

'I'm sorry, sir. We had some trouble on the way. The convoy was stuck for hours outside Serchhip. There were guerrillas spotted in the area,' the captain offered by way of explanation.

'You army boys scare easily,' the commandant sneered.

'It wasn't in my hands, Commandant. The convoy commander didn't want to risk it.'

'How long since you were commissioned into the army, Captain?'

'Just over four years, sir.'

'And a captain already? Don't you just love the army!' the commandant chortled. 'You know, Captain, if the army sends you to the Frontier Rangers on deputation, you'll strut in here as a deputy commandant. You know how many years it took me to work my way through the ranks to become a deputy commandant? Twenty years. Another ten before I was considered worthy of becoming a commandant. And this is it. I won't go any higher. The top posts in this force are all reserved for bright young army men like you, you see,' the commandant finished bitterly.

Caught off guard by this unprovoked rant, the captain smiled sardonically and said: 'The prisoner, sir. Major Mukherjee wanted me to assess if the information he had could help us nab Laldenga.'

The commandant paused for a moment, undecided if he should allow the captain to steer the conversation away from the path he'd set down. Then, letting it go, he said: 'We picked him up three nights ago in a raid on an MNF safe house, about thirty klicks south of here.'

'What do we know about him, sir?'

'Not much at the moment. But I think he's inconsequential. Just another misguided boy who got swept away by Laldenga's rhetoric. Which is why I'm surprised that the army sent you all the way out here to check him out,' the commandant replied. 'Anyway, I don't think he speaks English or Hindi.'

'I speak the local language, sir, which is why the Major sent me,' the captain said quickly.

The commandant eyed him curiously. 'You're the first officer I've met who speaks their language, Captain.' Then he leant forward and spat out viciously: 'You know why these chinkie bastards aren't made officers?' He paused for dramatic effect. 'They're fucking traitors, that's why. Thankfully, you're not a chinkie, are you?'

Startled by the commandant's outburst, all the captain could offer as a response was a feeble, 'No, sir.'

His authority over the captain established, the commandant's tone became business-like. 'Better start on him right away. You've got eight hours. My men are angry, Captain. Five of their brothers lost their lives in the raid. Three more were seriously wounded. Left to themselves, my men would have skinned this fucker alive. He's lucky. Your visit has bought him some time.'

'Yes, sir,' Captain Samuel responded uncertainly.

'My boys have softened him up. You won't have any problems with him. Ask him anything you like.' The commandant smirked conspiratorially.

The commandant's tone made Captain Samuel feel uneasy. He shifted uncomfortably in his chair.

Sensing his discomfort, the commandant softened. 'I hope you have the stomach for this, son. War is brutal business. Men die. We do what we have to do to get the job done – so that our men don't die. You get me?'

The captain nodded. The commandant pressed a switch that dangled on a wire beside his desk. A minute or two later, an orderly entered the room silently, standing at attention near the door.

The commandant turned his attention to the orderly. 'Escort the captain to the prison barracks. He is to be allowed to interrogate the prisoner.'

The orderly saluted smartly. 'Ji, sir.'

The commandant nodded towards the door and picked up the rotary dial phone on his desk. Captain Samuel stood up and saluted the commandant, who ignored him. The captain turned and followed the orderly out of the office.

One of the large tin sheds in a far corner of the garrison served as the prison. It was separated from the rest by a barbed-wire fence. A ten-foot-high metal gate, manned by two sentries, was the only way in. The orderly accompanied him to the gate and communicated the commandant's instructions to the sentries. One of them escorted the captain to the interrogation cell, which was ten feet wide and about twenty feet long. A rectangular metal table sat in the centre, two metal chairs on either side. The cell had two iron-grilled doors, that sat on a solid iron frame. The floor was roughly cemented. There were no windows, and the room smelt damp and musty. Hanging over the table from a wire in the ceiling was a thirty-watt bulb that threw large shadows on the walls. In one corner was a water pot made from clay, on a stand, with two metal tumblers.

Captain Samuel had just lit a second cigarette when the prisoner was dragged into the cell by two havildars, his hands and feet shackled in thick iron chains, a black woollen hood pulled tight over his head. He looked like a corpse – his hands and legs limp with no sign of life. The havildars hoisted him into the chair opposite the captain. The prisoner had been stripped down to his waist. His body bore the scars of the gruesome torture he'd been subjected to. When the havildars released their hold on him, the prisoner slumped forward, his head slamming down on the table, the hood still intact. A soft moan escaped his lips, the only sign that he was still alive.

Their job done, the havildars left, locking the iron doors behind them. The captain puffed nervously on his cigarette, unsure of how to proceed. The prisoner stirred, raising his head slowly and pushing himself back into the metal chair. As if exhausted by the effort, his head slumped down to his chest. The captain got up, poured water from the clay pot into the two tumblers and placed them on the table. Then he moved behind the prisoner and gingerly tugged at the hood, removing it and flinging it away. He walked back to his chair and took a long drag of his cigarette, forcing himself to look at the prisoner.

The man's face had been smashed in. His eyes were swollen shut; his nose was broken. His lips were cut and hanging wide enough for the captain to see he was missing a couple of teeth in his upper jaw. Streaks of blood from the wounds on his skull and forehead had splattered his face in grotesque hues of crimson, and ran through his long, matted, shoulder-length hair. The nauseating stench of blood, sweat, piss and shit that arose from the prisoner filled the room.

The captain felt the bile rise at the back of his throat. He staggered into a corner of the room and retched violently. When he was done, he returned to the table and glugged down the water from one of the metal tumblers. He threw himself back into the chair, waiting for the spasms to subside, avoiding any eye contact with the prisoner.

Then he thought he heard the prisoner say his name. Startled, and unsure if he'd heard right, the captain leant forward slowly.

Then he heard it again: 'Fucking Sammy!'

The prisoner's voice reverberated in Captain Samuel's head, like a gunshot. Stunned, the captain jerked backwards and then took a closer look at the prisoner. On his shattered lips, he saw the hint of a smirk. It brought new life and meaning to the prisoner's broken face.

'Sena!' the captain whispered hoarsely.

Once again, fate had dealt the captain a cruel, mocking hand, viciously ripping open the ugly scabs that had covered the painful wounds from his past, leaving him exposed and vulnerable, his army man's uniform offering him no protection.

CHAPTER 3

It was almost 3 a.m. by the time the reluctant doctor, summoned by the captain against his will, was done fixing up Sena. He'd done as good a job as he possibly could, cleaning and treating the open wounds. The dried blood had been wiped clean, the broken nose was reset and the torn lips were stitched up. Sena's long hair had been combed back from his face, gathered and secured at the back of his head with a rubber band. A fresh set of clothes had been procured for him, and his shit- and piss-soaked pants had been thrown away. After the doctor was done dealing with the wounds, he made Sena drink a litre of an oral rehydration solution – a cocktail of sugar, salt and water. And he fed him a plateful of rice and dal.

When the captain returned to the interrogation cell just after midnight, the man sitting across him bore little resemblance to the living corpse the havildars had dragged in for interrogation earlier that evening.

The captain took a close look at Sena. His face was filled with anger and hate. The captain, on the other hand, felt nothing, which surprised him. In the seven years since they'd last met, he'd often re-imagined the events of their last meeting. In his revised version, he'd fought back Sena's brutal assault, smashing his smug face into the floor again and again till he begged him to stop.

Now, when fate had delivered Sena to him with his hands and feet shackled, to do with him as he pleased, he felt nothing – there was no anger, no hatred, no regret and no compassion. But that feeling of nothingness gave him power over Sena. It let the captain see Sena for who he really was – another broken man, a victim of circumstances not entirely in his control, whose life had turned into a living hell.

'Take off his handcuffs,' the captain instructed the burly havildar who stood guard in the room.

'He's very dangerous, sir,' the havildar said. 'Better to leave them on.'

'Remove them and leave us alone.' His command was louder than he'd intended.

The havildar took off the handcuffs without further ado. But he showed his displeasure by cuffing Sena viciously on the back of his head with an open fist before exiting the cell and locking it behind him.

Sena and the captain stared at each other for a while.

The captain took out his pack of Charminar and a matchbox, and lit himself a cigarette. He slowly pushed the cigarettes and the matchbox across the table. Sena stared at him guardedly. Then he picked up the gauntlet, reaching for the cigarettes. He lit himself one and, with the cigarette hanging loosely from his freshly stitched lips, he settled back in the metal chair, looking up at the ceiling as he smoked.

The captain broke the silence. 'I'm sorry about what they did to you, Sena,' the captain said softly.

It was a mistake. Too much empathy, too soon. It allowed Sena to seize the upper hand. He flung his half-smoked cigarette away and, leaning forward, he banged his fists on the table, glaring at Sammy. 'You're sorry? You're sorry! I don't need your damn sympathy, arsehole. You destroyed Martha's life and ran away from Asakhua abandoning her. You're a fucking coward!' he spat viciously.

His words stung the captain badly. He reached across the table and slapped Sena across his disfigured face, sending him flying backwards, his chair toppling over. The sound of the metal chair crashing to the ground and the muted growl of pain that followed alerted the havildars outside. They rushed into the cell, their rifles drawn and pointed at Sena, who lay sprawled on the floor.

When Sena was put back in his chair and the havildars had left, the captain resumed his interrogation. He leant forward deliberately and sneered: 'You pathetic little rat. You think we're still in Asakhua and I'm afraid of you? Look at yourself, you miserable little fuck. Look at what you've become.'

Sena lunged across the table, swinging wildly at the captain. But his feet had been shackled, and that made his movements clumsy and awkward. All the captain had to do was lean back and he was out of the range of Sena's fists.

'Sit down,' he barked. 'The next time you try that, I'll break your hands. You hear me? I'll break your hands, I swear.'

That got Sena's attention. He sat back down in the chair, raising his hands in mock surrender. Then he reached forward slowly for the pack of cigarettes and lit himself another one.

The captain began again. 'No more games, Sena. I'm going to ask you some questions, and I need answers. That's what I'm here for.'

After what seemed like forever, Sena turned his face to meet the captain's gaze. 'I have nothing to tell you, you mixed-breed Indian dog,' he said coldly, not a trace of emotion in his voice.

The captain ignored his barb. 'Look, Sena, I hate you. I can't pretend I don't. But I'm the only one here who doesn't want to put a bullet in your head. So, you'd better talk. It's the only way you'll stay alive. Now, where is Laldenga?'

Sena looked at the captain incredulously. With a flash of anger on his broken face, he said: 'That fucking commandant has tortured me for days. He's had me hung upside down, beaten me, electrocuted me and made me drink my own piss. Yet, I told him nothing. And you think I'm going to talk to you? Why? Because you fed me some rice and dal, and offered me a cigarette?'

The captain felt guilty, as if he'd been responsible for the violence inflicted on Sena. He was also disturbed by the revelation that it was the commandant who'd personally interrogated him. Leaning forward sympathetically, he said: 'I'm sorry for what the commandant did to you, Sena. But I don't operate like him. I'm an Indian Army officer and I'm here to do my job. So, I'm asking you again, where is Pu Laldenga?'

Sena looked away disdainfully. The captain knew then that he wasn't going to get anything of value from Sena. He saw in him flashes of the boy who'd stood up courageously to his father in school. He hadn't broken then. He wouldn't break now. Even if Sena knew where Laldenga was, he would never give him up.

The captain changed tack. 'When I left Asakhua, you were studying for the civil services. What happened? How did you end up here?'

'That bastard who tortured me also asked why I became a guerrilla. I didn't tell him anything because I didn't want to give him any clues that could help him figure out who I was and where I came from. That would have put my family in danger. But now, he has you, doesn't he? You'll tell him all he needs to know about me, so that his men can hunt down my father and my sisters, and butcher them – like they have so many of our people. So, there's nothing to hide any more, is there?'

The captain shifted uncomfortably in his chair. Sena leant forward and helped himself to another cigarette. Then he began to speak.

'The Mautam destroyed our lives. There was nothing left for us in Asakhua after the rats came out of the jungle.

One day, we just packed everything we could into the Jeep and left. We were lucky. Hundreds of starving men, women and children walked along the road, desperate for food. Many of them died before they could reach the relief camps. The Indian government had years to plan. They knew the Mautam would come. They knew what would happen when it did. But they did nothing. When we were at our most desperate, India left us to die.'

'Yeah,' the captain said impatiently. 'What happened was tragic. But how does picking up the gun and going to war against India bring the dead back to life?'

Sena read the captain's impatience as callousness. 'What option did we have other than to pick up the gun and fight for our people, our dignity, our freedom?' he snapped. 'Did you think we'd just forget our dead and walk away? Do you think we're afraid of the Indian Army or these cowards from the Frontier Rangers? We're fighting for our right to be respected – never forget that. You Indians disrespected us when you turned your backs on us and looked the other way while thousands of Mizo men, women and children starved to death. But now, when we pick up the gun and demand our independence, we have your complete attention? Your Indian government has sent an entire brigade, thousands of soldiers, to crush us for daring to stand up to your tyranny.'

The captain was riled. 'What did you expect Delhi would do, Sena? Roll over and play dead? And allow every idiot in every part of India to grab a few guns and dream about a new nation? Did you really think there would be no reaction? No pushback? Are you really that stupid?'

Anger flashed across Sena's face. In a cold and dispassionate voice, he said: 'I would have expected your government to sit down at the negotiating table with our representatives and find a solution. Isn't that what they did when the Marathas wanted Bombay and their own state? Isn't that what they did when the Tamils revolted on the issue of Hindi, and burnt down buses and government buildings? But as far as you Indians are concerned, we're worthless savages, right? Savages who have to be shown who the master is! I'll tell you this, Sammy, do what you want, but we will not bow down. We will not give up. We will fight to the last Mizo man, woman and child. We will turn the Mizo Hills into India's Vietnam. You wait and watch.'

The captain smiled smugly. 'Sena, that's rubbish, and you know it. Yes, your attacks in March, last year, did catch the Frontier Rangers by surprise and you did make some quick gains – I'll hand you that. But once the Indian Army came in, we've pretty much smashed you into the ground. The MNF is finished. Most of your leaders have run away to Burma or to your handlers in Pakistan. Let's face it, you guys are no match for the Indian Army. You are certainly no Viet Cong. You don't have their guts or the backing of the Chinese. So, stop talking nonsense about turning these hills into Vietnam. You couldn't even hold Aizawl, man. We took it back in a week. You guys are just a bunch of amateurs – talking big, with nothing to show for it.'

Furious, Sena snarled: 'You took Aizawl? Your air force bombed the city, and killed innocent women and children who had nothing to do with this war. Our people died on the streets, strafed by your fighter planes. They died under collapsed, burning buildings, calling out for help from under the rubble. You wouldn't have dared do what you did in Aizawl anywhere else in India. But this isn't India, is it? This is some godforsaken land, too far for your media to bother to come to and report on what's really going on here.'

The captain was being baited into defending a position he didn't need to, losing sight of his objective. But he wasn't going to let Sena have the last word. 'The MNF is not some great defender of the Mizo people, Sena. You guys are nothing but a bunch of crooks, exploiting the misery of the people for your own gain. We know how much the handlers in Pakistan pay your leaders. We know who gives them the gold bars they smuggle into Thailand to buy guns. We know about the drugs that come in from Burma under the MNF's protection. The MNF looted government treasuries in Lunglei, Aizawl and everywhere else it could. Where did that money go? It went into the pockets of your leaders, that's where! You guys are as corrupt as anyone else in this country.'

It was first light and the captain had learnt nothing from Sena that was of any military use. Their heated debate had done nothing to win his trust either. It had only widened the chasm between them. Mercifully, the sound of the key turning in the lock brought the exchange to an end.

The havildars were back. 'Sir, would you like some tea?' the burly one asked.

'Get us two cups.'

The burly one didn't look pleased, but he replied with a dour, 'Ji, sir.' He returned a short while later and plonked two glasses of piping hot tea on the table, glared at the prisoner and left, turning the key in the lock once more.

The two men sat silently for a while, sipping their tea. Sena was still smarting from the captain's last barb, and he felt he needed to set the record straight. He said dispassionately: 'The money we took from the treasuries belongs to the Mizo people. It belongs to us. It is to be used to fight for our independence and to take care of the widows and orphans your army creates. You want to know where it went? Your fucking commandant stole trunks of it from the safe house where they trapped me. You want to know where it's gone? Ask that fucking thief!' Then, pushing himself back in his chair, he said: 'I'm donc talking to you, Sammy. It's pointless. You never understood us when you lived amongst us. How can I expect you to understand us now, when you wear that uniform?'

The captain was stunned by Sena's revelations about the commandant. Could Sena be lying? If he was, it wouldn't be the first time. But to what purpose?

CHAPTER 4

At 8 a.m., Captain Samuel was back in the commandant's office. The captain had showered, shaved and changed into a fresh uniform, his neatly combed hair oiled with scented coconut oil, his black shoes polished. Though he hadn't slept a wink, he looked like he was back from a vacation.

The commandant was sitting at his desk, his feet up on the oak table, a lit cigarette hanging from his thin lips. He was in a foul mood, and he came straight to the point. 'Are you a captain in the Indian Army or Florence fucking Nightingale?' He sprung to his feet and banged his fists down on the oak table.

'I beg your pardon, sir?' the captain asked, feigning innocence.

The commandant didn't buy it. He shot back: 'Don't you beg your pardon me, arsehole. I gave you permission to interrogate the prisoner only because I was ordered to by my boss. But you've gone and ruined all the good work my men did these past three days. We had broken that motherfucker down to the point where he would have given us the names and addresses of every guerrilla he knows. Then you show up. Why did you call the doctor to treat the prisoner without my permission? Why did you feed him? How dare you!'

'There's been a misunderstanding, sir. I didn't realize I needed your permission to call the doctor. I apologize. I would have asked, but I was told you were supervising an operation in Lunglei and unavailable. The prisoner was dying. If I hadn't moved quickly, we would have lost him,' said Captain Samuel, in as conciliatory a tone as he could muster.

The commandant puffed at his cigarette, the anger on his face impossible to miss. When he was done smoking, he stubbed his cigarette in the ashtray and settled back down in his chair. He didn't ask the captain to sit. The commandant then leant forward, his elbows on the oak desk, his fingers interlocked and held in front of his face, his thumbs resting on the bridge of his nose, his beady eyes peering at the captain. He asked: 'So what did you find out? Anything that can be of use to us?'

'Oh, yes,' said the captain. 'I think he's going to be of great use to us, sir. In fact, I sent a message on to Major Mukherjee this morning itself, asking for permission to bring the prisoner back with me to Aizawl, sir. The prisoner definitely knows where Laldenga is. He says he met him last month at a safe house near Thenzawl and that

Laldenga will cross over into Burma from Zorinpui later this month, sir.'

'I see,' the commandant said impassively. 'The prisoner told you all this last night? I'm impressed, Captain. He's told you more in one night than he's told my men over three days.'

The captain shifted uncomfortably in his seat. He pushed on: 'I think the kindness helped, sir. He trusts me. Which is why I think he shared so much information with me.'

'I see,' said the commandant again. 'But how do we know he's telling the truth? We must have some verifiable information before we can take him seriously. There's no way I'm parting with him unless we can verify at least one piece of information he's given us. Do you have anything?'

The captain was stumped by the question. He said nothing.

'I thought so,' said the commandant. 'You have nothing, son. It's best you pack up now and head back to Aizawl as soon as possible. The prisoner stays with us. When we're done with him, we'll send him up to Frontier Rangers' headquarters. They'll decide what to do with him.' The commandant stood up abruptly. The meeting was over.

The captain got to his feet slowly, carefully considering his options. He knew the only verifiable information he had about Sena would put his family at risk. It would put Martha at risk. But if he didn't take that chance, he knew Sena would die and with his death would vanish any hope he had of ever reconciling with Martha. His decision made, he said: 'There is more, sir. His real name is Sena and he grew up in the village of Asakhua, about twenty kilometres from here. His father is the headmaster of the local village school. That information can easily be verified.'

The commandant had walked into his own trap. He glared angrily at the captain.

'Sir, if you could organize an escort, I'll have the prisoner moved to Aizawl this afternoon,' the captain said quietly.

Three hours later, a Jeep and a truck were lined up outside the prison barracks. A squad of ten Frontier Rangers soldiers, led by Subedar Major Paul, had been assigned to escort Sena to Aizawl. Captain Samuel was anxious to get to Aizawl before nightfall, but the commandant had taken his time signing the transfer papers. It was only after Major Mukherjee called the commandant that the paperwork finally got done and Sena was brought out of the prison barracks, his hands and feet shackled. He wore a fresh set of oversized khaki-coloured trousers held up by a worn-out brown belt, into which was tucked a loose-fitting short-sleeved white shirt. On his feet he had on a pair of white canvas shoes. Two soldiers hoisted him up into the truck.

Subedar Major Paul climbed into the Jeep and sat behind Captain Samuel, who rode shotgun. With a casualness bordering on disrespect, the subedar major smirked, 'Chalo, sir. Let's go.' The captain pretended not to notice. He nodded to the driver. The Jeep pulled away slowly, followed by the truck.

In his room, the commandant sat with his feet perched on his desk, puffing slowly on a cigarette, looking pensively out of the window at the storm clouds gathering over the hills.

***

Three hours after the Jeep and the truck in which Sena was being transported to Aizawl had left the Frontier Rangers garrison in Lunglei, the spectacular 750-foot-high Vantawng Falls came into view, across a deep gorge. The captain craned his neck out of the Jeep to get a better look. Leaning across the front seat, Paul said: 'Sir, there's a side road up ahead, that leads down to a cliff from where we can get a superb view of the falls. Also, we need to give the soldiers a piss break.'

The captain concurred. Ten minutes later, the Jeep and the truck veered off the main road on to a disused jungle track that headed down into the gorge. Half a kilometre later, they arrived at a cul-de-sac, a short walk from a cliff that overlooked the gorge, that was just wide enough for the truck to be turned around in. The captain got down and walked to the edge of the cliff. The subedar major had been right; the view of the waterfall was stunning.

The soldiers got down from the truck and lined up by the side of the track to piss. Two stayed back to guard Sena. Paul asked them to bring him down. When Sena had been lowered, Paul unlocked the shackles on his feet but left his handcuffs on. He lit a beedi and handed it to Sena to smoke.

'We have another five hours to Aizawl. Stretch your legs and piss. We won't be stopping again.'

Sena strolled down the jungle track, with Paul following closely behind. Behind a rocky overhang, out of sight of the soldiers, Sena stopped and unzipped himself. He took a deep breath of the moist, clean jungle air. The distant roar of the waters of the Vanva River cascading over the Vantawng Falls, mixed with the sounds of the jungle, was a welcome relief from the jarring growl of the truck engine and the shifting of gears. Sena felt his body relax. He shut his eyes and pissed. For the first time in days, he felt totally at peace with himself.

Then Sena became aware of Paul standing just behind him, his pistol pointed at the back of his head. It struck him then: *This was the end, and he hadn't even seen it coming!* Looking back over his shoulder, he said: 'Paul, you motherfucker, if you're going to kill me, at least don't shoot me in the back like a fucking coward.'

Subedar Major Paul, his ego bruised, took a step back and sniggered. 'Take your time and enjoy your last piss, chinkie. When you're done, turn around and let's look deep into each other's eyes while I pump my bullets into your chest and watch you topple over the edge.'

Sena took his time. Then he slowly zipped up. Finally, he turned around. What he saw confused him, and the confusion showed on his face.

'Drop the gun, Paul, don't do it,' said Captain Samuel, his voice firm, his hands steady, as he pointed his pistol at the subedar major.

The world stood still for a moment. The voices of the soldiers chatting with each other floated down to them over the sound of the waterfall. Somewhere above them on the highway, a truck passed by, its engine straining as it made its way up the steep mountain road.

Subedar Major Paul didn't obey the captain's command. His pistol still pointing at Sena, he said: 'Captain, you don't understand. This man's name is Che. He's a cold-blooded killer who has murdered many of our own. He must be brought to justice.'

'You are mistaken, Paul. His name is not Che; his name is Sena. Now put your gun down. I won't tell you again,' said the captain, his voice firmer and louder.

Paul slowly lowered the pistol and turned to look at the captain. It was a mistake. Sena leapt at him in a flash, throwing his shackled arms around his neck. Then he dropped to the ground, pulling Paul down on top of him, wrapping his legs tightly around his torso, tightening the stranglehold on his neck. Paul thrashed around wildly on the ground, trying to get out of Sena's vice-like grip, his face slowly turning blue, his pistol still in his hands.

The horrified captain cried, 'Stop it, stop it, Sena, or I'll shoot!' But Sena didn't pay heed. Like a python crushing its prey, he tightened his stranglehold, even as the subedar major desperately tried to break free.

The crack of a pistol could be heard over the distant roar of the waterfall. The thrashing on the ground stopped as Subedar Major Paul's body went limp and a red stain spread quickly across his chest. Sena released the death grip he had on the subedar major and felt around in his pockets for a key. When he found it, he pushed Paul's limp body away and raced off down the jungle track. The captain was momentarily stunned by this sudden turn of events. Then he gathered his wits about him and fired a volley of shots in the direction Sena had taken off in. But it was too late. Sena was gone.

Hearing the gunshots, the soldiers thought they were under attack and dived for cover, throwing their half-smoked beedis away in a hurry. But when an entire minute had passed and nothing else happened, they scrambled back on to the jungle track. One of the more experienced soldiers, a havildar, took charge, assigning four of his comrades to guard the vehicles and ordering the others to follow him. They set off at a fast trot looking for their subedar major, the captain and the prisoner.

When the havildar cleared the rocky overhang in the path, he saw his subedar major lying crumpled on the ground, a huge blood stain on his back, with the captain standing over him, his pistol in his hand. Of the prisoner there was no sign. The havildar's bewilderment turned to anger when he surmised that it was the captain who had shot his subedar major. He stopped and raised his rifle to his shoulder.

The captain reacted instinctively. Bullets whizzing around him, he threw himself off the jungle path, crashing through the undergrowth and tumbling down a steep slope.

Meanwhile, Sena had stumbled upon a narrow shepherd's trail that led down into the gorge. He raced down the trail, nimbly leaping over the moss-covered rocks and pebbles that lay strewn all over – like a soldier trying to run through a minefield with his hands tied behind his back.

After slipping and sliding about twenty metres, through the thick undergrowth, Sammy found himself on the shepherd's trail that Sena had discovered. Scratched and bruised, he got back on his feet and scrambled down the trail, to put as much distance as he could between him and the soldiers he believed would soon come searching for him.

Up ahead, the inevitable happened. Sena slipped on the moss-covered rocks and fell in a heap by the side of the path, his legs twisting under him.

Even as he struggled to get back on his feet, Sammy had caught up with him. Enraged and out of breath, he pointed his handgun at Sena's head. 'I'll kill you! I swear, I'll fucking kill you,' he gasped, warily keeping his distance from Sena, who pulled himself to the trunk of a nearby tree and rested his back against it. Out of breath and in pain, Sena's right fist shut tight over the key he had taken off Paul. His shirt had ripped open, and there were fresh cuts and gashes all over – on his face, his chest and on his hands. Sammy's uniform too was torn in places and there was a deep laceration on his left arm. He sat down, resting against a rock, his pistol pointed at Sena.

Above them, the soldiers had given up the chase. A few minutes later, Sammy and Sena heard the Jeep and the truck start up and quickly pull away.

Each of them considered the possibility of what would happen next.

It was Sammy who finally broke the silence. 'I'm taking you back with me. You're still a prisoner.'

'You're unbelievable!' snarled Sena. 'There's no way I'm going back with you. I'd rather die.'

'That's a good idea. Maybe I should just shoot you right now and drag your body back. I'll be a hero. They may even give me a medal,' Sammy retorted.

'You should have thought of that before you pulled your gun on Paul.' Sena smirked. 'As far as they're concerned, you're now a traitor and a fugitive, just like me!'

For the first time, Sammy was forced to confront the reality of their situation. The last ten minutes had been a blur. He hadn't considered how his role in Sena's escape could be misconstrued. He realized he couldn't go back to the Lunglei garrison. In fact, he couldn't go anywhere near a Frontier Rangers' post. His only chance to extricate himself from the mess he'd landed himself in was to get to Major Mukherjee and tell him what had happened.

'I'm going to take you to Aizawl, to my commanding officer. I'll tell him what happened. He's a fair man. He'll understand,' Sammy said, the lack of conviction in his voice apparent.

'Are you crazy?' Sena asked. 'Why would I want to do that? Besides, it's a three-day march to Aizawl. There will soon be hundreds of Frontier Rangers soldiers looking for us. And the local police, too. We'll never make it.'

'We'll stay away from the villages and walk at night. What choice do we have?'

'We have a choice, Sammy. You let me go and I won't kill you. You walk back to the main road and get back to Lunglei. Paul is probably dead. You can tell them I killed him.'

'I'm not a traitor, Sena. Or a coward. You're my prisoner, and I'm taking you to Aizawl. That's what we're going to do; let's get going.'

Sammy got back on his feet and motioned Sena to do the same. He continued to point the pistol at Sena, who got to his feet reluctantly and set off slowly down the path. Sammy followed at a safe distance – just like it had been in their childhood. Except now, Sena led the way because he had a gun pointed at him and Sammy followed – not because that's how it had always been between them, but to make sure that Sena didn't hoodwink him and escape.

* * *

Three hours after he'd first learnt of the prisoner's escape, Commandant Aiyar, accompanied by a retinue of senior Frontier Rangers officers, stood by Subedar Major Paul's bedside in the field hospital at Thenzawl. The subedar major was hooked up to an intravenous line and looked like he was in great pain. While the bullet had passed clean through Paul's left shoulder and had caused no lasting damage, his throat had been badly bruised and cut by the iron shackles the prisoner had tried to strangle him with.

'Who did this to you, Paul?' the commandant asked.

'Captain Samuel, sir,' the subedar major whispered.

'Captain Samuel shot you?' the commandant asked incredulously.

'Yes, sir. He shot me and escaped with Che, sir,' the subedar major replied.

Commandant Aiyar's face was expressionless. He leant forward towards Subedar Major Paul and whispered: 'You motherfucker. I gave you a simple job and you fucked it up.' Straightening up, he said: 'The doctors say you're going to be fine, Paul. They'll discharge you tomorrow morning once the effect of the morphine wears off. You'd better get some rest.'

Without further ado, the commandant turned around and walked briskly out of the ward. In the corridor outside, he addressed the officers who were following him – amongst them his deputy commandant, Dilip Saikia, forty-five years old, built like a prize fighter, and a veteran of many skirmishes with the guerrillas.

'They have a four-hour head start over us. Saikia, stop all our other operations. Get our boys to hunt down these bastards.'

'Yes, sir,' the deputy replied.

'One more thing,' the commandant said. 'I want to know everything about our captain. Where he grew up, where he went to school, who his friends were, everything. Send a few of our boys to Asakhua to verify what the captain told us about the prisoner. It'll probably be false, but let's check it out just to make sure.'

'Yes, sir. I'll get on it right away,' the deputy replied. 'Is there anything else, sir?'

'Yes. Get the word out to all our informants. We're offering a reward of twenty-five thousand rupees each for the prisoner and the captain. Let's get those greedy MNF bastards to join our hunt.'

'Sir, won't we need permission from headquarters?' the deputy asked, nervously.

'That's my problem, Saikia; you follow your orders.' The commandant's tone was icy.

'Yes, sir.'

'Let's go, boys. Let's show these traitors what happens when you mess with the Frontier Rangers,' the commandant thundered, rubbing his hands together gleefully.

SAMMY'S WAR

CHAPTER 1

On the night of 14 April 1942, a child wrapped in a soiled woollen blanket was left on the doorstep of the Holy Child Orphanage in Kulikawn, near Aizawl. Tucked into the blanket was an old brown envelope filled with coins of many different denominations and an unsigned note scribbled on a sheet of paper ripped out of a child's exercise book. The note, written in neat, well-formed handwriting, read: 'The boy's mother died in childbirth, but I cannot do to him as our elder's desire. My heart is heavy with the burden of my sin. Please take care of him and may God bless and keep him always.'

The boy had got lucky. Amongst many tribes in the Mizo highlands, a child whose mother died in childbirth was considered a bad omen and buried alive with his dead mother. Sister Theresa, the nun in charge of the orphanage, examined the boy carefully. She noted his eyes didn't have the epicanthic fold that gave the indigenous Mizo people their distinctive almond-shaped eyes. 'A mixed breed,' she muttered to herself.

Sister Theresa opened her register and wrote down the circumstances of the child's arrival: 'A boy of mixed parentage; a day or two old; healthy and chubby; weighing about seven pounds; parents unknown; deposited at the orphanage by unknown person(s)'. After she'd carefully added up the value of each coin she'd found in the envelope, she dutifully noted in the ledger the eight-rupee donation that had been received from the anonymous donor.

Then Sister Theresa turned to her old and tattered Bible, and let the Holy Spirit guide her. Her frail eyes scanned the page that had opened, until they fell upon Samuel, a Levite, the son of Hannah – Hannah, who was barren, prayed to God for a child. When her prayers were answered, she named her baby Samuel, meaning: 'The Lord has heard.' Samuel grew up to be hailed as a seer and a prophet. Favoured by God, he also served the people of Israel as a priest, a judge and a military commander.

'Your name, my sweet, innocent child, is Samuel,' Sister Theresa whispered into the ear of the boy.

But the other children at the orphanage, they called him Sammy.

When Sammy was five years old, the Reverend Pastor Joachim Rego and his wife, Isabelle, chose to adopt him from amongst the thirty-three children at the orphanage. Unlike the other orphans, with his curly black hair, dusky complexion and eyes that didn't have an epicanthic fold, Sammy could easily pass off as their own. For Isabelle, who'd grudgingly consented to her husband's plan of expanding their family by adopting a child, that illusion was of utmost importance.

Reverend Joachim Rego's father, Aloysius Rego, was a devout Catholic and one of the richest men in Mangalore – a provincial town on India's west coast. He owned the 250-acre Bunny Hill Coffee Estate in Sakleshpur in the Western Ghats, and rubber, cashew and coconut plantations in the countryside around Mangalore. The money from his estates had been re-invested into buying prime land in town and, by the turn of the twentieth century, he was already Mangalore's biggest landlord. As his wealth skyrocketed, so did his power and his prestige, making him the pride of the Mangalorean Catholic community.

Unlike his siblings, who'd all joined the family business when they came of age, Joachim had other plans. After graduating at the bottom of his class in history, he'd spent six months backpacking across Europe – whoring, drinking, gambling and blowing up the money his father had generously gifted him to fund his European holiday. Then, all of a sudden, one bright winter morning, as he ate his scrambled eggs and toast, and sipped his glass of Chardonnay at a café on a cobbled sidewalk in Nice, he felt an overpowering urge to fall to his knees and give thanks to God. Which he did – babbling in tongues no one could comprehend, his face radiant and bright – much to the astonishment of the crowd that had gathered to watch the spectacle.

When he returned home to Mangalore, Joachim said to his father: 'I will dedicate my life to Christ, as a priest.'

The senior Rego couldn't have been more pleased! Joachim's decision would further cement his standing in Mangalorean society and give his very un-Christian, unabashed pursuit of wealth a spiritual legitimacy. Six years later, when Joachim was ordained a priest, Aloysius hosted a grand, week-long celebration that culminated in a lavish banquet to which all of Mangalore's rich and powerful were invited. Fawning speeches were made and full-page advertisements were taken out in the local newspapers congratulating the Rego family. The poor of the city were fed the leftovers from the banquet for an entire week.

Aloysius and the Rego family were the toast of the town. But it didn't last long. Two years into his new life as a priest, Father Joachim was appointed as vice-principal of The Sacred Heart School in the army cantonment town of Bangalore, where he met Isabelle Lazarado, daughter of Brigadier Vivian Lazarado, who taught music to the boys.

The dashing Father Joachim, with his ready wit, easy charm and an endless supply of tales from his time in Europe, and Isabelle – elegant, shy and a good listener – took an immediate liking to each other. At first, it was safe and light-hearted banter. They were of the same age, with similar interests, and an unconventional love for jazz. Besides, the school offered them no privacy. Their conversations were carried out in the open, in the staff room or in the corridors, in full view of the students and the teaching staff. It was only a year later, on a week-long school trip to Ooty, a hill station in the Nilgiris, for which Isabelle was hand-picked by Father Joachim to help him chaperone the boys, that love blossomed.

Word of the scandal soon reached Mangalore, and the Rego family became the laughing stock of the Mangalorean Catholic community. Aloysius rushed to Bangalore to confront his son, certain that the rumours were mere spiteful gossip that had to be nipped in the bud. But, by the time he got there, Joachim had already written to the Bishop of Bangalore confessing his sin and asking to be released from priesthood to marry the girl he loved.

Aloysius was livid. When father and son met, the father physically assaulted the son, hurling the vilest abuses and curses at him. 'You're a third-rate scoundrel and a disgrace,' he yelled. 'I'm ashamed to be your father! After all that I've done for you, spent on you, how can you embarrass me like this?'

Matters progressed quickly. The might of the Roman Catholic church was brought down on Father Joachim to get him to change his mind. 'The flesh may be weak, my son, but the spirit must be strong,' growled the Bishop of Bangalore.

'Son, it's not too late. Turn your back on Satan and return to the Lord. Pope Pius is praying for you. You will not disappoint him,' ordered a cardinal from Rome.

His mother played the most dramatic of her many emotional blackmail cards. 'Joachim, I swear, I will kill myself if you marry that wicked woman. I'd rather jump into the sea and drown than allow you to shame us all like this!'

His siblings descended on Bangalore to leverage what they could, collectively and singularly, of their weak bond. 'I knew you weren't cut out to be a priest. But now that you are, you owe it to yourself, and to all of us, to try harder. My wedding is in December. Can't you at least wait till then?' his sister Juliet pleaded.

But Father Joachim was adamant: 'The heart wants what the heart wants.'

Eventually, the church gave in, and Father Joachim Rego was laicised, defrocked and the doors of the Roman Catholic church shut firmly on him forever. As were the doors of the Rego family. Shortly after, Isabelle and Joachim were married at a poorly attended civil ceremony in Bangalore. Both the bride and the groom's families chose not to attend. Isabelle's family were devout Baptists. Her brother, Alan, was a Baptist preacher in Nellore, 400 kilometres east of Bangalore, where he ran a mission, educating and proselytizing the local population. Alan was the only one who supported Isabelle and Joachim, who found themselves unemployed and socially ostracized in Bangalore.

With no options left, the newlyweds moved to Nellore, where Joachim started teaching at the Baptist Mission School and Isabelle worked as a nurse at the Mission Primary Health Centre. But even though Joachim had been laicised by the Roman Catholic church, he continued to believe he was meant to dedicate his life to Christ. The forced celibacy that the Roman Catholic church demanded of its priests wasn't for him. The Baptists though, they didn't expect their spiritual leaders to be celibate. So, Joachim resumed the pursuit of his calling – now as a Baptist – and with dogged determination and another seven years of service and training, he was ordained a Baptist pastor and posted to the furthest outpost of the Baptist Church in India – the Pastorate of Asakhua, in the Mizo Hills.

Sammy's memories of the orphanage were hazy. His first real memory was the night India won her independence from the British. It was 14 August 1947. All of Asakhua had crowded into the Rego home that night to listen to India's first prime minister, Jawaharlal Nehru, on the reverend's radio, his prized possession – a Grundig, that played LPs and had an inbuilt multi-band radio receiver, a gift from his father on his twenty-first birthday. It was a miracle that the Grundig had arrived in Asakhua unscathed, given its 3000-kilometre road journey from Nellore to Lunglei in a goods carrier, and then a hike up the narrow forest track to

Asakhua, slung on a bamboo pole that was hoisted on the shoulders of porters. Sammy was too young to make any sense of what Prime Minister Nehru said that night, but the villagers clapped and cheered along, and it left an indelible memory in his young mind.

After the speech, Joachim rolled up the carpet and moved the furniture in the living room out of the way. He put on a Hoagy Carmichael record, turned up the volume on the Grundig and pulled Isabelle on the makeshift dance floor.

'Joachim, I haven't danced in years,' Isabelle cried, trying to pull away.

'Neither have I!' Joachim replied, giggling boyishly.

Finally, Isabelle gave in, and her husband and she began boogying to 'Huggin and chalkin', the smash hit of that year. The lyrics went like this:

I got a gal, who's mighty sweet,
Big blue eyes and tiny feet.
Her name is Rosabelle Magee,
And she tips the scale at three-oh-three!
Oh, gee, but ain't it grand to have a gal so big and fat,
That when you go to hug her, you don't know where you're at,
You have to take a piece of chalk in your hand,
And hug away and chalk a mark, to see where you began!

All their worries forgotten, their past firmly behind them, husband and wife danced with abandon while the villagers clapped and hooted in delight. The celebrations went on late into the night, and Isabelle rushed about serving their boisterous guests an endless supply of homemade wine and plum cake. At some point, Joachim hoisted Sammy on to his shoulders and with Sammy's older brother, Peter, clinging to him and Isabelle in his arms, they'd danced and laughed and cried, and it was all just wonderful and perfect!

CHAPTER 2

The Rego family lived in the old missionary bungalow within the compound of the Baptist Church in Asakhua, twenty kilometres south of Lunglei, the largest village in the region. Set amidst rolling rice fields with a network of narrow irrigation canals that were fed by a natural spring on the edge of the village, Asakhua was surrounded by thick oak and rhododendron forests and bamboo groves, and teemed with wildlife. The village didn't exist at the beginning of the twentieth century. The entire area was covered in undergrowth and bamboo groves, and had been cyclically farmed using traditional slash-and-burn techniques called 'jhoom' by a Paite tribe that lived in the area.

In 1920, Reverend John White, a missionary from England, arrived in Lunglei and set about working amongst the Paite. Within a decade, most of the Paite had converted to Christianity, given up their migratory lifestyles and jhoom, and settled down in the land around the imposing mission house Reverend White had built, giving birth to the village of Asakhua. By 1947, the village had grown to about forty homes. While many of the villagers were Paite, a fair number of Lusei, Ralte, Mara and Hmar families had settled down in the village as well, in keeping with the reverend's vision of a mixed, modern village built on Christian values.

Similar stories had played out across the region. Till the middle of the nineteenth century, the British had no interest in the inhospitable Mizo Hills that rose to over 2,000 metres, and were covered in thick forests and dense bamboo groves. They cared even less for the tribes who lived in these hills, referring to them generically as the 'Lushai' – literally, 'men who live in the hills', looking down upon them as savages who posed no threat to their mighty empire. It was only when the tribesmen began attacking their tea plantations in the foothills that the British turned their attention to how the 'Lushai' could be subjugated and colonized.

The foot soldiers encouraged by the British to 'civilize' the 'Lushai' were Christian missionaries, first from the Arthington Aborigines Mission in London and, over the years, from every major Christian denomination. Fired by evangelical zeal, and with the complete support of the colonial government, the missionaries competed against each other to win as many pagan souls as they could for Christ. As a result, Christianity spread quickly, with the Presbyterians establishing themselves in the north, around the town of Aizawl, and the Baptists dominant in the south, around Lunglei.

With money from donors around the world, Reverend White built the Asakhua Baptist Church on a spur on the hillside overlooking the village. Painted white on the outside, it had a wooden, slanting roof from which rose a bell tower – with a cross fixed atop it that could be seen from kilometres away – which housed a bronze bell. Inside, the church had twenty pews, made from hardwood oak, that could each accommodate about four adults and two children. Between the altar and the front pews was a wide-open space for the choir and the musicians, and for those in the congregation who felt the need to twirl or sway or dance to the songs.

The church's twelve stained-glass windows were a marvel – each a rectangle nine feet high and three feet wide, and each with a delicately etched artwork of one of Christ's disciples. On top of each window was a mosaic of coloured glass arranged in a neat semicircle. The windows had been sent from Belgium and had taken months to be shipped and carted up to Asakhua. On the walls of the church were rectangular wooden plaques, each featuring an intricately carved scene from one of the fourteen stations of the cross – Christ's journey from the time he was condemned to death by Pontius Pilate to his lifeless body being placed in the sepulchre.

The altar, on the other hand, was the antithesis of the church's intricate artwork. It was a plain marble slab about eight feet long and three feet wide, covered with a thick satin cloth, which rested on two large boulders whose tops had been chipped away and flattened. Set against this was a cross made from rough, unvarnished oak that ran from the floor to just below the ceiling, and it completely dominated the church.

Reverend White contracted malaria in 1945 and passed away in a hospital in Calcutta. Shortly after, the reverend's wife and children returned to England, their lifelong mission in the Mizo Hills prematurely aborted. For over a year, the 120-strong Baptist community in Asakhua were without a spiritual guide. Then, the freshly minted Reverend Pastor Joachim Rego arrived to take over the pastorate in January 1947.

At first, the new pastor was aghast by the intensity and fervour of his congregation, for whom singing and dancing were central to every service. Hymns in church were sung in two distinct styles. There were the traditional Western hymns that were sung by the congregation from the pews with great gusto. Then there was the *lengkhawm*, a distinct local flavour of singing, with two drummers who set the rhythm using traditional drums. The singing was led by a *hlahriltu*, a song proclaimer, who'd chant each line of the song that would then be repeated by the congregation. As the lengkhawm picked up in intensity, many in the congregation would step up into the open area near the altar and sway and dance in concentric, anti-clockwise circles, and as the Holy Spirit lay hold of them, they'd swoon and speak in strange tongues and collapse in a heap on the floor. They would need to be revived with another round of singing. In time, Reverend Pastor Rego learnt to let go of his inhibitions and encouraged his congregation to worship the lord in any way they chose to.

The church was central to Sammy's life in those early years. Every evening, as the sun began to set, he'd walk with his father, his tiny hand clutching his father's, to lock up the church for the night. It was just the two of them, father and son, and it made Sammy feel special and loved. 'You have a special bond with Christ, Sammy,' his father reminded him over and over. 'You are destined for greatness, and the Holy Spirit is in you. All you have to do is talk to Christ like you're speaking to a friend, share your fears and your dreams with him, and the Holy Spirit will do the rest. You'll never be alone, Sammy, if you walk with Christ. Your life will be joyful and blessed.'

Because he loved his father, Sammy believed him.

CHAPTER 3

In 1948, when he turned six, Sammy began attending the White Primary School, named after its founder Reverend John White, with thirty other children from Asakhua, all between the ages of six and fourteen. The school, built in a clearing in the jungle, on the outskirts of Asakhua, was no more than a rectangular shed about forty feet long and fifteen feet wide. Built with brick, the hall had a corrugated metal roof that was painted green, with a badly fitted wooden door, also painted green, and large wooden windows with vertical steel bars that allowed the hall to be lit up with natural light. Inside, bamboo mats were laid out on the cemented floor for the students to sit on, and a table and a metal chair were placed in one corner of the shed for the teacher. The whitewashed wall behind the teacher's desk sported a large, framed portrait of a stern-looking Reverend White. The other walls carried students' artworks from over the years. To have a painting go up on those walls, with the artist's name and year of study inscribed neatly on it by the headmaster, was an honour reserved only for a handful of students each year.

At one end of the clearing, a football pitch had been marked out, with white chalk powder, and wooden goalposts painted black. There was also a half-basketball court with a hoop nailed into an eight-foot-long wooden post. Adjoining the basketball court, a damp, dark rectangular shed had been created using old, corrugated metal sheets, nailed to bamboo poles sunk into the ground, with no roof, that served as an open toilet.

The school's headmaster – and its only teacher – Eoma, was a Mara tribesman. The teaching job paid him Rs 150 a month and provided free accommodation in one of the old mission bungalows. A strict disciplinarian with a strong sense of duty and commitment, Eoma was always on his feet. From teaching the alphabet to young children, to helping solve complex algebra problems for more mature students, the sheer range of subjects Eoma taught was breathtaking.

Eoma, whose wife had died of malaria, had three children – Christine, Sena and Martha – who studied in the school under his strict supervision. Sena, who was three years older than Sammy, hated the structure and enforced discipline of school, and showed little interest in developing his reading and writing skills. Despite Eoma's untiring efforts, he struggled.

Sammy struggled, too. His 'mixed-breed' status made him the butt of jokes. He was physically bullied by the older children, especially when Eoma wasn't around. The younger children took their cues from the older ones and mimicked their behaviour. Often Sammy went home bruised and bleeding, his clothes torn. This would make his mother furious. 'Why can't you stop fighting?' she'd berate him, twisting his ear and smacking him on the back of his head, even as Sammy tried to explain that it wasn't his fault.

His father was more understanding. 'It's going to be okay, Sammy. The other children just need time to adjust to you. It's going to be okay, you'll see,' he'd say gently, holding him close, as Sammy buried his face in his father's chest and sobbed. 'Remember how much Christ suffered, Sammy, when he was nailed to that cross? Can you even begin to imagine his pain? What is your pain in comparison to his? Be brave.' His father asked his son to pray for those who were tormenting him and to forgive them.

And because Sammy loved his father, he did.

But Sammy didn't feel like Christ, no matter how hard he tried. Every night, he'd get down on his knees and beg Christ to intervene, and stop the bullying and the beating. Then one day, just as his father had promised, his prayers were answered.

Eoma's constant presence during school hours served as a deterrent to the 'Mafia' – a gang of four older boys who took great pleasure in beating and abusing younger and weaker children. As a 'mixed breed' and without any friends to protect him, Sammy had always been a soft target for the 'Mafia'.

One Tuesday, when Eoma was ill and didn't show up, mayhem ensued. The 'Mafia' grabbed power and set about enforcing their writ over the other students. Eoma had used his thin, three-foot-long bamboo cane, only as a showpiece, a deterrent, aimed at discouraging unruly behaviour. It had sat for years, unused, balanced on two rusty nails that had been hammered into the wall, just above his desk. But the 'Mafia' took the cane down, and its members took turns summoning children to the front of the shed where the gang had established their staging post, for a caning. Sammy was singled out for special treatment.

When one of the gangsters asked Sammy to step forward, the anticipation of the terrible caning he was about to be subjected to was enough to make Sammy piss his pants. A warm stream trickled down his leg and formed a pool around his bare feet. Derisive laughter and hooting filled the shed even as one of the gangsters, a chubby boy named Rempuia, grabbed Eoma's cane and stormed towards Sammy.

The first blow landed on Sammy's back, sending him crashing to the floor, whimpering in pain. Rempuia then stood over Sammy, jabbing the damp area around his crotch with the cane. 'Hey, sissy boy, no pissing in class!' He smirked, causing the other children to burst into peals of laughter. As Sammy squirmed in discomfort, sobbing uncontrollably – more out of humiliation and fear than out of pain – Rempuia lifted the cane once more and was about to bring it down on Sammy's arse when Sena snapped.

Sena had watched silently while the gang had beat students, his anger steadily rising. He didn't care much for Sammy, but he didn't like bullies. The 'Mafia' usually avoided Sena not just because he was Eoma's son, but also because he was physically stronger than each of them.

When Rempuia raised the cane to hit Sammy again, Sena leant across and grabbed Rempuia's arm, twisting it behind his back till he yelped in pain and dropped the cane. He followed up that move with a full-blooded, vicious kick directed with great precision at Rempuia's knee, causing him to drop to the ground. A stunned silence filled the hall. Then all hell broke loose. The other members of the 'Mafia' rushed at Sena, who now held the cane. Though outnumbered three to one, Sena began to take out one boy at a time, even as the others kicked and punched at him. The tide soon turned in Sena's favour and, within the first minute itself, two of the gangsters were out of the fight. One of them had been badly kicked in his groin and he writhed on the floor, in Sammy's piss, with his hands between his legs. Rempuia limped away clutching his injured knee, tears streaming down his face. Seeing their friends in such agony took the fight out of the other gangsters, who turned tail and fled the shed.

As the awestruck students stared at him, Sena nonchalantly walked across to Sammy, wiping the dust off his pants and buttoning his shirt. 'You okay, Sammy?' he asked.

Sammy nodded. Wiping away his tears and the snot that ran down his nose, he stood up shakily. That's how Sammy's prayers were answered and the bullying stopped.

But there is always a price to be paid for standing up for the weak, and both Sammy and Sena learnt that lesson the hard way. When Eoma returned to school the next day, he called the students to assemble on the football pitch. For the first time since he'd become the headmaster, Eoma carried the bamboo cane in his hand. He stormed on to the podium at the front of the assembly and came straight to the point: 'I took a day off yesterday because I was ill. It was the first day I've taken off in over a year. I thought you would show me respect by maintaining discipline. But you disrespected me and made a spectacle of yourselves. One child was so badly beaten here in school that he had to be taken to the doctor in Lunglei. I want to know who was responsible. Who beat him up?'

There was pin-drop silence following Eoma's outburst. Not one child moved. No one spoke up. Furious, Eoma got off the podium and walked up to the nearest child – Rempuia. The sound of the slap rang out across the schoolyard. Rempuia burst into tears, even as Eoma grabbed him by his collar and shook him violently. 'Who was it? I'm asking you, Rempuia, who was it?' he yelled. Rempuia sobbed, but said nothing.

Three more boys were similarly slapped before Eoma came up to Sammy. 'I know you won't lie to me, Sammy. Who was it?' Eoma snarled, grabbing Sammy by the collar, just like he'd done with the other boys. Sammy burst into tears. 'S-s-s-Sena, it was Sena!' he stammered in terror, tears rolling down his face. 'But … it wasn't his fault!' Sammy offered weakly, sobbing, his breath ragged, his body tense, waiting for the slap he was certain would come.

Eoma was momentarily stunned by Sammy's confession. Then he pulled himself together and screamed: 'Sena, come up to the front at once!'

Sammy – shaken, fearful and embarrassed – turned around to look at Sena, who stood at the back of the assembly, staring down at his feet.

'Come here, Sena!' thundered Eoma, his voice louder and shriller than the children had ever heard before. Sena stepped forward and walked slowly towards the podium. As he walked past Sammy, their eyes met. The scorn and disgust on Sena's face was unmistakable.

When Sena got to the podium, Eoma berated him at the top of his voice: 'You are a disgrace to this school and to your family. Today I will teach you a lesson you will never forget. Step up on the podium.'

Sena stepped up slowly, his face turned away from the students.

'Turn around,' barked Eoma.

Sena turned around, his eyes staring at the ground defiantly.

Eoma's thin bamboo cane swished through the air. The dull thud as it slammed down on Sena's thighs – and the sheer violence of the act – caught Sena off guard, sending him crashing off the podium and on to his hands and knees on the gravel below.

'Get up,' snarled Eoma.

Sena, his knees scratched and bleeding from the fall, got to his feet slowly, the rage evident on his face. He climbed back on the platform, defiantly staring into the distance.

This time, though, Sena was prepared. He flinched each time the cane crashed into him, but he showed no emotion. Many of the younger children in the assembly sobbed uncontrollably, as did Sammy. But Sena didn't let out a sound and he didn't fall again. Twenty times the cane crashed into the back of Sena's thighs or on to his bum. Twenty times every child in the assembly flinched. But Eoma's rage didn't let up. Sena's refusal to break or ask for forgiveness made him angrier. That anger forced him to increase the intensity of the caning. On the twentieth blow, the cane gave way, splintering into two pieces. Furious, Eoma threw the stub at Sena and stormed away.

No one moved for a while. Then Sena stepped off the podium and limped away, impassively, blood trickling down the back of his thighs. The spell was broken. The assembly broke up and the children walked away, disturbed and shocked by the violence they'd just witnessed.

That night, Sammy didn't get down on his knees to pray. Instead, he buried his face deep into his pillow and wept bitterly. 'I'm a coward,' he sobbed. 'I hate myself. I wish I was dead.'

CHAPTER 4

While Sammy wept, Sena ran away from home. Eoma wasn't too concerned at first. When Martha told him that Sena hadn't come home from school, he said: 'He'll come back when he's hungry.' But when Sena didn't return at nightfall or the next day, Eoma began to panic. He went door to door in the village, to check if anyone knew where his son was. But no one had seen Sena after the caning in school. As word of the missing boy spread, the villagers formed search parties and set out to look for him in the surrounding jungle and fields. They even waded through the village tank, worried that he may have drowned. But Sena wasn't to be found.

In desperation, a delegation of villagers visited the Witch in the giant bamboo grove at the edge of the village, carrying with them offerings of her favourite *vawksa*, pork cooked with herbs, and *zu*, beer made from fermented rice. They asked her to divine the whereabouts of the missing boy. After the Witch had eaten the vawksa and drunk the zu, she settled down on the floor outside her shack and began to tap her head with an old shoe that belonged to the boy, swaying gently to a rhythm only she could feel, waiting for the spirits to speak to her. An hour later, just as the villagers were beginning to tire and grumble amongst themselves about her incompetence as a diviner, the Witch leapt to her feet and screeched: 'The boy's gone south to his mother!'

Sena's mother, Mapuli, was the daughter of the lal, or chief, of Tipa – a Mara village about 120 kilometres south of Lunglei. In his youth, Eoma, the son of a poor Mara farmer, had fallen in love with Mapuli. As happens in hierarchical societies, the romance between the commoner and the royal was frowned upon by the elders in the tribe. But, unlike the other men in his clan, Eoma was educated and ambitious enough to see a life for himself beyond the constraints of his village – a life that would be incomplete without the woman he loved. So Eoma's emissary, his uncle, went to the lal with a proposal of marriage, accompanied by expensive gifts for the girl and her family. The lal agreed to consider the proposal, but with a rider: it would be the spirits who would determine if he'd accept it.

That night, drunk on *sahma*, a local beer brewed from banana and rice, the lal dreamt that a thief with a bushy dog's tail and fangs as large as an elephant's tusks had sneaked into his pigsty and taken off with his fattest sow. The spirits had spoken: the marriage between his daughter and her spirited suitor would bring the lal bad luck.

Rather than rejecting Eoma's proposal outright and being forced to return the expensive gifts, the wily lal set an impossibly high *angkia*, the bride price he knew would be out of the young suitor's reach. But Eoma would not be put off. To raise the money, he surrendered his inheritance to his brothers. Left with nothing in the village, after their marriage, Eoma and Mapuli moved to Lunglei, where Eoma found a job as a teaching assistant in the local mission school.

Eoma, Mapuli and their three young children – Christine, Sena and Martha – had lived in Lunglei for seven years when disaster struck. Mapuli died of malaria. Eoma bore his loss with great fortitude and immersed himself in taking care of his children. A year later, the headmaster's position at the Asakhua school opened up. The pay was good and the offer of free accommodation in one of the spacious mission bungalows irresistible. It was a big step up for a family that lived in a one-room, cramped staff quarter in Lunglei. In the summer of 1944, two years after Sammy had been abandoned on the doorstep of the orphanage, Eoma and his children moved to Asakhua.

Eoma never spoke to his children about their mother. It was as if she'd never existed. Martha, who was just a year old when her mother died, had constructed an image of her mother in her imagination, based on her sister, Christine's, memories. It was an image of a beautiful woman with sharp features, with long black hair and piercing black eyes, one who was gentle and kind and loving. Martha felt the presence of her dead mother in her life, and when she was alone or troubled, she'd find herself talking aloud to her. 'What would you have me do, *Nu*?' she'd ask when she needed advice. A compassionate voice inside Martha's head, which she believed was her mother's, would reply with sensible advice – but Martha rarely acted upon it, choosing instead to follow her heart.

Christine, who was five years older than Martha, tried her best to fill the vacuum left by their mother. Though a child herself, it was Christine – and not Eoma – that Sena and Martha turned to when they were troubled. She listened patiently to them and offered them pragmatic advice. She could sense when her siblings needed a hug, or to be cuddled, and she reached out instinctively for them just as a mother would. In their home, Christine's word was law. Neither Sena nor Martha dared challenge her. By the time she was twelve, Christine practically ran the household. She was an excellent cook and a bundle of energy, distributing chores amongst the three of them. Christine bore the burden of ensuring Sena and Martha never suffered for the absence of their mother, or a father, who, though present, was too broken to engage meaningfully with his children about anything other than their studies and their Christian faith. It was a burden Christine bore without complaint, even though it had forced her to abandon her own childhood and behave and think like an adult much before her time.

When Sena disappeared, Martha was distraught. She blamed Eoma for publicly shaming him. Though Christine comforted her, telling her that Sena was safe and that he'd return, the voice in Martha's head told her otherwise. 'He's dead, he's dead,' the voice screamed over and over, causing her temples to throb and her chest to tighten. Then her hearing began to get affected by a strange, persistent, high-pitched hum, like she was alone in a forest with millions of cicadas all around her. At night, Martha tossed and turned in her bed, her head buried under her pillow in an attempt to drown out the debilitating hum that peaked at night, leaving her sleepless and tired. When a week had passed by and there was yet no news of Sena, Martha decided she'd go to the Witch herself, to find out if he was alive. Or dead – like the voice in her head said he was.

The next morning, with a small bowl of *bai* – a soup cooked with pork, bamboo shoots and mixed vegetables – stolen from their kitchen, Martha sneaked out of her home and scrambled down to the clearing in the giant bamboo grove where the Witch had built her dilapidated shack. There she squatted, hidden in the bamboo, fearful but determined, waiting for the Witch to emerge. When she did, Martha called out timidly, '*Chibai!*'

The Witch, who'd just returned from foraging in the surrounding forest for herbs for her potions, spun around – surprised and angered by the intrusion. When she'd located the little girl hidden in the bamboo, she stormed up to her and yanked her out of her hiding place. The frightened girl held up the bowl of bai high above her head as an offering. Amused, the Witch softened. She reached down and took the bowl the girl had offered her and sniffed at the pleasant aroma of freshly made bai. Then she sat down on the ground, and placing the bowl beside her, she said: 'You shouldn't be here, child. What do you want?'

Tears poured down Martha's face, causing her to cover her eyes in shame, even as her frail, little body shuddered, wracked in spasms of grief. Moved by the child's tears, the Witch pulled her close, hugging her tight, swaying back and forth gently. When Martha had stopped crying, the Witch sat her down in front of her. Placing her fingers gently under the girl's chin, she lifted her face, so that she could take a good look at her. Then she asked: 'What is troubling you, child? Why have you come to me?'

'My brother's dead! And I don't know what to do!'

'Is your brother the one they call Sena?'

'Yes, that's him,' Martha whimpered.

The Witch smiled and patted her gently on her head. 'The boy isn't dead. He's gone south to his mother. He's safe and no harm will come to him.'

'But my mother's dead, too!' Martha cried. 'She got a terrible fever, and she died when I was little. My father said so.'

The Witch was disturbed by this news, and it showed on her face. But she quickly gathered her wits about her and snapped: 'No, she isn't. She's alive. And the boy is alive. I've seen it and it's true. My visions are never wrong!'

Martha was confused by the Witch's conviction. But it filled her with hope. The voice in her head – her mother's voice – was wrong. For the first time since Sena had gone missing, Martha smiled. The Witch smiled back at her – a toothless smile that lit up her face and revealed to Martha its gentleness and the great loneliness in her eyes.

A week later, a messenger arrived in Asakhua from Eoma's brother-in-law, Lalmalsawma, the lal of Tipa. The messenger brought good news: Sena was safe and with his uncle in Tipa. No one knew how the boy had survived the long trek from Asakhua on his own, but, somehow, he'd pulled it off.

'Could our mother be alive as well?' Martha asked Christine, after she'd told her aghast sister about what she'd learnt from the Witch.

'You must never go there again!' Christine cried. 'You don't know how lucky you are to be alive. Don't you know the Witch turns children into ogres? It's why no child ever goes near the bamboo grove.'

'But she was kind, Christine,' Martha replied. 'And she didn't turn me into an ogre, did she? She was right about Sena, too, wasn't she? Maybe she knows things we don't. Should we tell Pa what she said? About Nu?'

'No!' said Christine firmly. 'It would only cause him more pain. Don't you see he never talks about Nu because he's sad that she's gone?'

Martha nodded. 'You're right. We won't tell him.'

'Martha, you must never go near the bamboo grove again.' Christine's voice was stern. 'Promise me! It's not safe for you over there.'

'I won't, Christine, I promise. I'm just happy Sena is safe. I was certain he was dead,' Martha replied, hugging her sister.

Christine laughed. 'I was, too. But I had to be brave for you! I'm so glad he's okay and that he'll be home soon.'

Eoma set off for Tipa on a pony early the next morning, eager to be reunited with his son. The journey took him two days. But, when he got to his brother-in-law's hut, he found Sena dead set against returning home with him. Sena told his uncle how his father had unjustly and mercilessly thrashed him in public, and that if he was forced to return home, he would run away again. As a compromise, his uncle offered to keep the boy for a few months till he was ready to return. Heartbroken and wracked with guilt for how he'd treated Sena, Eoma accepted his brother-in-law's offer, on the condition that Sena would enrol at the primary school in Tipa.

Sena wouldn't return to Asakhua for another two years. Those two years would change who he was as a boy and shape who he would become as a man.

CHAPTER 5

Although Sena wasn't around, Sammy was no longer bullied in school. But the other children wanted nothing to do with him, a 'mixed breed' and a coward to boot. At first, Martha too avoided Sammy, blaming him for the injustice that had been done to her brother. But, in time, she forgave him and, feeling sorry for the way he was being treated by the other children, she befriended him.

Sammy and Martha walked together to school every morning and back home in the afternoon. Sammy was happy to finally have a friend his age, someone who wasn't ashamed to be seen with him.

The path to school began at the village tank, across from where Martha lived, and wound through the fields before descending through a patch of jungle to the clearing in which the shed stood. Their routine was the same each weekday. At 8 a.m., Sammy, wearing a freshly washed and crisply ironed uniform, and shiny black shoes, his hair plastered in Mangalorean coconut oil and combed back neatly, would wait by the tank for Martha. She was never on time. Sammy would watch fascinated as she'd come running up the path, out of breath, looking like she'd just rolled out of bed, scruffy and unkempt. Her white school uniform was always crumpled, her shoes muddy, and her short hair knotted and tangled. She'd storm right past Sammy, never acknowledging his presence. Undeterred, Sammy would hurry to catch up with her and they'd run as fast as they could to get to school before the bell for assembly sounded.

The afternoons were more relaxed. At three, when the school bell rang, Sammy would hurry out of class and wait patiently by the gate till Martha showed up. She'd take her time leaving, loitering about school, chatting with her friends and saying her goodbyes. Sammy didn't mind. He had nowhere else to go.

Sammy and Martha didn't speak much to each other, even on the walk back home. The one-and-a-half kilometre walk would often take them over an hour. Sometimes, on Martha's prodding, they'd take a detour to the bamboo grove, where the Witch had her shack, peering furtively through the bamboo stalks hoping they'd spot her. When they did, Martha would shout out 'Chibai!' The Witch would wave at her, a big grin on her wrinkled face. But because she'd made a promise to Christine, Martha never ventured back into the grove to meet her.

When the weather was good, Martha and Sammy would stop by the village tank and sit at its edge watching the fish or trying to skim flat pebbles on its surface like they'd seen the older boys do. It was the only time Martha allowed Sammy into her world and showed any interest in his. They'd talk about the small things that mattered to them. About their dreams and fears. 'I miss Sena a lot,' Martha said one day to Sammy, as they sat by the tank feeding the fish with the leftovers from their lunch boxes. 'I hate my father. Why did he have to beat Sena so much?'

Sammy stared moodily into the water, his guilt and shame re-surfacing. Then he whispered softly, his voice breaking: 'I'm sorry, Martha. It's all my fault.'

Martha said nothing, but when Sammy looked at her, he could see she was crying. He looked away, unsure of how to react. Wiping her tears, she said, 'No, it isn't.' They sat in silence for a while before Martha got up. Offering Sammy her hand, she yanked him to his feet. They walked home together, holding hands, nothing more said.

Sunday morning was the only time Sammy saw Martha neatly dressed and all cleaned up – her hair combed and plaited, her shoes polished. The villagers gathered at the Asakhua Church at 9 a.m. for mass. The Rego household would be up much before that. Joachim would be up by six, putting the finishing touches to his sermon. 'I don't want anything. I don't want to be disturbed. Can you all just stay out of my way for a couple of hours?' he'd growl impatiently when asked if he needed anything.

The reverend took his sermons very seriously, using stories from the Bible and interpreting them in the context of current events and real people. Mahatma Gandhi was his hero, and he would find some way of including an aspect of the Mahatma's life or his teachings into every sermon. 'Christ is the Mahatma and the Mahatma is Christ,' he liked to say, although it made the more traditional members of his congregation cringe.

While Joachim prepared his sermon at his worktable upstairs in the attic, Isabelle would begin work on lunch. The Rego family ate frugally through the week, but not on a Sunday! On Sunday, the Rego home would fill with the aroma of slow-cooked pork, fresh mutton stew and fried fish – all prepared the way Isabelle's mother had taught her. Every Sunday, Isabelle would invite one of the village families to join them for lunch. The house would echo with laughter, the dining table overflowing with food, and homemade wine and zu poured at the open bar in a corner of the living room, while Peter played the piano and Joachim led the singing. When the sun was out, the dining table would be set up on the lawn and lunch would extend all the way till four in the afternoon, till it was time for Sunday School, when the parish community would descend on the Rego home for community singing, Bible reading and the sharing of personal spiritual experiences.

By 8.30 a.m. on Sunday mornings, Reverend Pastor Joachim Rego would position himself at the entrance to the church, personally greeting every member of the congregation. The church choir would already be in, practising the hymns for the service. By 8.45 a.m., the opening hymns would begin, just as the first members of the congregation were settling down in the pews.

The high point of the Sunday service was Joachim's sermon. It usually ran about twenty minutes long, but depending on how the congregation was reacting, he would extend or cut it short. Joachim made sure he had different versions, of different lengths, from fifteen to about thirty minutes. He was a good preacher, who began each sermon with a story that set up a moral dilemma that would only be resolved at the end. This structure created an air of suspense and had the congregation hanging on to his every word. He wasn't afraid to take on controversial subjects like domestic violence, alcoholism and teenage pregnancy. But Joachim wasn't overly moralistic or harsh, and he knew how to mix the bitter with the sweet, creating a powerful tonic that the congregation willingly swallowed each week. The exceptions were his sermons about unity and peaceful coexistence.

When India won her independence in 1947, the state of Assam was a huge, sprawling land mass that spread across northeast India and had its capital in Shillong. Its mountains and forests were home to a cocktail of tribes, each with their own distinct cultural identity. In the decades preceding Independence, these tribes were actively encouraged by the British to see themselves as being distinct from Indians and India. As a result, at Independence, many tribal communities in the region were dead set against joining the Indian Union. The Indian government turned a blind eye to their demands, refusing to negotiate, which caused many who lived in India's northeast to feel betrayed and embittered.

Pastor Joachim Rego's sermons on unity and national integration were simplistic, lacked a deeper understanding of politics and ignored local sentiment. In one sermon, the pastor had thundered, holding up his hands: 'India is like the ten fingers of our hands. Each finger has a different shape and size and a different purpose. But when they work together, we Indians can create magic. There is strength in our diversity. India is home to thousands of different tribes, hundreds of languages, regions and ethnicities. If each community demands independence from the other, how will India survive? Is this not what our Mahatma, who was martyred because he fought for India's unity, taught us to resist? Will we let his sacrifice be in vain?'

Unhappy with what he felt was Joachim trivializing and disrespecting the growing local sentiment of the people of the Mizo Hills, against their integration into the larger Assam state, Eoma stood up in protest. 'Let's go,' he barked. Christine and Martha slid out of their pew obediently and followed their father out of the church, hurriedly, even as a murmur of protest rose in the congregation.

Meanwhile, the pastor, his ego bruised by Eoma's walkout, thundered on: 'Those who want us to separate from Assam, nay even from India, do us all a disservice.

They strengthen our enemies who want to see India fail as a nation. Those who make common cause with those enemies are traitors. They are anti-national. And they will be punished by God.'

By the time the sermon was done, most of the congregation had decided to support Eoma's walkout. The church was empty, except for the Rego family and a handful of others who stayed out of pity for their pastor and were embarrassed by the humiliation he'd been subjected to.

CHAPTER 6

After Mapuli's death, Eoma consciously distanced himself from his tribal roots, opting instead for a Western cultural identity built around a Christian moral framework. It was what helped him land the headmaster's job in Asakhua. This wasn't uncommon in the Mizo Hills in those days. Influenced by Christian missionaries, tribal traditions and customs increasingly came to be looked down upon by the Mizos as backward and regressive, and were replaced with those more compatible with a Western-Christian moral and cultural structure. Children were given biblical names; Western suits and dresses replaced tribal outfits; traditional spring and harvest festivals became less important than Christmas and Easter; and tribal music gave way to Western music. It would be decades before the tribes of the Mizo Hills would come to realize that their tribal and Christian identities weren't mutually exclusive.

But in the 1940s, even as great changes were taking place across the Mizo Hills, time had stood still in the village of Tipa. Sena's uncle, Lalmalsawma, the lal of Tipa, was a firm believer in the traditional Mara way of life. Under his tutelage, Sena was re-introduced to the Mara language, its customs, traditions and folklore – all of which his father had turned away from after his mother's death. Sena watched as his uncle settled disputes between villagers, delivering his judgements only after careful consideration. Watching him, Sena learnt that a leader must listen more and speak less, but be prepared to act swiftly and decisively when required.

There was nothing Sena loved more than to accompany his uncle on hunting and fishing expeditions. His uncle taught him about the forest and its many secrets: how to read the weather and the tracks of wild animals; which leaves, berries and mushrooms were good to eat and which had deadly toxins that could kill a man. Under his guidance, Sena became a superb marksman and learnt how to wield a bow and arrow, a slingshot and the dao, a traditional sword. He also learnt the art of the hunt – to lay traps and stalk his prey; to think like the animal he was stalking and to kill without hesitation or fear.

In Tipa, Sena stumbled upon a terrible truth. One morning, a barefoot, haggard, middle-aged woman, her long, matted hair tied in a bun at the back of her head, and wearing a tattered *thihni* – an exquisitely embroidered skirt typically worn only by women in the lal's family, that too only on ceremonial occasions – showed up at his uncle's hut. The woman smoked a thin pipe and her ears were embellished with heavy brass earrings. She had a noble face with sharp features, but time and circumstance had been unkind to her. When she saw Sena, her face lit up, and the tears in her eyes weren't fake. She pulled him close and whispered: 'My son, my son.'

Mapuli hadn't died of malaria as Eoma had told his children. She'd eloped with another man when Sena was a child. Eoma could have demanded that Mapuli's father return the substantial angkia he'd paid for her, but he chose to let Mapuli go in peace, hiding from the world the shame and anger he felt at her betrayal. Pretending his wife was dead, he had turned his attention to bringing up his three young children and giving them a good education.

When Mapuli heard that her son was in the care of her brother in Tipa, she'd set off on foot from her village over fifty kilometres away, where she lived with her husband and their five children. For Sena, his mother's sudden appearance left him with mixed emotions. Already reconciled to her death and with no previous memories of her, Sena found himself unable to reciprocate the love and affection the woman, who called herself his mother, showered on him. He squirmed uncomfortably, repulsed by the stale smell of tobacco and sahma on her breath, and the stench of her unwashed garments, as she ran her hands through his hair and over his face.

Through the week that Mapuli stayed in her brother's hut, she tried her best to forge a bond with her son, asking him questions about Christine and Martha, his life in Asakhua and Eoma. But Sena had no space in his heart for his prodigal mother and, while he answered all her questions politely, he kept his distance from her. At the end of the week, when it was time for Mapuli to return to her village, she wept bitterly, hugging Sena close and begging him to forgive her for the pain she'd caused him. But Sena was indifferent to her pleadings and was relieved to see her go.

Towards the end of Sena's second year in Tipa, his uncle was mauled by a tiger while on a hunting expedition. The hunting party had carried their lal back to the village on a makeshift bamboo stretcher, but by the time they got him to Tipa, he'd lost too much blood to have any hope of surviving.

The dying lal was laid out on the floor of his hut. His right arm had been chewed off by the tiger and his body was covered in deep gashes. Sena was distraught when he saw his uncle and revolted by the sight of the blood, the loose flesh and the shattered bone in his arm. When his uncle saw Sena cowering in the corner of the hut, he asked for the boy to be brought to him. With Sena kneeling by his side, he said: 'Be brave, Sena. You are a warrior unlike any other. Remember all that I have taught you and never forget who you are.'

The elaborate funeral befitted a man of Lalmalsawma's stature. After he'd passed, his body was washed in warm water and dressed in his finest ceremonial clothes. The dead lal was placed on a mat in a reclining position, as if sitting up and greeting all those who came to pay their last respects. Above him, on a wooden shelf, were placed rice, meat and eggs as offerings to the gods. For three days Lalmalsawma's body lay in state, while the mourners drank, sang, danced and feasted in his honour. On the evening of the third day, he was buried in a grave dug by the young men of the village just outside his house. A wooden post, with the heads of the animals the lal had killed in his time on earth, served as a tombstone.

CHAPTER 7

A month after his uncle's death, Sena reluctantly returned home to his family in Asakhua. In the two years that he'd been away, the legend of Sena had grown. He was now the undisputed leader in school – and that wasn't just because he'd grown taller and more muscular than all the other village boys.

'He's grown so tall and strong because he was fed beef and pork twice a day by my uncle,' Martha told Sammy proudly. But Sena struggled to adjust to life in Asakhua, which revolved around school and church, unlike in Tipa, where he spent all his free time honing his shooting, fighting and hunting skills under the guidance of his uncle. In Tipa, Sena had developed a cynical view of the idea of an omnipresent god. In Asakhua, such cynicism was taboo.

Eoma believed that the key to Sena's future was a good education, and it hadn't helped that he'd fallen behind after two years of lax academic supervision in Tipa. He pushed Sena hard at school to catch up academically with the other children his age and there was no let-up at home. Eoma took great pride in the home library he'd painstakingly built over the years. He loved the classics and poetry, and had a collection of over 200 books that he'd picked up from old-book sellers in Aizawl. 'You must read, Sena. You don't know how lucky you are to have a library at home. Why do you think I keep buying these books? For show? I haven't seen you read a single book since you got back from Tipa. Can't you at least try?'

Unrelentingly badgered by his father, Sena grew increasingly sullen, resentful and aggressive. When he returned from Tipa, Sena found it difficult to relate to the other village boys his age, who bonded over Western music and fashion, both of which Sena cared little for. With no friends and a father he despised, Sena grew increasingly isolated and lonely. The only people Sena found he could be himself with, and who loved him for who he was, were his sisters, Christine and Martha. But even they couldn't make up for the emptiness he felt inside after his uncle's death.

'I was thinking of putea,' Sena said wistfully to Martha, as they sat on the rocks one summer afternoon, dipping their feet in the village tank. 'I wish you'd met him, Martha. You would have loved him. He was the bravest and wisest man I've ever met.'

Martha reached out and squeezed Sena's hand. 'I know how much he meant to you, Sena. I'm glad you had time to spend with him and to learn from him. But don't be sad that he's gone. He'll live forever in your heart, and he'll always look out for you and protect you.'

When Sena had returned to Asakhua, he was surprised to discover that Martha and Sammy had become inseparable friends. Sena was at first annoyed by Sammy's constant presence by Martha's side. But, when he saw how much Sammy meant to her, he thawed, forgiving Sammy's betrayal and accepting his fawning friendship. Sena tried to teach Sammy how to shoot, stalk prey and hunt, just as his uncle had taught him. But these weren't skills Sammy had a natural inclination for, and he made little progress. However, with Sena as a friend and a role model, Sammy grew more confident of himself.

In Sena, Sammy found the brother Peter never was.

For the first six years of his life, Peter had been the only child at home – never having to compete for his parent's attention or time. Sammy's arrival changed all that. Unlike Sammy, who was untidy, underconfident and painfully shy, Peter had always been well-groomed, confident and extremely precocious around adults. He played no sport, hated the outdoors, and spent his free time reading and playing the piano. When he was eight, Peter was shipped off to St. Edmund's School in Shillong, then the capital of Assam, because his mother didn't think that the village school in Asakhua was good enough for her beloved son. The school was run by the Irish Christian Brothers, who believed nothing shaped a boy's character better than strict discipline, sport, academic excellence and a sound public thrashing if the child dared show any signs of disobedience, independent thought or question the authority of those in charge. Peter would always associate Sammy's arrival with his exile to boarding school, where the harsh discipline and emphasis on sport made him miserable. It made him resent Sammy bitterly, and that bitterness he would never outgrow.

On Sammy's tenth birthday, Peter, who had come home from St. Edmund's on vacation, incensed by the affection and presents that were showered on his sibling by his parents and burning with jealousy, revealed to Sammy the secret his family had carefully shielded him from: 'You aren't really a part of our family, Sammy. You were adopted. Mamma and Pa brought you home from the orphanage.'

Distraught, Sammy rushed to confront his father. 'Is it true, Pa? Am I adopted?'

Joachim had always known Sammy would one day ask him this question, and yet, when it came, he wasn't prepared for it. So, instead of telling Sammy the truth, he offered him a sermon: 'Your mother and I love you very much, Sammy – as much as we love Peter. You're a blessing, a gift from God that we will always be grateful for. I see a similarity between you and your namesake in the Bible, Samuel. He was adopted by Eli, the priest, and raised to be a prophet. Like him, you too are destined to serve God and do great things.' Then he put his arm protectively around his son and pulled him close.

'Am I adopted, Pa?' Sammy asked once again, pulling away.

There was to be no escaping the question the son was asking of his father. And so, Joachim told Sammy all that Sister Theresa had told him and Isabelle – that his mother had died in childbirth and that he'd been abandoned at the doorstep of the orphanage. No one knew who his real parents were or where he'd come from. Joachim told his son that it was Jesus who'd saved his life and brought them together as a family.

But Joachim's words, and Peter's subsequent apology, did little to calm the storm that raged in Sammy's heart. From that day on, Sammy felt terribly insecure, overcome by the irrational fear that his parents would stop loving him and return him to the orphanage. This caused him to become more guarded, submissive and secretive, bottling up his real feelings, and going out of his way to be the dutiful son – so as never to give his parents any excuse to stop loving him.

When Sammy told Martha and Sena what he'd discovered, they looked uncomfortable. Then Sena said: 'We know, Sammy. We've known all along. Most people in the village know. It's why the children taunt you and call you a mixed breed.'

Stung by Sena's words, Sammy burst into tears. Martha reached out to comfort Sammy, pulling him close and gently patting his back as he wept. Then, glaring at Sena, she said: 'How could you be so mean? Why did you have to tell him that?'

'It's the truth.' Sena was defensive. 'Isn't it better he knows the truth?'

'He didn't need to hear that. How does it matter?'

'Sure. Nothing matters,' Sena snarled, his anger rising. 'Let's all cover up the truth. Let's all lie. It's easier for everyone that way. Our father is an expert at it. Do you know he lied to us about Nu? She's alive, Martha. Not dead! She left him and married another man. I met her in Tipa, Martha. We too have been living a lie our entire lives.'

Stunned silence followed Sena's outburst. Even Sammy stifled his sobs, silently wiping away the tears from his face. It was early evening and the shadows had begun to lengthen. The cacophony of crows settling down in the trees for the night filled the air. Sena, Sammy and Martha sat on the rocks beside the village tank, peering moodily into its dark waters, nothing said between them. Then Martha broke the silence: 'I know,' she said, matter-of-factly. 'I've known for a long time about Nu. The Witch told me.'

* * *

When Peter was seventeen, he passed the Trinity School of Music eighth-grade piano exam with distinction and was offered a full scholarship to pursue a diploma in London. It could have been the stepping stone to a career as a classical musician. Instead, Peter chose the National Defence

Academy, or the NDA as it is more familiarly known, and the life of an army man just as his mother had wanted.

Isabelle's father, Brigadier (Retd.) Vivian Lazarado, was a decorated war hero who had won a Victoria Cross at the Battle of Megiddo, in Palestine, where the British Army defeated the Turks in the First World War. As her father rose through the ranks, each promotion brought with it a bigger bungalow and a larger retinue of batmen, gardeners, cooks and helpers that made life quite easy for Isabelle and her seven siblings. Besides, life in the cantonment had its own charm. The gymkhana was the hub of the Lazarado family's social life, where the children met and socialized with other young men and women their age. From golf and tennis to dances and picnics, the Lazarado children were happy and secure in their little cocoon, sheltered from the harsh realities of India. They turned a blind eye to the sacrifices, suffering and hard work the brigadier had put in to get to a position where his wife and children could enjoy the perks of his rank and status, protected from the millions of impoverished Indians who'd grown tired of British rule and were hungry for independence.

While Isabelle desperately wanted Peter to live the idyllic cantonment life she'd had as a child, his life would be far from idyllic. There would be wars to fight, injuries to suffer, and months spent recuperating alone in military hospitals as he worked his way up slowly through the ranks, even as the old order gave way to the new – in which the army and its officers didn't have the same privileges in independent India as they did when the British ruled.

Unlike his wife, Joachim was a pacifist who hated the idea of Peter joining the army. He'd hoped Peter would follow in his footsteps and choose a life dedicated to God, or even become a concert pianist or a composer – anything but the army! But Peter loved his mother more than anyone else in the world and would do anything to please her. And so, to the army he went.

CHAPTER 8

The years passed by quickly. As Sammy and Martha entered adolescence, and Martha transformed into a woman, their friendship that had endured over the years, began to unravel. As far as Sammy was concerned, Martha wasn't just the most beautiful girl in the world. She was kind, gentle and funny, and she understood him better than anyone else did. He loved her. And he wanted her to love him back. But Martha had outgrown her childhood friendship with Sammy and, while she cared for him deeply, she wanted something more.

When Sammy turned fifteen, he secured admission to the Baptist Higher Secondary School in Lunglei, along with Martha and four other children from Asakhua. The group left the village early each morning and walked for an hour through the forest to get to the Aizawl–Lunglei Road, from where they'd be ferried to school in an ancient Land Rover, packed with children from villages on Lunglei's outskirts. Their return journey unfolded similarly. One of the boys in the group was Rempuia, two years older than Sammy, and captain of the school football team. Rempuia, who had viciously bullied Sammy in their childhood, had grown into a good-looking, well-built, extroverted lad – the sort of boy any girl would fall in love with. And Martha did.

Sammy was sure it wouldn't last. He was certain it was just a silly crush and that Martha would soon see Rempuia wasn't the one for her. Then things would go back to the way they had been between them, before he showed up. Besides, Rempuia had a reputation for not sticking with any one girl for too long. *Why would he when he can have any girl he wants?* Sammy thought. *Martha will get her heart broken!*

But as the weeks turned into months, it seemed that for Rempuia, Martha wasn't just a passing fling. Now, Martha and Sammy hardly saw each other any more, except on the long walk to school in the morning and back home in the afternoon. But even those walks were torturous for Sammy. Martha and Rempuia walked together, laughing, joking and often holding hands. There was no space for Sammy in that relationship. And, as the distance between them grew, Sammy's resentment and jealousy began consuming him. Some nights, he'd lie awake thinking of ways in which he could attract Martha's attention. To get her to see how unfairly she'd treated him – her true friend, the real love of her life. Sammy even thought of running away from home – like Sena had – leaving her a note telling her that he'd run away because of her. But he couldn't bring himself to do that. Instead, he chose to wallow in self-pity and let his teenage heartbreak overwhelm him. Like Gandhi, Sammy opted for satyagraha and non-cooperation, ignoring Martha and refusing to speak to her.

While Sammy battled his teenage angst, Sena joined a residential coaching program in Lunglei, preparing for the Assam State Civil Services exam. He'd return to Asakhua only on the weekends, when Sammy would visit him at home and they'd spend time together. It was on these visits that Sammy would sometimes run into Martha. But when Martha tried to engage him in conversation, he'd ignore her. Upset by his rudeness and indifference, Martha shut him out of her life.

But it didn't last. Or rather, Martha and Rempuia didn't last. A year into their romance – that Martha had thought would last forever – Rempuia dumped Martha for Ang Arte, the captain of the girls' basketball team. When Sammy heard the news, he felt vindicated. *I knew all along that Rempuia was an arrogant, selfish pig and that he'd break Martha's heart*, he told himself smugly.

With Martha now the butt of vicious jokes in the village, it didn't take long for the predictable showdown between Sena and Rempuia to come to a head. It came at a football game, where Rempuia and Sena were on opposing teams. At some point, Rempuia was racing down the pitch with the ball when Sena brought him down with a vicious tackle. A furious Rempuia got back to his feet and took a wild swing at Sena, catching him flush on the nose. Blood spurted out of Sena's nostrils, dripping down his face and on to his T-shirt.

The blow released Sena from any pretence that the fight was about anything other than Martha. 'You fucking loser, you cheated on her! I'll kill you,' he snarled as he hurled himself at Rempuia and threw him to the ground, punching him in his stomach and face again and again. Soon, members of both teams had entered the fray and a proper brawl ensued, while the referee desperately tried to restore order and the spectators watched the unfolding action with glee.

The dark cloud that had hung over Sammy all year lifted that day. The old Sammy was back. The brooding, miserable fool was gone. His father was the first to notice. 'Someone seems to be in a good mood today,' he joked, when Sammy flopped down next to him on the sofa in the living room after school, instead of storming up the stairs to his room in the attic.

Sammy kicked off his shoes and threw his arms around his father. 'I know I've been selfish. I'm sorry, Pa.'

'It's okay, son. It's tough being a teenager.' His father smiled.

That evening, Sammy walked across to Martha's home with his hair neatly combed, a brand-new pair of jeans, leather boots, a checked-blue shirt and cowboy hat, and wearing a week's quota of his father's 'Chanel Pour

Monsieur' deodorant. It would be awkward, he knew, but he was determined. He had been given an opening back into Martha's life, and he wasn't going to let it go.

Eoma was clipping the bougainvillaea that ran up the walls of the old mission home when Sammy walked in through the front gate. Eoma looked down at him quizzically. 'Haven't seen you around in a while. Going to a party?'

Sammy squirmed awkwardly. 'No, sir. No party,' he mumbled. 'Is Sena home?' He was suddenly conscious of the fact that he was overdressed for his supposedly casual and unannounced visit.

'No, he isn't,' said Eoma, returning to trimming the bougainvillaea. Sammy waited, unsure of what to do next. 'Sena and Christine have gone to the dentist in Lunglei. Christine had a tooth that needed to be pulled out. They'll be home for dinner. Martha is home if you'd like to meet her.'

'Yes, I'll go say hi,' said Sammy, trying to sound as casual as he could. He hurried past the ladder Eoma was perched on. It was dark inside – the evening lamps hadn't yet been lit.

Sammy walked up the dark stairs to Martha's room. The door was shut, but he could see a sliver of light shine from under the door. He paused. He'd ignored Martha, not spoken to her in months, and now here he was, outside her door, with no prior notice. *What will I say to her?* he wondered. *Will she even want to see me?* But it was too late now to slink away. So, he knocked on Martha's door firmly.

'Who is it?'

'It's me, Martha. Sammy,' he said, trying to sound confident.

'Sammy? What are you doing here? What do you want?' She didn't sound pleased at all.

'I've come to meet Sena. Any idea where he is?' Sammy lied, his confidence wavering.

Sammy heard Martha shuffle across the wooden floor. Then there she was, in the doorway, a silhouette lit up by the gas lamp behind her flickering on her table. She wore her home pyjamas and an old flannel shirt. She looked like she'd been crying. Her hair was dishevelled, her eyes swollen. She looked vulnerable and broken. Sammy felt a surge of love overwhelm him. He wanted to pull her close and tell her how much he loved her. And that she was safe and everything would be all right.

Martha took a step back towards her table, her hands folded across her chest, as Sammy walked into the room and shut the door behind him. 'Sena's not at home and I'm a little busy right now,' she said, sounding impatient, but her voice cracked ever so slightly, giving away her true emotional state.

That was enough for Sammy – a tiny opening. A moment that may never come again. He grabbed hold of it as if his life depended on it. 'The truth is, Martha, I didn't come to see Sena. I came to see you. I know we haven't spoken to each other in a long time. And I'm sorry, I've behaved like an idiot with you. But I've missed you. You're my best friend. I love you and I've been really lonely without you.' Sammy raced through what he had to say before he lost his nerve.

Martha didn't say anything. Sammy shuffled uncomfortably, waiting for her to respond. When she didn't, his confidence began to falter and he looked away, unable to hold her gaze, fearful of the anger that would be unleashed upon him.

After what seemed like forever, Martha broke her silence. 'I think you should sit down,' she said, nodding towards the bed, on which were piled stacks of her clothes, books, and her old guitar. The bed looked like it hadn't been made in days. Sammy sat uncertainly at its foot, staring at the floor, unsure of what to do next. *Maybe she thinks I've gone mad,* he thought.

Then, Martha walked across and sat down beside him. Her scent washed over Sammy, bringing with it an overwhelming sense of peace and joy, like he'd never felt before. She placed her head on Sammy's shoulder and slipped her fingers through his, as if reassuring him it was okay. That she wasn't upset with him. And that maybe, just maybe, she could love him back just like he loved her.

CHAPTER 9

If the forties in the Mizo Hills were defined first by the havoc caused by the Japanese war machine as it hacked its way through the jungles of Burma and Assam during the Second World War, and later the promise of a new beginning, offered by Independence, the fifties would be a decade of wasted opportunities.

In Asakhua, as in most of the northeast, esoteric terms such as 'the temples of modern India' held no meaning and were heard only on All India Radio news broadcasts. The development of the region and its problems were of little consequence for the new ruling elite in Delhi, who referred derogatorily to the indigenous people of the northeast as 'chinkies'. In turn, the indigenous people referred to those of non-mongoloid stock simply as 'Indians' or '*Vais*' – to clearly establish that they didn't consider themselves Indian and had little in common with India.

Although Sammy had lived in Asakhua all his life, as far as the village boys were concerned, he'd always remain a 'mixed breed', a 'Vai', and would never be one of theirs. Over time, Sammy had become indifferent to their taunts and stopped trying to befriend them. Instead, he'd developed a caustic and self-deprecating sense of humour, which he used as a weapon to defuse situations with the potential to spiral into violence. The only one who stood up for Sammy and treated him with respect was Sena. When he was around, Sammy felt safe.

Sena was a natural leader. While he was a superb footballer, and the village boxing and wrestling champion, it was his hunting and shooting skills that set him apart from everyone else. Learnt from his uncle in Tipa, much to Eoma's disgust, Sena was a natural at tracking animals. As far as Eoma was concerned, hunting was for the savages. But for Sena, who'd struggled all through school, hunting allowed him to express himself in ways algebra and poetry never could. Sena was an instinctive hunter, who could patiently stalk his prey for hours, waiting for the perfect opportunity. When it came, he didn't hesitate, going for the kill with clinical precision.

Every New Year's Eve, the village boys would set out to hunt a wild boar that would be served at the dance that evening. The tradition was a coming-of-age ritual – an opportunity for the older boys to prove they were worthy of being called men. If they returned empty-handed, they would be subject to ridicule and scorn by the entire community.

On New Year's Eve in 1958, it fell upon Sena to lead the hunting party. In previous years, Sammy hadn't been allowed to join the boys on the hunt. But this year Sena was in charge and Sammy begged him to let him tag along. Sena looked concerned. 'Are you sure, man? Could get dangerous out there.'

'I'm ready, Sena. I've been practising with Pa's rifle for months now. I've become a good shot. It will be fine,' Sammy said earnestly.

'Okay,' Sena conceded. 'But you stick close to me and you do exactly like I tell you.'

Sammy was thrilled. He'd dreamt of being part of the hunt for as long as he could remember. *Maybe I'll be the one to shoot the boar!* he thought.

'Absolutely not. Not him!' thundered Rempuia when Sammy showed up on the morning of the hunt with Sena. The other boys were concerned, too. 'Look at what he's wearing! He's obviously never hunted before,' said Lairozama, one of the older boys.

Sammy squirmed uncomfortably in his blue denim jeans, red sneakers and a long-sleeved, bright-orange flannel shirt. His jet-black hair had been oiled with coconut oil and neatly combed back. He carried his father's Daisy .22 rifle over his shoulder.

'I think he's ready for tonight's dance,' chortled Rempuia, falling to his knees with exaggerated whoops of laughter. The others broke out into big grins. Sammy felt small and humiliated.

'I'll take responsibility for him. Besides, we've all got to get into our hunting gear, so he's obviously not wearing that. Let's get on with it, or we'll have bigger problems than him if we come back empty-handed,' growled Sena, firmly putting an end to the rebellion.

Half an hour later, the boys set off into the forest at a brisk pace. Sena led the single file, Sammy following close behind. Sena had painted the boys' faces in green and brown stripes to help them blend into the foliage. He'd made them all strip down to their waist and forced them to splatter their bodies and hair with wet mud to get rid of any smells that could give their presence away to the wild animals in the jungle. Each of them held a weapon – bows and arrows, machetes, old muzzle loaders. Sammy's .22 was the only modern weapon in the hunting party. Sena, his shoulder-length hair held in place with a bandana and leather sandals on his feet, carried an ancient muzzle loader.

The hunting party had been marching silently through the thick jungle, in sweltering heat, for over three hours when Sena suddenly stopped. Sammy, drenched in sweat and out of breath, was grateful for the break. He immediately flopped down under a giant banyan tree, his rifle clattering on the rocks beside him. 'Get up,' hissed Sena, 'and don't make a fucking sound.'

Sammy staggered to his feet and picked up his rifle. Sena, crouching low, left the narrow path they'd been walking on, pushing his way through the dense undergrowth. He made no sound. The others followed him, Sammy now bringing up the rear, his rifle clutched tight in front of him.

Ten minutes later, they came to the edge of a clearing and saw what Sena had sensed. A massive lone boar was digging up the jungle floor, looking for tubers and roots. It was oblivious to their presence.

Still crouching low, Sena turned around and said, 'We're going to have to fan out and surround him. I don't want a single sound from any of you till we're in position. If he hears us, he'll make a break for it. Got it?' The boys had hunted together before and knew the drill well. Wordlessly, they began to move off in twos and threes to encircle the boar.

Sammy set off behind Sena, trying to blend into the foliage. He could feel his heart thud and sweat pour down his face. He was nervous and afraid, unlike Sena, who moved through the undergrowth like a shadow. As they walked into a smaller clearing, Sena began to load his gun and search for a spot from where he could get an unobstructed view of the boar.

Just then, the stillness of the jungle was broken by Rempuia's voice: 'Spread the circle wider. Stop behaving like a sissy.'

The advantage the boys had was lost. The sound carried to the boar. It snorted angrily and stomped its feet. Then it made a break for it, racing into the jungle, headed straight towards Sena and Sammy.

Sena sensed the approaching danger and leapt to one side. But Sammy hadn't seen the boar charge and was late to react. Before he could move out of the way, the boar was upon him and had sent him flying like a rag doll into a thorny thicket. Sammy was wounded in his thigh and bleeding, but he'd escaped being gored. As he emerged unsteadily from the thicket, his body shaking uncontrollably in terror, Sammy found himself face-to-face with the boar, that had stopped in its tracks and was stomping and snorting angrily, its hackles up.

Sammy froze. He lost control of his limbs, and a warm stream of piss began to flow down his legs as he begged his God silently: *Please, Jesus, please, please, please …*

Tired of waiting for Sammy to make his move, the boar let out a loud snort and charged, its head lowered, its tusk aimed straight at Sammy's groin.

Just then, a gun went off. The boar squealed in pain, veering away at the last moment and racing past a trembling Sammy, who collapsed in a heap on the floor of the forest. Then Sammy saw Sena, his old muzzle loader still smoking, step forward and walk quickly to him. 'Sammy, Sammy, are you okay, man? Don't move. I've got you,' he said with an unusual softness.

Tears poured down Sammy's face. 'It almost killed me, man. It got me in my leg!'

Sena put his arms around Sammy and helped him to a clump of rocks. There was a deep gash in his thigh where the boar's tusk had grazed him. 'It's an ugly gash, Sammy, but it won't kill you,' said Sena, as he unsheathed his hunting knife and cut away Sammy's jeans from around the wound. 'I'm going to get something to stop the bleeding. Sit tight and don't move.' Sena strode off into the jungle.

He was soon back with a handful of herbs that he mashed into a paste with wet mud. He applied the paste to the wound and wrapped it up with his bandana. 'You're going to be fine, man. You're lucky. This could easily have been bye, bye, Sammy!'

Sammy said nothing, embarrassed by the wet patch around his crotch and his tears.

Just as Sena had finished bandaging the wound, the forest came alive with the excited whooping of the boys who were carrying the dead boar, now hanging from a bamboo pole. Hugging Sena, Langfuia said: 'It's your kill, man. You shot him straight behind the head. He was dead even as he ran. He just didn't know it!' The other boys laughed.

Sammy watched them sullenly, thinking: *If only I'd seen the boar first, I would have shot him and been the hero instead of Sena.*

The boys examined the dead boar and marvelled at its size. Then their attention turned to Sammy. Rempuia walked up to him and chortled at the wet patch: 'Hey, guys, Sammy's pissed his pants again!'

Humiliated and upset, Sammy struggled to get up to his feet, trying to cover the telltale wet patch with his hands.

Rempuia wasn't done. 'Pissed your pants again, eh, Sammy? Hunting isn't for sissies like you. Go back to India, man.' He pushed his face so close to Sammy's that Sammy could smell his foul breath. All the boys began to laugh. Tears began to well up in Sammy's eyes again.

Sena stepped forward and grabbed Rempuia by the collar; pulling him away from Sammy, he flung him to the ground. 'Shut up, Rempuia. Don't talk to him like that, man. He's one of us,' he snarled.

Rempuia, furious at being humiliated in front of the other boys, leapt to his feet, his fists ready for battle. 'Just because he's your friend, don't make him one of us. He's a mixed breed, a Vai. He can never be one of us,' he spat back.

One of the older boys, Rian, stepped in before it got ugly. 'Come on, guys, we've got to get this little piglet back for the feast tonight. You guys can fight later.'

Four of the boys hauled the bamboo pole with the boar up on to their shoulders. The party set off in a single file back to the village – Sammy limping at the rear end. As they marched back to Asakhua, the hunters chanted a *hlado*, a chant to celebrate a successful hunt.

On the day the rich man performs a great feast,
The village sounds with joy and laughter.
But we poor men achieve great fame,
When the hills echo chants of our hunted victory.

CHAPTER 10

A full moon peeped through the light winter mist that hung over Asakhua that night. Bathed in the diffused moonlight and lit by hundreds of oil lamps placed on the boundary walls, walkways and windowsills, and its old brass bell tolling in the night, the Baptist Church of Asakhua stood like a beacon of hope, a symbol of God's great love and compassion for mankind. The New Year's Eve service was a thanksgiving for keeping the villagers safe through the year.

By ten that night, when Reverend Pastor Rego began the service, the chapel was packed, with only a little standing room at the back of the chapel. Every man, woman and child in the congregation was formally dressed. All the men wore deep-blue, grey or black suits with ties and bows of different colours and formal black shoes. The women wore puans in muted tones of black, blue or red, with heavily embroidered blouses accessorized with matching shoes, gloves and shawls as protection from the cold.

But for Sammy, the only person who stood out was Martha. She wore a strapless, deep-blue tube gown in satin, a narrow belt at the waist and a big bow at the low back offset by a black bolero. To complement her outfit, she wore an understated mother-of-pearl pendant set in silver with matching earrings, her long hair combed neatly for a change and a thin plastic headband holding it all in place.

All through the service, Sammy looked furtively back across the aisle at Martha, hoping to catch her eye. And when he did, her face lit up, acknowledging his presence with a shy smile, leaving Sammy feeling over the moon, helping him forget the pain from the wound the boar had inflicted and the embarrassment of the morning.

Sammy and Martha had kept their love for each other a secret. Martha preferred it that way, unsure of how Eoma would react when he found out. But that night, Sammy had decided he wasn't going to hold back. He no longer cared what anyone thought. His thigh had been heavily bandaged and he'd swallowed a couple of painkillers to dull the pain. His head felt woozy, but he wouldn't have missed the dance for anything in the world. He wanted the whole world to know how he felt about Martha.

Despite the solemn air of the thanksgiving service, the congregation was restless in anticipation of the night's festivities. The pastor knew this and he kept his homily short: 'Tomorrow, we begin a new year. But before we lose ourselves in celebrating it tonight, let's take a moment to give thanks for the year gone by – for our loved ones, for our friends, for all the blessings we've received this year. Let us pray that in the new year, God strengthens our families, our community and our nation, and that we may continue to submit ourselves to his will. Amen.'

When the service came to an end, the congregation lined up at the exit, as was tradition, to thank their pastor. Sammy stood beside his father, who insisted on dragging out each exchange, ignoring the growing impatience of those at the back of the line waiting to get out.

When Eoma and his children stepped up, Joachim singled Sena out for special attention. Putting an arm around him, he said, 'Thank you for saving Sammy's life, Sena. If not for you, tonight may have been a night of mourning for us instead of a celebration.'

Sena was caught off-guard and stammered: 'No, no, it was really nothing, pastor. Nothing would have happened to him.'

'That's not what I hear,' Joachim shot back, quickly switching subjects so as not to embarrass Sena or Sammy further. 'How is your preparation for the civil services exam going?'

'I've been working really hard, pastor. I think I will make it this time,' mumbled Sena.

'I'm sure you will, son. Never give up. It doesn't matter how many times you fall. All that matters is whether or not you get up again,' Joachim said, patting Sena on his back affectionately.

While Joachim and Sammy wished each member of the congregation, Isabelle and Peter – who had come home on vacation – stationed themselves behind a solid wooden table in the chapel courtyard on which were heaped mounds of plum cake and shot glasses filled with homemade wine. The wine was extremely popular and would disappear as soon as the glasses had been re-filled. Soon, groups of tipsy, boisterous villagers were navigating their way down the steep village path to the dance.

The event was organized under a giant tent set up on the football field. A wooden platform served as the dance floor. At its edge was a stage, large enough for a five-piece band that would perform through the night. Spreading out from the dance floor, like spokes from a hub, were rectangular tables that could seat eight, each reserved by a family.

When Sena and Sammy got there, they headed straight to the bar that had been set up outside the tent and was the staging post for the young men of the village. The boys from the hunting party were already there, laughing at a very drunk Rempuia's jokes. Rempuia waved Sena and Sammy over, calling out loudly, 'Hey look, it's the mighty Sena with his little Vai, together as always!'

Sena ignored him and walked to the other end of the bar. Sammy quickened his pace, trying to avoid Rempuia. But Rempuia was still smarting from the humiliation of the morning, and alcohol had only made him more resentful. He staggered across to where Sena and Sammy were collecting their drinks. Putting his arm around Sammy's neck, he pulled him close in an uncomfortable bear hug and whispered seductively into his ear: 'How are you, sissy Vai boy?'

'Leave him alone, Rempuia,' Sena snarled. Rempuia tightened his grip around Sammy's neck instead and kissed him on the cheek. The boys who had gathered around them burst out laughing.

Sena slammed his drink down on the bar and yanked Rempuia's arm from around Sammy's neck, pushing him away. 'Leave him alone and piss off, Rempuia. You're drunk.'

'What is he to you?' taunted Rempuia, 'Why are you always protecting him?'

Sena didn't reply. Instead, he herded Sammy away from the bar and into the tent.

Rempuia called out after them: 'Hey, sissy Vai boy, save a dance for me!'

Sammy could hear the boys laugh even as Sena and he walked into the tent.

The Rego family had one of the tables closest to the dance floor. Joachim, Isabelle and Peter were already seated by the time Sammy got there. Eoma, Christine and Martha had settled down a few tables away. Joachim walked over to their table. 'Thank you for the wonderful job the parish committee has done, Eoma,' he gushed.

Eoma accepted Joachim's compliment with humility and told him that Sammy had also contributed as a volunteer. 'He's a wonderful young man, your son. So kind and thoughtful,' Eoma said, waving Sammy over. Sammy walked across and stood beside his father.

'I've hardly seen Sammy this Christmas vacation. He's at your home with Sena more than he is at ours,' said Joachim, laughing.

'He's family, pastor. He's always welcome in our home,' replied Eoma.

With less than half an hour left for the countdown to the new year, the band struck up a rock'n'roll song. There was a flurry of activity as everyone scrambled for a partner. Martha walked over to Sammy and asked: 'Want to dance?'

'Yes, sure,' Sammy replied, feigning nonchalance.

Sammy led Martha to the centre of the packed dance floor, where he knew it would be difficult for her family to keep an eye on her. He'd never danced with Martha before. The wound in his thigh hurt and, at first, his dance moves were laboured and clumsy. To cover up his awkwardness, he tried engaging Martha in conversation. But the music was just too loud, and she couldn't hear him over it. A few songs later, the band switched to a slower number, triggering an exodus of couples from the dance floor. Martha looked at Sammy uncertainly, but when he stepped up and held out his hand, she took it without any hesitation and slipped easily into his arms. Only a handful of couples were dancing now and Sammy could see they were attracting attention. 'Your family is watching us,' Sammy whispered, as Martha nestled her head on his shoulder.

'I don't care,' she shot back. 'I think they know how I feel about you.'

'Does Sena know?'

'I haven't spoken to him about you. Why, has he said something?'

'No, he hasn't,' Sammy said. 'But I'm going to have to speak to him soon. He's my friend and I don't want to keep any secrets from him.'

'Let me speak to him first,' Martha replied. 'It will be better that way.'

A little before midnight, an enthusiastic master of ceremonies took to the stage. 'It's almost time. Get on the floor, everyone. You don't want to be standing alone when the clock strikes midnight,' he screeched into the microphone. The announcement triggered a mad dash back to the dance floor. No one was left behind. Families huddled together, forming closed circles, their arms intertwined. Joachim, Isabelle, Peter and Sammy hugged each other tight as the countdown began: 'Ten, nine, eight, seven, six, five, four, three, two, one … Happy new year 1959! Happy new year!'

As fireworks went off in the night sky, the band struck up '*Auld Lang Syne*'.

Should auld acquaintance be forgot
And never brought to mind?
Should auld acquaintance be forgot

And the days of auld lang syne?
For auld lang syne, my dear
For auld lang syne
We'll drink a cup of kindness yet
For the sake of auld lang syne.

Soon, the dance floor was transformed into a mass of boisterous people wishing each other a happy new year. For those few minutes, the villagers of Asakhua were one people, celebrating the endless possibilities that the new year offered.

Sammy grabbed Martha's hand and they slipped out of the tent unnoticed, racing across the empty football field – away from the glare of the lights, the laughter and the blaring music – to a darkened patch at the other end in the shadow of a giant oak tree. They rested against the tree to catch their breath. Sammy reached out for Martha. He ran his fingers through her hair, looking into her brown eyes. She stared right back at him, her breath increasingly ragged. Then she reached up and pulled his face to hers, kissing him. Sammy kissed her back hungrily. When they finally pulled away, she whispered: 'Happy new year, Sammy. I hope you have a good one!'

Sammy kissed her forehead, then cupping her flushed face in his hands, he whispered back: 'Happy new year, Martha.' They stood there for a while, holding each other, listening to the music and the sounds of laughter floating across the field.

'I think we should go back before your family sends out a search party for you,' Sammy said, grinning from ear to ear. Martha nodded, smiling, slipping her arm through his as they walked back to the tent, two teenagers hopelessly in love and at peace with the world.

CHAPTER 11

Sammy's seventeenth birthday – 14 April 1959 – began inauspiciously. The villagers of Asakhua were roused at dawn by an anguished, full-throated wail that pierced through the dense fog that hung over the village. When minutes went by and the wailing hadn't stopped, the villagers began stepping reluctantly out of their bamboo huts, into the cold of dawn, to see what the commotion was all about. Soon, the entire village had gathered – huddled in little groups outside each hut, peering into the fog, searching for the source of the disturbance, unsure of what to do next.

Then someone shouted: 'It's the Witch! It's the Witch, wailing!'

The villagers let out a collective sigh of exasperation. They'd grown tired of the Witch's, or as she was known locally, the Dawi Thiam Pitar's, frequent shenanigans and many of them cynically dismissed her early morning wailing as another one of her attention-seeking ploys. The cynics retreated into the warmth and comfort of their huts to try and eke out a few more minutes of sleep. The more adventurous clambered down the slippery, slush-covered path that led to the giant bamboo grove at the edge of the village.

When the villagers got to the periphery of the giant bamboo grove, in which the Witch had built her shack, the first rays of the early morning sun had begun breaking through the giant bamboo stalks and the fog that had enveloped the village began to lift. It was only then that the villagers saw that the bamboo had flowered overnight. From each node on every plant grew, spiky pale-yellow flowers, thin-stemmed and without petals. Backlit by the rays of the early morning sun, the sudden flowering of the bamboo presented a stunning spectacle that filled the villagers with awe. But the elders were filled with a sense of foreboding. They remembered the last bamboo flowering, forty-eight years ago, and the devastation it had wrought on the Mizo Hills. They knew that the flowering signalled the beginning of the Mautam.

'What is the Mautam, Pa?' Sammy asked his father.

'An old tribal superstition, Sammy. They say when the bamboo flowers, it bears fruit and dies. Then swarms of rats come out of the jungle to eat the bamboo fruit and seeds, and what follows is a terrible famine. That cycle is called the Mautam,' the pastor replied.

When the Witch had been shooed back into her shack and her wailing had stopped, the villagers began to disperse.

As Sammy and his father trudged home, Zofakzuala, the postman, called out to them: 'Sammy, a registered letter for you! It must be important. Hope it's good news!'

Sammy's heart skipped a beat. He knew what it was, but he wasn't sure he wanted to open it. The pastor looked at Sammy disappointedly. Zofakzuala handed over the letter and got him to sign for it. Sammy quickly slipped the letter under the waistband at the back of his pyjamas and pulled his sweater down over it.

'You don't have to do this, Sammy,' Joachim said. 'You have lots of other options.'

'I know, Pa. But this is something I really want to do,' Sammy said, even though he knew that wasn't what Joachim wanted to hear.

When they got home, Isabelle was waiting for them at the dining table with plum cake and hot coffee, to celebrate Sammy's birthday. But Sammy didn't care about his birthday. All he could think about was the letter. 'It's come, Mamma,' Sammy said, handing the letter to his mother. 'Open it, for luck!'

Isabelle couldn't contain her excitement. She ripped open the envelope and took out the letter. Sammy looked over her shoulder as a big smile slowly spread across his mother's face. Isabelle got up from the dining table and turned around to face Sammy, the letter still in her hand. Her voice quivering, she said: 'You've made it, Sammy! I'm so proud of you! The NDA!'

For the first time in his life, Sammy felt that he'd truly achieved something noteworthy. He'd worked hard to prepare for the National Defence Academy exam and to achieve the levels of physical fitness he needed to get selected. And now that he'd made it, he felt proud of his achievement – more so because it had brought his mother great happiness.

But Sammy's selection into the NDA left his father with mixed emotions. He didn't think Sammy – gentle, kind, soft-spoken Sammy – was suited for a life in the army. He knew Sammy had applied to the NDA only because he thought it was what his mother expected from him, and that Sammy would do anything he could to win her love and to show her he was as good a son as Peter. The pastor had tried to talk Sammy out of taking this path, speaking to him of the many options he had before him given his academic excellence. But Sammy was adamant and eventually his father gave in – though he knew that the path his son had chosen would bring him great hardship and sorrow.

Once breakfast was over, Sammy raced to Martha's house and walked in as he usually did, hollering, 'Hey, anyone home?' But there was no response. Sammy took off his jacket and slung it over a chair in the kitchen. He helped himself to a glass of water, wondering if he should wait or come back later. Then he heard the strains of '*Lonely Boy*' by Paul Anka drift down from the room on top of the stairs. It was one of Martha's favourites!

Sammy bounced up the stairs with a spring in his step and pushed the door open without bothering to knock. Martha was writing at her desk, the music on the wind-up gramophone turned up loud. She didn't notice Sammy enter till he turned down the volume. 'Sammy! What a lovely surprise. I was making you a card. Happy birthday!' she exclaimed as she walked across the room and threw her arms around him. Then she slipped an amulet she'd bought him as a birthday present around his wrist. It had her name inscribed on it. 'This is so that you never forget my name even when you grow old,' she chortled.

'I'll never forget you, Martha,' Sammy said, kissing her hungrily.

Sena, Eoma and Christine had driven down to the weekly market in Lunglei. They wouldn't be back till late afternoon. Martha had feigned an illness hoping to spend the day with Sammy on his birthday. And he had turned up, as if he'd read her mind!

'Martha, I have something really exciting to tell you!' Sammy burst out, unable to contain his excitement.

'What?' murmured Martha, as she held him close.

'I've got into the NDA!' The exhilaration in his voice was palpable.

Martha took a step back, pushing Sammy away, stunned. 'The army? You're joining the Indian Army?' she asked, her voice breaking. 'When did you apply? You never told me that you'd applied, Sammy. And now you spring it on me out of the blue? How can you be so insensitive?'

Tears welled up in her eyes, and she turned away from Sammy.

Until that moment, Sammy hadn't even considered how Martha would feel about his decision to join the army, or whether their relationship would survive him going away to the academy. He hadn't told her that he was applying to the NDA, because he was fearful of not making it and didn't want to embarrass himself. He'd decided he would tell her only if he got accepted and had assumed she would be pleased for him then. But he'd never once asked her how she felt about the idea. Regret washed over him; he realized he should have been more respectful of her feelings. However, there was no going back now. All Sammy could do was to try and explain why he'd chosen the life of an army man.

Sammy told Martha about his grandfather and his Victoria Cross; about his family's tradition of serving in the army; about his mother's life as a young girl in an army cantonment and her dream of her sons following in their grandfather's footsteps. Sammy told her how hard he'd worked to pass the entrance exam and the physical tests, and that it was an honour to be selected from the thousands who'd applied.

Martha didn't react at all, sitting impassively on her bed, listening to him. She only seemed to relent when he told her he loved her and that the NDA wouldn't change anything between them, nor would it change how he felt about her.

They sat in silence for a while, then Sammy walked over to the gramophone and flipped the 78-RPM record over. 'Dance with me,' he begged Martha.

Hurt, but no longer angry, Martha got off the bed and slipped into his arms. She softly sang along to Paul Anka's 'Put your head on my shoulder'.

People say that love's a game,
A game you just can't win.
If there's a way,
I'll find it someday,
And then this fool will rush in.
Put your head on my shoulder….
Whisper in my ear, baby.
Words I want to hear, tell me,
Tell me that you love me too.

As they swayed slowly to the music, Sammy told Martha over and over that he loved her and that he wanted both of them to be together forever. Sammy asked her to wait for him. He promised he'd never forget her or let her down. Because she loved Sammy, Martha believed him.

When the song ended, they held each other even as the needle on the turntable kept tracking the dead wax of the record, filling the room with a continuous loop of static and staccato blips as the gramophone slowly wound down. In that moment, paused in time, Martha and Sammy went from being innocent teenagers in love to lovers. Their fingers moved wordlessly as they took off each other's clothes. Martha yanked the bedspread off her bed, sending her books and clothes flying across the room as she and Sammy tumbled down and slipped under the sheets. Sammy had been brought up to believe that sex before marriage was a monumental sin. But Sammy didn't feel wicked or immoral or weak in that moment. He felt alive, blessed and loved, and he knew Martha felt the same.

When they were spent, they lay under the sheets in each other's arms – Sammy's eyes shut tight, not sure what he should say. He could tell she was looking at him. She ran her fingertips slowly and gently over his face, like a blind person drawing a tactile map to remember him by, in case she never saw him again. Sammy didn't stop her.

Though it was still early afternoon, the rain clouds had rolled in. The sky had turned dark. A storm was coming. Sammy started to stir again and turned to face Martha. She giggled shyly when she felt him and opened herself to him again. The occasional flash of lightning lit up the sky and the thunder grew louder as the clouds gathered over the hills of Asakhua. Which was why neither of them heard the Jeep pull up outside.

When Sena saw Sammy's jacket hanging on the chair at the dining table, in the darkened house, he knew instinctively that all the ugly rumours he'd been hearing from the boys in the village about Martha and Sammy were true. Furious, he raced up the stairs to Martha's room.

Sena kicked the door open with such ferocity that it nearly flew off its hinges. The sudden violence of the act caused both Martha and Sammy to leap up, startled. Martha grabbed the bed sheet to cover herself, while Sammy stood on her bed stark naked, paralysed with fear.

The sight of a naked Sammy on Martha's bed triggered Sena's terrible temper that had lurked under the surface of his every interaction – a consequence of years of pent-up anger, frustration and betrayal. It blinded him to the possibility that his sister and his best friend were in love, and that Sammy hadn't manipulated him just to fuck his sister. Instead, all Sena felt was a primal rage that rose to the surface like a tsunami, one that would destroy everything in its path.

Sena snarled: 'You fucking Indian dog – how dare you?'

Before either Martha or Sammy could react, Sena had grabbed Sammy by his leg and yanked him off the bed, sending him crashing to the floor. As Sammy scrambled to his feet, Sena picked up the heavy wooden chair from under Martha's desk and slammed it across Sammy's back, causing the chair to splinter and sending Sammy stumbling into the wall.

Sammy staggered towards the door trying to get away from Sena, even as Martha pleaded: 'Stop it, Sena! Please stop it. I love him!'

Martha's pleas infuriated Sena even more. He picked up one of the legs of the broken chair and clobbered Sammy viciously with it. Sammy fell to the ground, writhing in agony. But Sena wasn't done. He kicked Sammy over and over, as he lay there cowering and naked, curled up like a foetus in its mother's womb that was about to be ripped out of its safe haven, trying to protect his head with his hands, even as Sena continued to scream: 'You fucking Indian dog! I'll kill you!'

In those few moments of violence, the trajectory of each of their lives was altered irreversibly, sending them hurtling into a dreadful abyss of despair from which there would be no coming back.

CHAPTER 12

At nightfall, the Rego family was gathered at their dining table. Joachim sat at the head, with Isabelle by his side. Sammy sat at the foot of the table, holding his head in his hands, weeping bitterly. He looked like he'd been mauled by a wild animal – his eyes bloodshot, his face swollen, and covered in cuts and bruises.

Earlier that evening, an enraged Eoma had barged into the Rego home and accused Sammy of raping Martha. He was going to Lunglei to file a police complaint, he'd said, and that he wanted Sammy arrested and punished for his terrible crime.

'I didn't do it, Pa, I swear! You can ask Martha. She'll tell you the truth,' Sammy sobbed. 'You have to believe me. Martha and I … We love each other. I want to marry her.'

Isabelle looked at Sammy with undisguised disgust. All evening, she'd refused to make eye contact with him, even as she'd bandaged his wounds, applied cotton wool dipped in Dettol on his cuts and rubbed towels soaked in cold water to the bruises on his face, back and legs. As upset as she was with Eoma's accusations, she was even more upset that Sammy's actions had ripped the family name to shreds. But when she heard Sammy say he wanted to marry Martha, she snapped. 'You're not marrying anyone, you foolish boy, least of all that tribal girl!'

She then turned on her husband. 'Joachim, I said nothing when that man came into my home and accused my son of rape. I watched while you sat there like a mouse letting him rubbish our family name. But I won't tolerate it any more.'

Joachim was taken aback by her outburst. All his years as a preacher hadn't prepared him for a crisis like this, and he was clearly out of his depth. Not Isabelle, though. Once she'd decided that Sammy was innocent, she took charge of the situation and, like a general strategizing a counterattack, she laid out the plan for her family. 'Sammy, you're leaving tonight. Your father will drive you to Aizawl. Go to your room and pack a bag,' she said firmly, catching Sammy off guard.

'Where am I to go, Mamma?' Sammy asked quizzically.

'You're going to your Uncle Alan in Nellore, from where you'll go up to Poona, to the NDA, when it's time.'

Sammy hadn't been prepared for this sudden turn of events. His mind tried to process what it would take for him to compress an entire lifetime in Asakhua into a single suitcase and leave his home – maybe forever – that very night? Impossible! Sammy looked to his father for support and his father stepped right up, uncharacteristically banging his fists down hard on the dining table. 'No son of mine is going to run away in the middle of the night like a thief!' Joachim thundered.

There was pin-drop silence at the table. Then Isabelle said, in a cold, detached, dangerous voice: 'Joachim, I've suffered ridicule and humiliation from the day I married you. I left my home and my family for you, because I thought it was God's will. Now, I see it wasn't God's will at all. All along, it's been *your* will. Now you want to use this false accusation of rape to keep this boy here and derail his going to the NDA? You want him to rot over here, like you and I are, in this godforsaken part of the world, where they hate us and want us gone? I won't allow it, Joachim. This boy will leave here tonight and nothing will come in the way of his going to the NDA.'

When she was done speaking, Joachim had been broken and Sammy's fate had been sealed.

That night, Sammy packed his suitcase into which went the few clothes he owned, and a tiffin with some cake and sandwiches for his journey. The three hundred-rupee notes his mother handed him, he slipped into his wallet with his identity card. The small black-and-white photograph of him, Martha and Sena, that he'd tacked to the wall in his bedroom, that the photographer at the New Year's dance had clicked of them, he slipped into the pocket in his jacket. The Bible that his father gave him, Sammy flung away in anger.

Before they left home, Joachim, his voice breaking under the weight of the emotional storm that had engulfed their family in the past few hours, said a prayer over Sammy, asking God to keep him safe from all harm, protect him from his enemies and that he be blessed with a good life. Isabelle wept bitterly as she hugged Sammy and said goodbye.

But Sammy didn't shed a single tear. He had no more tears to cry. No more prayers to recite. All he wanted was to get away from Asakhua as quickly as he could, to never look back, to never again feel the pain he felt then, as he got into the car and his father drove him away from his home, his family and the girl he loved.

THE WAILING OF THE BAMBOO

CHAPTER 1

Over half of the bamboo that grows in the Mizo Hills is the *Melocanna baccifera*, known locally as the mautak. It's a running bamboo whose rhizomes, or creeping root stalks, spread rapidly underground like tentacles, sprouting shoots that mature into bamboo poles on average thirty feet tall, two inches in diameter and a quarter-inch thick, in just a few months. A single grove of mautak can easily spread over hundreds of kilometres, surviving and thriving in some of the harshest terrains on the planet.

In the spring of 1959, after a gap of forty-eight years, the mautak across the Mizo Hills began sprouting long, wispy spikes of flowers that soon transformed into green, pear-shaped fruit with a hard, yellow pulp and a white seed about the size of an avocado pit. Soon after the flowers had borne fruit, the mautak died, covering the Mizo Hills in grotesque, dried stumps of bamboo, some as high as eighty feet. When the fruit ripened, its protein-rich seeds fell to the ground like manna from heaven, drawing rats out of the jungles by the hundreds of thousands. The dying of the bamboo, the ensuing plague of rats and the inevitable famine that followed – this set of events is collectively referred to as the Mautam.

The rats were mostly of the common black variety, *Ratus ratus*, which were responsible for the bubonic plague in the fourteenth century. But some villagers in the Mizo Hills also claimed to have seen the chawmnu, with a white spot on its head and a white tail, that was the size of a young pig sow, that could only be killed by slicing off its head with a dao!

A female rat can bear up to a dozen pups in a single litter. A month later, it can be pregnant again. Besides, rats become fertile when they are just three months old. So, if the male doesn't eat its young, a pair of rats can account for over 14,000 pups every year. When the Mautam came to the Mizo Hills in 1959, the males stopped cannibalizing their young, preferring instead the bamboo fruit and its protein-rich seed that lay scattered in abundance across the land. When all the seeds had been eaten, the rats invaded the fields, chomping and gnawing their way through the standing crops. When the crops were gone, they turned their attention to the homes and granaries in the villages and hamlets across the Mizo Hills.

It's not that the tribesmen didn't try to fight back. They did, with their traditional iron traps, and some ingeniously designed ones that crushed a rat with a log of wood or simply garrotted it when it came to eat the bait. They even tried to poison the rats with zinc phosphide and used long bamboo tubes to blow tobacco smoke into burrows hoping it would kill the rats nesting inside. But what could they do against an army that gave birth to new soldiers every day? Eventually overwhelmed, entire villages were abandoned – people fleeing on foot to the towns where they hoped the government would take care of them.

It was raining heavily in Asakhua the day Eoma, Christine, Sena and Martha decided to give up their battle against the rats and move to Aizawl, where Eoma's brother lived. They packed a few suitcases with clothes and valuables, fastening them firmly on to the soft canvas roof of their Jeep with bamboo ropes. All along the dirt track, they saw the old and the young, the weak and the hungry trudging in the pouring rain, soaked to the bone, carrying their meagre belongings in jute sacks and bamboo baskets balanced on their heads. Many never made it. They fell by the wayside, too weak to carry on.

A few miles from Serchhip, the rain had triggered a landslide, blocking the road to Aizawl. Desperate, Eoma and his family sought refuge in a relief camp that had sprung up in the playground of a government school. The camp hosted a hundred or more temporary shelters made of bamboo frames, covered in black tarpaulin sheets – these had been donated by relief agencies, but were being sold on the black market for ten rupees a sheet. Everything in the camp, including the right to build a shelter and rations, came at a price. Eoma had the money to ensure that his family were well taken care off in the camp. But there were many who weren't as lucky.

A tribesman with a large crucifix around his neck shivered in the damp and the cold in the shelter next door, too weak to sit up. His wife was cooking a thin potato soup on a small fire she'd got going in the middle of the shelter. Their four young children looked longingly at the soup. All of them looked terribly undernourished and sickly. The family had walked for nine days from their village in the highlands, surviving their forced march by eating leaves, shoots and roots that they'd foraged from the jungles along the way.

One of the children whimpered, 'I'm hungry, Nu.'

His sister put her arms protectively around him. 'Be brave. We'll all eat soon. Be brave.'

The tribesman wailed from the corner of the shelter, tears flowing down his face, 'My god, my god, why have you forsaken us?'

Wracked with guilt for the relative comfort their money had bought them, Martha asked Eoma for five rupees to buy their neighbours food.

'Who all will you feed, Martha?' Eoma asked, grudgingly handing her the money. 'Look around you. Everyone is in the same boat.'

'We aren't,' Martha said firmly.

* * *

Even as an inferno of hopelessness and despair engulfed the Mizo Hills, the Indian government was clueless about the scale of the devastation. Their relief efforts were ham-handed and inadequate. The relief camps quickly turned into a quagmire of disease and sickness. As the government scrambled to try and get food to those in need, everything appeared to be an insurmountable challenge – the terrain, the remote villages and the rain that turned the unpaved jungle tracks into strips of slush in which vehicles carrying relief material and food got bogged down.

After the rats had eaten everything – the seeds of the bamboo fruit, the crops in the fields and the food in the abandoned villages – they began dying by the millions. Their role in the Mautam played to perfection, the rats faded into oblivion. But the suffering in the Mizo Hills had yet to peak.

The start of a new decade – 1960 – should have been a year of abundance. After all, the rats were gone and there was plenty of dead bamboo that could be used as mulch for crops. But the monsoon failed that year, leaving the people hostage once more to the government's incompetence. The next year, 1961, the dead bamboo and dry forests were like a tinderbox. Massive fires were reported across the Mizo Hills that summer, destroying vast swathes of forest and fields, and even entire villages. Again, the harvest was below average, further exacerbating the suffering of the people, whose patience had thinned, and whose simmering anger was beginning to find expression.

In Aizawl, a young and powerful orator was beginning to get noticed by the Mizos. He articulated the betrayal and hopelessness that the people felt with great flair and offered them an enemy to direct their anger at – the Indian Republic. His name was Pu Laldenga, or 'one who was born on a Sunday'.

Pu Laldenga was the fourth child of devout Baptist parents. Born in the South Mizo Hills near Lunglei, he was a school dropout, but was enlisted in the army as a havildar-clerk. When he was decommissioned in 1953, at the age of twenty-seven, Pu Laldenga moved to Aizawl, where he found a job as a cashier in the District Council. In those early years in Aizawl, Pu Laldenga maintained a low profile. On most evenings, he'd amble across to the 'Liar's Association', where the town's intellectuals and elite would gather to spin yarns and tell each other outrageous stories. That was where Pu Laldenga honed his public-speaking skills and made important friends, his circle of influence growing steadily.

When the Mautam struck, Pu Laldenga was quick to grab the opportunity that presented itself in the form of an incompetent Indian government, forming the Mizo National Famine Front (MNFF) in September 1960. The MNFF soon became popular with the youth. They signed up as volunteers delivering rice and other essentials to villages that were difficult to reach. One of those volunteers was Sena.

In October 1961, the organization dropped the term 'Famine' from its name and became the Mizo National Front (MNF) with Pu Laldenga as its president, signalling that he was ready to make his move. 'Mizoram for the Mizos' was his powerful rallying cry. With the sheer power of his oratory and the force of his conviction, Pu Laldenga lit the fire of rebellion amongst the Mizo youth and sold them the dream of an independent nation. Thousands of young people stepped forward to serve a cause greater than themselves, for which they were willing to give up their lives. At night, campfires would be lit around Aizawl and the youth would gather to sing songs of freedom and dream of a new nation. At the time, nothing seemed impossible to them. No sacrifice was too big to make and no effort too small.

When Sena told his family he was going to join the MNF, Eoma was livid. 'You young people have been mesmerized by Laldenga. You think the Vais will give us our independence just because we want it? There will be a bloodbath. Thousands will die. Don't you know what's happening in the Naga hills?' he thundered.

'Better to die trying than to live in fear as second-class citizens in our own land,' Sena shot back.

'You forget that you are a Mara. How foolish of you to think the Lushai will accept you as one of their own!' taunted Eoma.

'All of us who live in these mountains are brothers,' Sena replied. 'It was the British, and now the Vais, who drove a wedge between us. We have no quarrel with each other. Our dream is the same – freedom.'

'We should never have come to Aizawl,' bemoaned Eoma. 'It would have been better if we had starved in Asakhua than to see you ruin your life like this.'

Christine too tried to talk Sena out of joining the MNF, fearful that he would put his life in danger. 'Don't do it, Sena,' she begged. 'What will become of us without you? Let's go back to Asakhua. There's so much to be done there.'

Martha was the only one who supported Sena's decision. 'If you've set your heart on this path, then go. Don't worry about us; Christine and I will take care of Pa. We'll be fine. But always remember, we love you and we'll be here for you – no matter what happens.'

His mind made up, one stormy night with the rain pouring down as heavily as it had when they'd fled Asakhua, Sena slipped away to join the MNF. There were no dramatic farewells or tearful goodbyes. He made no promises to his family that he would write or stay in touch. He just walked away when they were asleep, knowing in his heart that he'd never see them again.

CHAPTER 2

Sena's superior fitness and extraordinary marksmanship soon singled him out for special attention from the MNF leadership. He was amongst the first batch of recruits sent across the border to the Chittagong Hill tracts in East Pakistan, where the Pakistan government had set up a military training camp for the MNF. Over the next two years, Sena was trained in the art of guerrilla warfare. Speed, surprise and secrecy were critical to a guerrilla's battle of attrition against a better-armed and much larger enemy.

In the training camp, Sena studied the guerrilla's bible – Mao Zedong's *On Guerrilla Warfare*, written in 1937 after the Chinese Revolution. He also got his hands on an early English translation of *La Guerra de Guerrillas*, a military handbook written by the hero of the Cuban revolution, Che Guevara. Sena read the book numerous times and could quote extensively from it. He even grew his hair long, sported a beard, and wore an olive-green army jacket and a black beret with a brass star, like his hero Che did. His obsession with the famous Cuban revolutionary soon led to Sena being nicknamed 'Che' by the other trainees in the camp. The name stuck.

When the first battalion of guerrilla fighters was assembled by the MNF in 1964, Che was appointed a captain. Pu Laldenga, who had become increasingly paranoid about his safety, handpicked fifty of the best fighters and set up the Special Force (SF) to guard him round the clock. One of those selected was Che. SF troops would shadow Laldenga on his tours and were always present when he met the public. They were also chosen to execute special missions that were considered far too dangerous for regular guerrillas.

In the winter of 1964, a squad of MNF recruits led by Che was sent on a dangerous mission across the border to collect a massive shipment of arms sent by the Pakistani military. The shipment included automatic rifles, pistols, mortars, grenades and ammunition, and was to be collected from Ruma Bazar in East Pakistan. It took Che and his squad weeks to smuggle the arms into the Mizo Hills, walking only at night and using old jungle trails that only local villagers knew, to evade Indian border patrols. When the arms cache was safely delivered by Che and his squad to the MNF leadership, they had it buried in a field in Bungtalang, on the edge of the jungle, its precise location known only to a handful of senior commanders.

The successful mission enhanced Che's reputation. His professionalism and courage had been noticed by

Pu Laldenga and his guerrilla commanders, and he was increasingly assigned to lead dangerous high-stakes missions, which included the assassination and kidnapping of those identified as 'traitors' by the MNF leadership. As a result, the legend of Che grew amongst the Mizo people. They said he operated like a ghost, a master of disguise and subterfuge, who could easily hoodwink the police and escape the nakabandis and patrols they sent out to capture him. It was also said that he was ruthless and unforgiving with those who betrayed him or the MNF. Across the Mizo Hills, 'Wanted' posters with Che's image began appearing in public places and on bulletin boards. But these only served to enhance his image as the 'Mizo Robin Hood', fighting the Vais for justice for the Mizo people.

One evening, about six months after the arms cache had been buried, the MNF received a tip-off from an informant that a massive Frontier Rangers convoy with over a hundred soldiers, led by Commandant V.C. Aiyar, had left the Lunglei garrison for Bungtalang. The informant claimed that the commandant had been provided with a map pinpointing the site of the buried arms cache by a traitor within the MNF leadership. The convoy would halt at Thenzawl for the night, offering the MNF a tiny window of opportunity to try and retrieve the arms before the Frontier Rangers found them.

At nightfall, Che and a squad of handpicked SF men left their hideout in two Jeeps and a Bedford truck. The headlights were turned off as the vehicles raced up and down the treacherous mountain tracks in pitch darkness towards Bungtalang, over 120 kilometres away.

As dawn broke over the hills, Che's squad was still an hour away from their destination. Then, disaster struck. The front-right tyre of the Bedford burst, sending it careening into a shallow ditch. The truck was a wreck, leaving Che with a difficult decision to make. Should he abandon the mission? Or should he continue the race against time to try and dig out the arms cache before the Frontier Rangers got there, and use the two Jeeps to ferry it to safety – leaving his men to escape on foot, putting their lives at risk?

It didn't take him long to make up his mind.

Bedford abandoned, the guerrillas raced towards Bungtalang in the Jeeps, with the pickaxes and shovels they would need to dig out the arms. An hour later, the guerrillas were stripped down to their waists, digging furiously. 'Faster, faster, you motherfuckers, faster,' growled Che.

Meanwhile, the Frontier Rangers convoy had arrived at Bungtalang. 'Saikia, we need to move fast,' Commandant V.C. Aiyar snapped at his deputy. 'I want a tight cordon around the entire area. No one is allowed in or out till we're done. Got it?'

'Yes, sir.' The deputy saluted the commandant.

At the dig, metal boxes covered in mud were being pulled out of the ground and loaded quickly into the Jeeps. Drenched in sweat, the men finished the operation in under an hour, and as soon as the Jeeps were loaded, they were driven through the freshly ploughed fields towards the jungle – the men running alongside, crouching low, weapons drawn, using the vehicles as cover. The guerrillas had barely scrambled a few hundred yards towards the jungle, when the bullets began to fly.

A section of Frontier Rangers soldiers that had circled around through the jungle, faster than their comrades in the over-stretched cordon, broke into the clearing. They stopped at the edge of the jungle to watch as two olive green Jeeps, with men in Frontier Rangers uniforms running alongside, moved through the fields towards them.

It was Sepoy Paswan who first noticed that the men approaching them had long hair and unkept beards, and looked nothing like Frontier Rangers soldiers. He screamed, 'Open fire, open fire, it's the MNF!'

Caught in a hail of bullets in an open field, the drivers halted the Jeeps and leapt out, ducking for cover.

'Get those Jeeps moving, you motherfuckers!' Che screamed.

When neither of the cowering drivers responded to his command, Che crawled into the lead Jeep and, getting behind the steering, he started up the engine and pushed the pedal to the floor. But the Jeep was overloaded, and when it stopped, it had sunk into the soft mud. Now its wheels spun, with no traction.

'Push,' Che screamed. 'Push, or we're all dead!'

Even as bullets ricocheted off its metal body, the guerrillas got behind the stuck Jeep, pushing desperately to free it. Finally, it lurched forward, and picking up speed, it lumbered towards the Frontier Rangers soldiers who had taken cover in the undergrowth at the edge of the forest. Following his captain's example, a young lieutenant got the second Jeep moving.

At the sight of the two Jeeps flanked by the guerrillas racing towards them, Sepoy Paswan panicked. 'Get back into the jungle, back, back!' he hollered, lumbering towards the safety of the trees, his men following close behind. As the soldiers fled, they became sitting ducks for the guerrillas, who cut down three of them before they could get to the jungle. Sepoy Paswan had almost made it to safety, when a bullet ripped into his arse, sending him sprawling to the ground, screaming in agony.

By the time Commandant Aiyar got to the site of the skirmish with reinforcements, it was all over. The jeeps and the guerrillas had disappeared into the jungle, the arms cache safely recovered.

Sepoy Paswan whimpered in pain as he was bundled on to a stretcher, face down, the blood stain on his arse spreading rapidly. When he saw the commandant, he called out: 'It was Che, sir. I saw him. He was driving one of the Jeeps.'

The blood drained from the commandant's face. The terror that had haunted him for months, that he'd tried so hard to blank out, returned, overwhelming him, sending him crashing down to his knees, his eyes shut tight. In his mind's eye, he saw the blurry face of the bearded, long-haired man with the black beret, on which was emblazoned a brass star, who'd peered at him through the shattered windscreen of his Jeep.

'Are you okay, Commandant?' Deputy Commandant Saikia asked.

'Yes, I'm fine,' the commandant whispered, getting slowly back to his feet. 'Just a dip in sugar levels. I'm fine.'

CHAPTER 3

Just before midnight on 28 February 1966, the recently promoted Major Che and his company of armed guerrillas waited impatiently in the jungles bordering Lunglei for the fireworks to begin. Earlier that day, they'd received confirmation that Operation Jericho, an armed insurrection by the MNF against the Indian Republic that had been in planning for months, would launch simultaneously at midnight in the towns of Aizawl in the north, Lunglei in the south and Champhai in the east. Complete independence was what the MNF was seeking and Operation Jericho was the first step in that direction.

In preparation for independence, which they believed was within their grasp, the MNF had designed a flag, composed a national anthem and even drafted a constitution for the yet-to-be-born nation, which began as follows: 'The Lord Jesus Christ is the Supreme Head of Mizoram, and the Holy Scriptures will be the Cornerstone of the Law.' With Operation Jericho, Pu Laldenga finally had a chance to test the resolve of his volunteers, and the quality of their training and planning. If the operation was executed as planned by his military commanders, on the morrow, Pu Laldenga would raise the flag of an independent Mizoram in Aizawl.

'You will wait for my signal,' Che told his men. 'The element of surprise is on our side. We cannot afford any mistakes.' The men acknowledged his instructions with a quiet nod, slipping away into the darkness to take up their positions. At midnight, on Che's signal, the guerrillas broke cover and raced towards their target – the Lunglei treasury, a brick-and-mortar building protected by a twelve-foot boundary wall. The wall had inverted L-shaped iron brackets sunk into it at six-foot intervals, through which were strung coils of barbed wire. A massive iron gate, locked from the inside, was set in the wall. A single sentry secured in a wooden pillbox on the inside of the compound guarded the gate.

In the days leading up to the attack, the guerrillas had chalked out a precise plan that they now put into execution. Tall bamboo ladders were used to get to the top of the wall, and metal cutters were used to slice the barbed wire. Then, one by one, they dropped silently into the compound below. One of the guerrillas moved stealthily towards the pillbox, dagger in hand. The bored, sleepy sentry, chewing on tobacco to stay awake, was caught by surprise and had no time to react. His throat slit, his lifeless body slumped in the pillbox.

As soon as the sentry was down, Che cried out, 'Attack!'

A group of guerrillas raced towards the treasury, while another circled around to the back, where the Frontier Rangers' company tasked with guarding the treasury had pitched camp. When the camp had been encircled, petrol bombs were hurled at the canvas tents. The panicked soldiers who rushed out to escape their burning tents were mowed down by the guerrillas.

Che and his men combed the treasury, meeting little resistance. At the back of the building was a large room with thick walls and no windows. The only access was through a locked metal grill.

'Blow it up!' Che barked.

One of the guerrillas placed an explosive charge on the grill while the others took cover.

'Do it!' Che commanded.

On cue, the explosion blew the metal grill off its frame, filling the room with smoke. When the smoke had cleared, the guerrillas entered the room that was stacked with locked steel trunks. Che shot the lock off one of the trunks and flung its lid open. It was filled with Indian currency notes, neatly sorted in bundles of different denominations, each held together by a thick rubber band.

'There's more than a lakh of rupees in this trunk alone. Enough to make us all rich!' an excited guerrilla exclaimed, peering over Che's shoulder.

'We're not thieves!' Che snapped at the guerrilla. 'Now, get these trunks out of here. Move!'

The sound of fierce gun battles underway all across Lunglei filtered to the treasury as the guerrillas dragged the steel trunks out and loaded them into the back of the Bedford truck that had been driven in through the now-unlocked gates. Just as they were done loading, a Jeep, its headlights blazing, raced into the compound and pulled to a stop about a hundred yards from the truck.

As the guerrillas scrambled into the back of the Bedford, the men in the Jeep opened fire. They were reinforcements sent from the Frontier Rangers' garrison in Lunglei by the commandant, who had correctly anticipated that the treasury would be an obvious target for the insurgents. Che leapt into the front seat and screamed: 'Go! Go! Go!'

The eight-ton Bedford truck, powered by a P6 Perkins diesel engine that delivered eighty-three horsepower at twenty-four hundred RPM, rammed into the Jeep at about fifty kilometres an hour. The impact hurled the Jeep into the air, killing the two soldiers seated in the front on the spot and severely injuring the other three in the back. Path cleared, the badly damaged Bedford careened through the gate and lumbered off into the darkness.

* * *

All across the Mizo Hills, MNF guerrillas overran the smaller towns, arresting government officers and policemen, ransacking offices, confiscating equipment and weapons that their movement would need. Champhai had capitulated quickly, its garrison overrun, and a large number of officers and soldiers taken prisoner. But it would be days before Lunglei fell – the Frontier Rangers refused to surrender, despite being heavily outnumbered, suffering massive casualties, and their food and water supplies cut off. They were counting on reinforcements arriving from Aizawl, but the guerrillas had blocked off all routes into Lunglei.

In Aizawl, Operation Jericho stuttered. Despite their early success in capturing the telephone exchange and cutting off all communication between the Mizo Hills and the rest of India, the MNF guerrillas couldn't access the vault inside the Aizawl treasury and eventually had to settle for a little under Rs 20,000. Worse, the MNF's expectation that the garrison in Aizawl would fall within hours was wildly off the mark. The soldiers, caught off guard at first by the ferocity and suddenness of the attack, suffered massive casualties. But, like in Lunglei, they quickly regrouped and pushed back the attackers.

A few hours after Operation Jericho launched, Pu Laldenga released a two-page 'Declaration of Independence' that stated: 'India is unworthy and unfit to rule over us, the civilized Mizo people.'

At the MNF headquarters, the adjutant general of the Mizo volunteer corps announced the formation of the MNA with about 2,000 volunteers, who would henceforth be known as soldiers, organized along the lines of the Indian Army, with eight battalions divided into two brigades.

In Aizawl, even after three days of incessant attacks, the Frontier Rangers' garrison refused to surrender. With time running out, on 4 March, a large squad of MNA soldiers was ordered to charge the garrison. It was a suicide mission. The attack began early that morning and went on all day. A swarm of guerrillas charged forward, firing machine guns and lobbing grenades over the walls of the garrison. The soldiers, fighting for their lives and for the lives of the women and children holed up inside the garrison with them, counter-attacked with great courage, eventually forcing the MNA to retreat, leaving fourteen of their dead behind.

Though their primary objective of capturing the garrison had eluded them, the guerrillas now controlled Aizawl. MNA troops took up positions in abandoned houses and buildings all over the town, anticipating the arrival of the Indian Army. Their plan was to engage the army in an urban guerrilla battle, in which they held the advantage. Pu Laldenga had hoped that a long-drawn-out guerrilla war with guaranteed army casualties would be politically problematic for New Delhi and make the Indian government amenable to a truce. But he hadn't bargained for what the Indians did next.

A few hours after the suicide attack on the Frontier Rangers' garrison had been repelled, Indian Air Force fighter jets swooped down, strafing and bombing Aizawl to free it from the guerrillas, razing entire sections of the town to the ground.

Che was rushed to Aizawl with reinforcements when the bombing began. When he arrived, the scale of the destruction stunned him. The town was in flames, and the bodies of civilians and guerrillas lay scattered all over. Che could hear the desperate cries for help of those trapped under the rubble of collapsed buildings.

As Che and his guerrillas rushed about trying to get the injured to safety and free those buried under the rubble, they came under fire from a Frontier Rangers' patrol. Che was separated from the rest of his men in the crossfire, and took cover in the ruins of a bombed-out building. As he scrambled through the ruins, looking for a vantage point to fire at the soldiers from, he heard a whimper in an alcove just behind him. He spun around to see a young Mizo lad, about sixteen years old, wearing oversized combat fatigues and a camouflage helmet slung loosely on his head, cowering in a corner, holding an automatic rifle. The boy was bleeding badly from a shrapnel wound in his stomach. Che moved quickly towards him and grabbed him by the throat. 'Shut up! You're going to get us both killed.'

'I don't want to die,' the boy whimpered.

'You won't die,' Che said softly. 'Don't make a sound, and we'll get out of here alive, I promise.'

The boy wiped his tears. 'You're the one they call Che, aren't you?' His face lit up in recognition.

'Yes, I am,' Che said, reaching out and adjusting the boy's helmet.

Then a grenade went off close by. The boy shut his eyes tight and covered his ears with his hands, tears flowing down his face. Che rolled out from behind the alcove and opened fire with his carbine at two soldiers who'd crawled up on them. The firing alerted the other guerrillas to his location, and they rushed to back him up. Che raced out of the building and into the open, taking cover behind a mound of rubble, dodging bullets, firing and screaming out instructions to his men. But the tide of the skirmish was beginning to turn decisively in favour of the soldiers.

Almost out of ammunition, Che was pinned down in the rubble, his escape routes blocked off and most of his men dead. The dragnet the soldiers had formed began to tighten around him. Che was out of ideas. Lying back in the rubble, he turned to look up at the sky. The sun flitted through the dark smoke billowing upwards from the buildings burning all over Aizawl. 'God have mercy on me and forgive me my sins,' he whispered, as he placed the barrel of his carbine under his chin and jabbed his thumb on its trigger.

Then a volley of shots rang out. It was the boy. Badly wounded and weakened by the loss of blood, he staggered out of his hiding place. The soldiers ducked for cover as the boy made his way slowly up the mound of rubble, firing indiscriminately. It was the last stand of a hero fighting to redeem himself. But it didn't last long. A bullet slammed into the boy's chest, sending him crashing to the ground. A soldier ran up to the boy and shot him in the head, to make sure he was dead. Then, as if to honour the death of the fallen hero, the unmistakable roar of fighter jets filled the sky. The soldiers scrambled to save their lives, leaving Che to his fate, as the Indian jets began strafing and bombing the town once more.

Che didn't run. Weeping bitterly, he climbed the rubble and, picking up the dead boy in his arms, carried him away before the hellfire, that the Witch of Asakhua had prophesied would rain down on the Mizo Hills, could consume his lifeless body.

CHAPTER 4

Towards the end of March 1966, on the back of the bombing of Aizawl, the Indian Army marched into the Mizo Hills. In a few weeks, it had regained all the territory that the MNF had laid claim to, forcing its leadership to flee across the border into East Pakistan and Burma. But Che never left the Mizo Hills. He went underground in the Lunglei region with a small band of trusted guerrillas, launching raids, sabotaging electricity and water works, and hitting soft targets in the government – just as his namesake, Che Guevara, had done during the Cuban Revolution. The boldness of his attacks and the fearlessness of his band of guerrillas enhanced his reputation amongst the local people. The Mizos came to see him as a symbol of resistance and Mizo pride, who would not bow down before the powerful Indian Army.

In April 1967, Che received word that the MNF leadership had summoned him to an urgent meeting at a guerrilla camp in Burma. It took him two weeks to trek to the meeting and, when he got there, he was thrilled to meet many of his friends in the MNF who were alive and well, and eager to strike back against the Indian Army. But that would have to wait. What the MNF needed more than anything else was to replenish its stock of arms and ammunition, which had run low in the aftermath of Operation Jericho. With the operation not going to plan, the MNF's support in the Pakistan military had dwindled as had the supply of weapons, forcing the leadership to improvise to keep the movement alive.

The money looted from the Lunglei treasury and other government departments during Operation Jericho, and funds that had been collected earlier, had been distributed and hidden in MNF safehouses around Lunglei. The money was of no use to the MNF in the trunks it was stored in. It needed to be laundered into gold bars, that could then be smuggled across the border to Thailand, where it would be used to purchase automatic weapons, mortars, grenades and ammunition. The MNF leadership had identified a trader in Calcutta who was willing to sell them the gold in exchange for cash. Che was put in charge of the operation.

Three weeks later, the trader from Calcutta arrived in Lunglei to hammer out details of the deal, and how the gold bars would be delivered and cash exchanged. The trader hadn't been given a location for the meeting. He kept waiting for a week in a guest house in Lunglei, his every move watched by Che's men. He was kidnapped from the guest house late one night by the guerrillas, bundled into the back of a Jeep and driven to an MNF safe house to meet Che. Over the next few hours, the two men negotiated the price of the gold bars and where and when the delivery was to be made.

But, unknown to the guerrillas, the abduction of the trader during the unscheduled power cut the previous night, and his subsequent return early the next morning, hadn't gone unnoticed. Later that day, the Jeep the trader was travelling in was stopped an hour out of Lunglei by the Frontier Rangers. A few hours later, the tearful trader was seated in the interrogation cell in the Lunglei garrison, his face badly bruised and swollen from the beating he'd been given. Across from him sat the commanding officer of the garrison, Commandant V.C. Aiyar.

That night, a platoon of heavily armed soldiers, led by the commandant, made their way towards an isolated bungalow in a village in Chengpui, on the outskirts of Lunglei. The old single-storeyed bungalow, built of stone, with a corrugated metal roof, was once owned by a missionary couple who'd returned to England after Independence and had been bought by a local businessman. Surrounded by open fields, it had been built in a clearing in the jungle. The soldiers had parked their vehicles three kilometres short of the village and trekked silently through the jungle to keep their presence in the area a secret. It was a moonless night, and once they'd surrounded the bungalow, the men began moving in slowly towards their target.

The first shot was fired by a guerrilla Che had posted as a lookout in a thlam – a jhum bamboo hut on stilts – in the field adjoining the house. Soon, the night was filled with bursts of heavy automatic fire as the Frontier Rangers' soldiers charged toward the bungalow firing, and Che and two of his guerrillas holed up inside returned the fire. With the element of surprise lost, the soldiers charging across the open field became easy pickings for the guerrillas, who fired on them from the inside, constantly changing positions.

Although the guerrillas fought bravely, there were too many soldiers converging on the bungalow from all sides. Che knew there was no escape, but there would be no surrender. His two comrades knew this, too. This would be their last stand. Death was preferable to the terrible torture that would be inflicted on them, if taken alive.

Then, one of the soldiers flung a grenade into the living room through an open window. The explosion killed Che's comrades instantly. In the adjoining bedroom, Che was stunned by the blast. As he struggled back on to his feet, disoriented, his ears ringing with the sound of the explosion, the butt of the commandant's automatic rifle crashed into his skull, knocking him unconscious.

EVERY MAN HAS TO DIE

CHAPTER 1

Sena knew Sammy's plan to trek to Aizawl was unrealistic and naïve. There was little hope of them being able to trek over a hundred kilometres while evading the Indian Army, the Frontier Rangers and the local police force, who would all soon be looking for him and Sammy. Left to himself, he may have been able to pull it off. But with Sammy in toe, holding a gun to his head, while his hands were bound in shackles, the idea had an almost surreal, farcical quality to it. But it was only a matter of time. Sena knew he would soon be presented with an opportunity to free himself and to melt into the countryside on his own. For now, he marched on sullenly.

The sun was beginning to set when Sammy called for a break near a gushing stream. They were both tired, hot and thirsty, and the cold water was a welcome respite. Sena dropped to his knees and started to drink, his hands still in shackles. When he was done, he dunked his entire body into the stream. Sammy walked downstream, placing his pistol on a rock within easy reach, and splashed his face with water from the stream, washing away the sweat, before settling down to drink, watching Sena warily all the while.

Soaked to the bone, Sena settled down on a dry patch of grass on the bank of the stream, resting his back against a rock. He couldn't resist the temptation of mocking Sammy. 'What's up, brave army officer? Afraid I'll get my hands around your neck? Why so far away? Come sit next to me, man.'

Ignoring the barb, Sammy settled down against a rock fifteen feet away, his hands wrapped around his pistol. Sena, who hadn't slept a wink since the day he'd been nabbed by the Frontier Rangers, fell into deep sleep almost immediately, his head rolling down on to his chest. Sammy lit himself a cigarette and watched Sena sleep – vulnerable, flawed and broken, a pale shadow of the hero he'd idolized as a boy. He thought about their childhood, and the idyllic, innocent life they'd led in Asakhua before the troubles. His thoughts turned fuzzy as he dozed off, letting his guard down, the pistol by his side.

Sammy had been asleep for about half an hour, when the tinkling of a bell, drawing close, woke him up. He jumped up and strode quickly over to Sena, kicking him awake. Sena staggered to his feet, groggy, instinctively looking for the best place to take cover. But it was too late. An old man limped unsteadily across the stream right towards where they were, leading his cow, a mangy thing with its bones sticking out, that looked as old as the man himself. The bell around its neck tinkled with every step. Sena and Sammy looked at each other, uncertain of what to do next. Then Sena sat back down, twisting his body so that his shackled hands couldn't be seen. Sammy followed his cue, quickly slipping the pistol into his waistband, trying to appear casual and relaxed.

The cow knelt beside the stream and drank its fill before settling down to chew cud on a patch of grass. The old man wore a weather-beaten army camouflage jacket, tattered woollen pants and an old pair of canvas shoes, their laces missing. He had a frayed cloth bag strung across his shoulders. He looked the two strangers up and down, and quickly judged that Sammy, who didn't look like he was from the hills, was the more powerful of the two. He limped up to him and sat down on his haunches. The old man could only be described in cliches – wizened, stoic, full of character. His hair was winter-white and he'd lost all his teeth, but not his curiosity. He took out a pack of beedis and a matchbox, and lit himself one. Then he offered the pack and the matchbox to Sammy, who helped himself to a beedi. They sat smoking for a while, no words exchanged between them. Then the old man spoke up. In Mizo, he said: 'My cow is driving me crazy. She's becoming more and more stubborn with age.' Then he giggled wickedly and added: 'Just like my wife! Do you have a cow?'

Ignoring the smirking Sena in the background, Sammy answered in rusty Mizo: 'I used to. But not any more.'

The old man was quick to grab the opening. 'How do you manage without a cow?'

'He ate his cow,' piped up Sena before Sammy could reply. Sammy glared at him, angrily.

The old man was intrigued. 'Would you like to eat my cow too? You can have her for five rupees,' he said, holding up his right hand to show Sammy five wrinkled fingers.

Sammy wasn't interested. 'I don't want to eat your cow.'

But the old man wasn't willing to be fobbed off so easily. He was a shrewd businessman, and he'd sensed the opportunity for a deal. He deftly changed tack. 'You don't have any money? Do you have a bottle of rum?'

Sammy was stumped. Sena guffawed loudly. 'What do you have in your bag?' Sammy asked.

'My wife had packed me some sanpiau and chhangban, but I didn't eat today. My tummy hurts,' he said, running his fingers gingerly over his stomach. 'My wife, she's old, but she cooks well.'

'I'll pay you two rupees for your bag and your food,' Sammy offered.

The old man considered Sammy's proposition, then held up his five wrinkled fingers once again.

'Okay, fine. Five rupees,' said Sammy, reaching into his pocket and pulling out his leather wallet. He handed the old man a brand-new five-rupee note. The old man carefully held it up to the fading light to make sure it wasn't counterfeit. Satisfied it was the real thing, he handed over the frayed bag to Sammy.

The cow got back on to her feet and set off for home, determinedly. The old man neatly folded his new five rupee note and placed it in the front pocket of his jacket. Waving Sammy and Sena goodbye, he set off, limping as quickly as he could, in pursuit of his cow.

'There must be a village close by,' Sena said, getting to his feet, looking worried. 'That man will tell his entire village about us. We should get going.'

Sammy nodded. The two of them set off again – Sena leading, Sammy following about ten paces behind, still clutching his pistol, up a path into the mountains, as the light faded and darkness set in.

* * *

Commandant Aiyar sat at his desk, puffing on a cigarette, when there was a sharp knock on his door. 'Come in,' he barked impatiently.

Deputy Commandant Dilip Saikia saluted his boss smartly before striding across the room. He sat down in one of the metal chairs across from the commandant without waiting to be asked.

'Two calls from Mountain Brigade headquarters, sir, from Major Mukherjee. He's heard rumours about a skirmish involving Captain Samuel. The Major wants to speak to you right away,' he said, with a hint of nervousness.

'I'll call him once I have something concrete to report,' the commandant replied. 'Any news from Asakhua, Saikia?'

'We made contact with our informant, sir,' the deputy commandant replied. 'The captain told you the truth. Che's real name is Sena, and he did grow up in Asakhua. His father, Eoma, is the headmaster at the village school. His two sisters still live in Asakhua, with their father, but Che hasn't been seen in the village since the Mautam.'

The commandant had assumed the captain had lied to him. Now that it appeared he hadn't, the convoluted conspiracy theory he'd been developing in his head over the course of the day came crashing down. 'What did you find out about our captain?' he asked his deputy.

The deputy opened the file he'd been carrying. 'Captain Samuel's grandfather was Brigadier Vivian Lazarado. He won the Victoria Cross in the First World War, in the Battle of Megiddo. Captain Samuel's brother, Peter Rego, was a Captain with 3 Cavalry. He was killed in the Battle of Asal Uttar, in the 1965 war. Captain Samuel's father is a Baptist pastor. The captain studied at the Baptist Secondary School here in Lunglei. Then he went to the NDA from where he graduated in 1962. Nothing spectacular about his performance there. Graduated from the Indian Military Academy in 1963 – nothing notable from his time there either. Commissioned as a second lieutenant in 7 Bihar. Was promoted to lieutenant and saw action in the 1965 war. Was promoted to captain and posted to Brigadier Kabraji's staff a few months ago as the brigadier wanted an officer who could speak the local language and understood local customs.'

The commandant pondered over the information his deputy had brought him. He wondered aloud: 'Why would the captain help Che escape, Saikia? What are we missing here?'

'Could Che have bribed him, sir? We know we didn't recover all the money that was looted by the MNF in the raid. There has to be more of it hidden in safe houses around Lunglei. It's the most plausible explanation, sir,' the deputy replied, unconvincingly.

The commandant looked troubled. 'For a moment, let's suppose you're right. What does that mean for us?' Aiyar stood up and turned to the large contour map on the wall behind him. 'This is where they escaped,' he said, marking a cross on the map. Marking a second and a third cross in quick succession, he said: 'This is Asakhua, and this is us here in Lunglei. What are his options then, Saikia?'

The deputy walked over and used his finger to trace the map. 'Either they can head north towards Aizawl or south towards Lunglei. My guess is, if they're coming back for the money, they'll head towards Lunglei. Besides, the river gorge is a natural boundary to the west and the mountains to the east are too formidable for two men to cross without any supplies.'

Aiyar considered his deputy's analysis carefully. 'I don't think they'll head towards Aizawl, Saikia. Makes no sense if they're on the run. Too many Army and Frontier Rangers patrols in that area. You're right. I too would put my money on them trying to get to Lunglei, an area Che knows well, and where he'll have enough local support to be able to disappear for a while.'

'I concur, sir,' Saikia replied.

'Well then, let's tighten the noose around them,' the commandant said. 'Checkpoints every five kilometres from Thenzawl all the way to Lunglei. I want every vehicle stopped and searched.'

'Yes, sir.'

'I also want units heading inwards from all these points,' said the commandant, drawing arrows at four different places. 'We've got to cut off their escape routes and hem them in.'

'Roger that, sir. I'll action it right away,' the deputy said enthusiastically.

The commandant lit up another cigarette and stood by the window smoking in silence. Saikia began to gather up the file. Aiyar turned to his deputy and asked: 'Saikia, this Asakhua, is it on the list of villages to be regrouped?'

'I don't believe it is, sir,' the deputy replied.

'Well, get the paperwork done and put it on the list ASAP. They have to pay a price for harbouring anti-nationals, don't they?' the commandant asked.

'Yes, sir, certainly.' The deputy commandant looked smug.

CHAPTER 2

Sammy and Sena had found it difficult to navigate the steep mountain trail in the darkness. Sammy had struggled, but he'd kept pace with Sena, never letting his guard down even for a moment. He knew if he did, Sena would attack him, as he had attacked Paul, and disappear into the darkness. Neither prospect appealed to him. When the moonlight finally broke through the thick cloud cover and lit up the mountainside, the two men stopped to take stock of where they were. In the distance, Sena spotted a cave in the mountainside, below the trail they'd been trekking on, and scrambled down towards it.

The cave appeared to have been recently used. Its mud floor had wood ash and sheep droppings scattered all over it, bearing testimony to the many fires shepherds had lit in the past to keep them warm and protect their flock from predators. Sena set himself up in a corner of the cave, on an old bench shaped from a tree trunk. He knew he had to get away from Sammy. But he couldn't afford to make any more mistakes.

Sammy built a fire with the twigs and branches he had collected from around the cave. He sat on a large flat rock and opened the old man's bag. Inside it was a metal tiffin box with *sanpiau* – rice porridge mixed with meat and vegetables – and a few rolls of *chhangban*, the local bread, wrapped in an old newspaper. A recycled glass Coca-Cola bottle, with a wooden stopper, was filled with zu. Sammy pushed the sanpiau and chhangban towards Sena. 'Eat,' he said. Sena shrugged and helped himself to the food. He was famished. Other than the rice and dal the prison doctor in Lunglei had fed him the previous night, he hadn't eaten in days. Sammy pulled out the cork stopper and sipped the zu, watching Sena gobble down the food. When the food and the beer were finished, Sammy lit up two cigarettes and cautiously passed one to Sena.

'Who is Che?' Sammy asked. 'Why did Paul say you were Che, a cold-blooded killer?'

Sena looked up at Sammy sharply. 'That's funny coming from a man who was about to shoot me in the head in cold blood.'

'You haven't answered my question.'

'Che is one of my comrades, a guerrilla commander. I'm surprised you haven't heard of him before. He's famous in these parts. I don't know why Paul would think I was Che. My guess is he was just making excuses to murder me.'

'I haven't heard of him.' Sammy said. 'Clearly, there's a lot I have to catch up on.'

'Maybe you should start by surrendering at the Lunglei police station, where there's an FIR registered against you for raping Martha, which has been pending for over eight years now,' snarled Sena.

'Shut up, Sena. You know I didn't rape her. I loved Martha. And she loved me. You knew that. And yet, you lied.'

Sena shuffled nervously on the wooden bench, puffing on his cigarette. He finally said: 'If you were innocent, you wouldn't have fled like a thief. You would have stayed and fought for her. That's what a man in love does. You didn't love her. You were just using her. She figured that out for herself when you ran away.'

The smoke from the fire and the emotional turmoil he felt talking about Martha caused Sammy's eyes to well up. Sena watched him wipe away the tears with the back of his hand. Then Sammy said: 'I was young and afraid. My mother forced me to leave Asakhua. She was trying to protect me. But you're right. I never should have left Martha. It's a regret I'll carry the rest of my life.'

Uncomfortable with the conversation and wanting to bring it to an end, Sena threw away the stub of his cigarette and lay down on the wooden bench, settling down for the night.

Sammy swept away the ash from around the fire with his foot and, folding the old man's frayed cloth bag into a pillow, he lay down on the mud floor, the pistol by his side, thinking about Martha and how much he missed her. In a few minutes, he'd dozed off.

Sena unlocked the handcuffs with the key he'd pocketed from Paul. Then he moved quickly and stealthily across the floor, hurling himself at Sammy, his right hand wrapped around a rock he'd found under the wooden bench. In a matter of seconds, the power equation between the two of them had changed irreversibly. Sammy lay knocked out on the floor, handcuffed, blood oozing from the wound on his head where Sena had hit him with the rock, while Sena sat nonchalantly beside the fire, smoking one of Sammy's cigarettes, the pistol in his hand.

* * *

In the village of Sailam, about two kilometres from where Sammy and Sena had taken shelter for the night, Lance Naik Kamlesh Paswan stepped out of his tent to piss. Six feet tall, with an impressive handlebar moustache and a paunch so large he looked positively obese, the lance naik was from Champaran in Bihar. His family name, 'Paswan', had Persian origins and loosely translated to 'bodyguard'. The Paswans were members of the Dusadh community, considered to be lower castes, though not untouchable, because they refused to work as manual scavengers. They traced their roots to Rajasthan, from where they were driven out to the east of India, by the Mughals. A demotion in caste and the consequent loss in social status was the price they were forced to pay to make space for themselves in the new land they'd moved to. Legend has it that to strengthen their army before challenging the mighty Siraj ud-Daulah, the last independent nawab of Bengal, the British recruited hundreds of young Paswan men, who'd been socially oppressed and exploited by the upper castes. In the Battle of Plassey, on 23 June 1757, the British army under the leadership of Robert Clive, crushed the nawab and his French allies, laying the foundation for the British Empire in India. The victorious British rewarded the Paswan men for their loyalty by appointing them chowkidars and police informers with monthly salaries.

Lance Naik Paswan, who took great pride in his ancestry, was a violent man. He brooked no indiscipline from the squad of nine sepoys he was in charge of. For the past couple of months, he and his men had been assigned to man a remote outpost just outside the village of Sailam. His superior officer in Thenzawl had repeatedly reminded him that the outpost was of great strategic importance, though what that strategic importance was, he hadn't bothered to say. And the lance naik hadn't asked because it made no difference to him. This was their 'duty'. The 'why' mattered not.

The nine sepoys in his command were rotated, three sepoys to a shift, eight-hour shifts, seven days a week, manning the three pillboxes set up at vantage points in different parts of the village. The sepoys were nervous and unhappy. MNF guerrillas seamlessly blended in with the locals and were impossible to spot till they whipped out a gun, which left the sepoys perpetually on edge. They were unhappy, because none of them had been home in months, and they hated the food and the weather. To make matters worse, Lance Naik Paswan was a cruel taskmaster, who believed that constant humiliation and repetitive, meaningless tasks were critical to keeping his unit sharp and focused.

It was just past nine. The lance naik had eaten a plate of mutton and rice and glugged a bottle of Khoday's rum when he felt the urge to piss. He stepped out into the cloudy night and ambled off a few paces from the canvas tent he shared with four of the sepoys, scratching his balls while using a splinter of wood to pick out the little pieces of mutton stuck in the many cavities in his paan-stained teeth. As he unzipped himself and released an unsteady stream of piss into the night, he became aware of a flickering light up on the mountain. At first, he thought he'd imagined it, but when he stared harder, he saw it clearly. Someone had lit a fire. It couldn't be the shepherds – they'd been banned from straying out of the village between sunset and sunrise, on pain of being branded MNF sympathizers and shot. *Could it be the escaped prisoners about whom they messaged us on the wireless from headquarters*, he wondered. The rum had made him feel light and happy, and he'd been looking forward to a good night's sleep. Now this! He called out to his men, lolling around in the tent, listening to Hindi film music on the radio. 'Turn off that radio, you motherfuckers,' he yelled out in Hindi, 'and get your lazy arses out here, on the double.'

* * *

Before first light, Lance Naik Paswan and six sepoys set off to investigate the fire they'd seen up on the mountain in the night. The men were fully armed and dressed for action, wearing camouflage uniforms, black waterproof boots and green berets. Lance Naik Paswan was a large man, with poor aerobic capacity, who'd thrice failed to be promoted to the rank of lance naik. Each time, he had passed the written test with top marks but failed the physical test and been disqualified. His promotion from sepoy to lance naik only happened because he'd been shot and badly injured in a skirmish with MNF guerrillas, which automatically got him an out-of-turn promotion. Lance Naik Paswan believed in leading from the front. And, as long as he led from the front, the patrol moved along at a snail's pace.

When dawn came on the mountain, Sammy shook himself awake. His head ached terribly. And his hands were shackled. Sammy was angry and bitter. He hadn't expected Sena to turn on him as unexpectedly and viciously as he had. Besides, he'd saved Sena's life twice in the past couple of days, putting his own life and career at risk to do so. *I should have let him die*, he thought bitterly to himself as he got to his feet shakily.

Sammy saw Sena walk back from the stream that flowed just past the shed. He'd filled up the old glass Coca-Cola bottle with water. 'Here, drink this,' he said, handing the bottle to Sammy, who accepted it grudgingly. He gulped down the water, then shuffled across to the wooden bench and sat down on it. Sena smirked. 'You went down like a sack of potatoes when I hit you. Boom! And lights out.'

Sammy glared at Sena. He didn't find Sena's description of his vicious attack funny at all, but he couldn't afford to antagonize him. He needed to think clearly. He'd been wrong in assuming Sena would be grateful to him for saving his life. Or that he'd play fair. Or that he wouldn't attack him. Sena couldn't be trusted. But the power was now in his hands and Sammy was pragmatic enough to accept this.

'What you did to me last night was unfair, Sena. I've saved your life – not once, but twice, these past couple of days. And how did you repay me? By smashing my head in with a stone?'

'Oh really?' Sena snapped back. 'And what choice did I have? You had a gun pointed at me. And kept me handcuffed. And that idiotic idea of yours – to walk to Aizawl? What about that? Are you fucking crazy? It was the stupidest idea anyone could come up with. You're a fucking moron.'

'I saw what you did to Paul,' Sammy said, sullenly. 'I was afraid you'd do the same to me, which is why I left the handcuffs on. And I was right.'

Sena lit himself a cigarette from the pack he'd taken out of Sammy's pocket. 'If I wanted to kill you, you'd be a dead man already.' Then, almost as an afterthought, he lit another cigarette and offered it to Sammy.

'Look, man, we've got to agree on the way forward. I can either leave you here handcuffed and take off, and you can pray that the guerrillas or the Frontier Rangers find you before the wolves or the leopards do. In either case, you're a dead man. Or,' Sena paused dramatically, 'I take off your handcuffs and let you go; you go your own way in peace, and we never see each other again.'

Sammy said nothing. If he went back to Aizawl without Sena, he knew he'd probably be court-martialled. It would be his word against Paul's – if he was still alive – and the other sepoys who had seen him flee with Sena. He didn't want to be left alone on the mountainside, handcuffed, either. So, he tried to play the middle ground. 'Look, without a gun and all alone out here, I won't make it. You know that. So, if you want to kill me, do it now. Shoot me and get it over with.'

Sena's first instinct was to call Sammy's bluff. He raised Sammy's pistol and pointed it at his head. 'Fine,' he said, 'if that's what you want, so be it.'

For a moment, Sammy thought he was a dead man. Then Sena guffawed. He lowered the gun and said: 'Okay, this is the best I can do. I will take off your handcuffs. You can walk with me till Serchhip. It's a twelve-hour trek, and we'll only get there by nightfall if we walk fast and don't run into any patrols or villagers. From there, you'll be able to hitch a ride on a bus or an army truck back to Aizawl. But any tricks from you, any bullshit, I swear, Sammy, I'll kill you. You better believe it.'

Sammy nodded. This was a far better outcome than he could have imagined. Sena threw him the keys to the handcuffs. Sammy unlocked them and let them drop to the floor. Then he rubbed his wrists to get the circulation back and gingerly felt the wound on his head. Sena tucked the pistol into the back of his trousers and said, 'Let's go.' Then he set off at a fast clip up the trail. Sammy scrambled back on to his feet and hurried after him.

* * *

It was almost seven by the time the Frontier Rangers' patrol got to the cave in the mountainside. The remnants of the fire that Sammy and Sena had lit the previous night were still warm. In one corner, the men found a frayed cloth bag with an empty tiffin box that had the distinct aroma of sanpiau. But what got the lance naik's attention were the handcuffs his men found lying on the floor, near the wooden bench. It confirmed his theory that the escaped prisoners were in his area. The lance naik chastised himself silently. The previous night's rum and mutton had made him lazy, and that laziness may have cost him fame, a cash reward and another out-of-turn promotion. *I should have set out to investigate the fire as soon as I spotted it,* he thought angrily. *But maybe all is not lost. Maybe we can still catch them.*

'Come here, you motherfuckers,' he yelled out to his men. When the sepoys had lined up, the lance naik barked out his instructions. 'You three,' he said, pointing to the three sepoys at the head of the line. 'Run down to Sailam and inform headquarters on the wireless that the prisoners have been spotted in our sector. You are to come back here with rations and ammunition for all of us for the next three days. Do you understand?'

'Ji, sir,' said the men in unison, nodding furiously. The lance naik dismissed them with a wave of his hand, and the three sepoys scampered away to do their leader's bidding.

The lance naik hollered after them: 'You motherfuckers, don't go wasting your time shagging on the way. I want you back here in two hours, or I'll take the hide off your bottoms.'

Turning to the other three, he barked: 'Spread out and stay alert. These bastards may be around here somewhere. They're armed, so be extra careful. They're dangerous men.' Instructions issued, Lance Naik Paswan took off his shirt, kicked off his shoes, farted with aplomb all the gas that the mutton and rum fermenting in his belly had built up through the night, and lay down on the rough bench to snooze the rest of the morning away.

CHAPTER 3

Sena and Sammy had been making good time on the trail to Serchhip, though they'd twice been forced to get off the path and hide when they'd spotted villagers approaching in the distance. They'd walked in silence all morning. With the fear of a surprise attack from Sena out of the equation, Sammy felt more relaxed and at ease. The hike began to remind him of their time in Asakhua, trekking through the jungle without a care in the world. Even then, it had always been Sena who would walk ahead and set the pace, chart the route, and look out for any signs of danger.

From the shepherd's shelter, the trail had wound its way through lush green jungle with the elevation barely changing. Then, as if it had got bored with its own consistency, it veered sharply up towards the ridgeline. Now, the going got tougher and the path rockier. Sena's pace didn't flag, but Sammy was struggling. His lungs were bursting and his muscles were beginning to cramp. Yet, he pushed on gamely, his fragile ego not allowing him to ask

Sena to slow down. Soon, they were above the tree line and the track wound around the side of the mountain, like a ribbon tied loosely around a gift packed by inexperienced hands, with no consideration for its contours. One side of the track was a sheer, jagged, granite rock face, the other a steep precipice, with thick, thorny shrubs and bushes that had managed to survive and thrive in the little islands of soil between the rocks, growing below the precipice, like a frayed safety net hung around the sides of a skyscraper under construction.

Sammy's body finally gave in to exhaustion. He bent over gasping. Nauseated and dizzy, he dropped his hands down on his knees to stop himself from keeling over, too exhausted to walk any more, his mind foggy and unfocused. In his delirium, he heard an ambulance race towards him, rushing to his rescue. *How is that possible?* he wondered, breaking into a demented grin. He heard someone shouting out to him over and over, even as the clanging of the ambulance bell grew louder. Then, something slammed right into him, hurling him into the air. He landed at the very edge of the precipice, stunned. As he struggled to get back to his feet, he felt himself tottering. He moved his foot back to steady himself and regain his balance, but strangely there was nothing there, just thin air. Then, the centre of gravity shifted decisively, and his body began to topple over the precipice even as his brain tried to make sense of the fact that his foot was treading thin air. He fell over backwards, his arms flailing helplessly, crashing down into the thorny shrubs and bushes that grew into the rock face, below the precipice. Luckily for him, they broke his fall before he crashed on to a rocky ledge, saving him from certain death.

After what seemed like forever, but in reality was no longer than a minute, Sammy stirred. Instinctively, he knew he was in grave danger. He looked around to consider where he was. The ledge was large enough to hold him if he didn't do anything stupid. Sammy stood up slowly, his back hugging the wall of the mountain, and took in his surroundings. Terror washed over him, for beyond the ledge, there was nothing. One false move and he'd fall to a certain death. Paralysed by fear, he felt his entire body begin to tremble. Then a wretched, embarrassingly warm flow of piss trickled down his leg and flowed over his boot and off the edge – like a waterfall to eternity.

'Sammy, Sammy,' Sena called out to him, his voice betraying his worry. 'You all right, man?' Sena lay flat on his stomach, peering over the precipice cautiously.

Sammy didn't dare look up. His eyes were shut tight. The vertigo he thought he'd conquered, jumping off high platforms at the NDA, returned, making him feel dizzy. He called out weakly to Sena, 'Please help me!'

Sena realized Sammy was panicking. 'Don't worry, Sammy, I have you, man. I'll get you out of there. Stay calm, okay?'

Sena scrambled to his feet. Two men were running towards him. They were mule drivers, who'd finally managed to get hold of their runaway mules. They looked terror-stricken; the lead mule had slammed headfirst into Sammy and sent him over the precipice. 'I need a rope,' Sena shouted out to them urgently in Mizo, grabbing one of the men by his shoulders.

'I have one. It's on my mule. I'll get it for you,' the man said, racing off to fetch his rope.

'Is he alive?' the second man asked Sena nervously.

'Yes, but barely,' replied Sena. 'He's fallen on a ledge. If we don't get him up quickly, he'll fall to his death.'

The rope wasn't very thick – just strands of jute rolled together, about twenty feet long, that was used to fasten sacks on to the mule. It would have to do. Sena tied one end around his waist. Once again, he lay down on his stomach and then threw the rope over the edge.

'Tie the rope around your waist,' he shouted down to Sammy. 'We'll pull you up!'

Sammy grabbed the rope and tied it firmly around his waist, tugging on it to signal that he was ready to be pulled up. Then, he felt the rope tighten around him, as Sena and the two mule drivers began hauling him up, off the ledge. Sammy held on to the rope firmly and used his legs to push himself off the rock face, like he'd been trained to do, as he was pulled steadily upwards, through the shrubs and bushes that had broken his fall. When he was back on the path, he collapsed in a heap, as the rush of adrenaline subsided and he slowly revived. Luckily, he had suffered no serious injury – just some cuts and bruises from when he'd crashed through the thorny bushes and on to the ledge. One of the mule drivers fetched a bottle of water and a wad of rough cotton from his saddle bag, and tended to Sammy. The men marvelled aloud at his fortuitous escape, even as they reprimanded him for foolishly standing in the middle of the track instead of getting out of the way of their mules.

'Mules are very stubborn; they don't stop for anyone,' one of the men told him in Mizo. 'The bell is to warn everyone to get out of their way.'

After the men and their mules had left, Sammy and Sena sat down on the track, to rest, their legs dangling over the edge. Sena was worried about the two men. The accident with Sammy and his dramatic rescue was too irresistible a story for them to not share at the first opportunity. Word of two strangers in the mountains would spread quickly and, by the time they got to Serchhip, there could be men from the Frontier Rangers, the local police force, or even the Indian Army, waiting for them. Sena concluded it was safer for them to get off the track once they crossed the ridge line and bivouac for the night in the jungle below. In the morning, he'd need to find a path that skirted around the town. He couldn't let Sammy go either. *What if Sammy gives away my position?* he thought. *No, we're going to have to stick together for another day.*

***

By the time the three sepoys returned to Lance Naik Paswan, each carrying two large rucksacks filled with dry rations, utensils, ammunition and foldable sleeping mats, it was eleven. The rations, enough to sustain the patrol for the next couple of days, were redistributed amongst the six sepoys. The lance naik had woken up from his mid-morning snooze, feeling rested and ready for action.

'Come on, motherfuckers, let's get going. We don't have all day to sit around shagging,' the lance naik barked in Hindi, waddling back on the track.

The patrol had been walking for a little over four hours when they heard the clanking bells of mules charging down the track. The lance naik yelled out anxiously to his men, 'Get to one side, you motherfuckers. These animals are unpredictable. Don't mess with them.' The sepoys moved quickly to the inside of the track, leaving enough space for the mules to pass them without incident.

Then, two Mizo men, running hard, trying to keep pace with their mules, came into sight. The lance naik stepped into the middle of the track, blocking the men's path, bringing them to a halt. The mules raced away unsupervised. The first man, agitated and out of breath, tried to explain to the lance naik that the animals posed a clear and present danger to anyone on the track and that he should be going after them. The lance naik looked at the man sympathetically, then threw his entire weight behind the open-handed slap that caught the man flush across his face and sent him crashing to the ground. The lance naik rubbed his hands together, a sneer on his face, then he reached down and grabbed the cowering man by the collar of his frayed cotton shirt and pulled him close. He could smell the man's putrid breath and his fear. The second man took a step back, terrified, silent, not wanting to draw any of the lance naik's attention to himself. 'Chinkie, we're looking for two escaped prisoners. Have you seen them?' the lance naik asked the man softly in Hindi.

CHAPTER 4

Engines straining, a Frontier Rangers' convoy of ten trucks led by a Jeep made its way slowly up a narrow dirt trail on the outskirts of Lunglei, leading to the top of a steep hill. In the Jeep, Commandant Vinay K. Aiyar rode shotgun next to the driver, his deputy bundled in at the back. As the convoy crested the hill, the Asakhua Baptist Church – with its white walls, its distinct wooden roof and towering steeple – came into view, the setting sun bathing it in diffused orange hues, putting it in nature's spotlight.

As the convoy moved down into the valley, the commandant was pensive. He was thinking of Malti. In a few weeks, it would be their thirtieth wedding anniversary. He smiled to himself thinking of the day they were married, in Madurai, just the two of them, with his best friend, Bala, who served as witness, and the corrupt temple priest who had to be bribed to conduct the ceremony quickly. Their wedding had been the culmination of a whirlwind romance – one that had begun when he had gone back to his ancestral village for his grandfather's funeral. Malti and he had been introduced to each other by Bala at the Meenakshi temple, at the prayer ceremony that marked the end of the mourning period. Two weeks of furtive meetings, stolen kisses, desperate fumbling and long conversations in the groves around the village pond and by the banks of the Vaigai river that flowed close to their village was long enough for him to know that she was the one. But his time in Madurai was almost done. His widowed mother wanted him back home, in Assam, where they lived in a tea estate, earning a daily wage plucking tea leaves and pruning tea plants.

A few days before he was to return to Assam, freshly bathed and powdered, his hair well-oiled, wearing a new white, short-sleeved cotton shirt, a freshly starched *veshti* – a white unstitched cloth wrapped around the lower body – and a new pair of Hawaii rubber chappals, with his father's elder brother in tow, he'd visited Malti's home to formally ask her father for her hand. It didn't go well. He was just eighteen years old, with no money, no job, no property, and he lived in faraway Assam. No sensible parent would have agreed to such a preposterous proposal. But Vinay was in love, and he was sincere. And that was enough for Malti.

When the day arrived for him to return, she slipped away from college during the lunch break and rode at the back of Bala's scooter to the Thiruparankundram Murugan temple – dedicated to Lord Muruga, the son of Lord Shiva.

At the temple, Bala bribed the priest twenty rupees to get them married without asking too many questions. He had selected the temple because it was close to the railway station. Marriage solemnized, they were on a train that very afternoon to Madras, and then onwards to Assam. Malti never saw her family ever again, and Vinay made sure she never regretted it.

Malti had proved lucky for him. Within days of returning to Assam, Vinay received word that he'd been selected as a sepoy in the Frontier Rangers. Now he had a permanent job and a regular income, and he could take care of Malti. But in those early years, life had been anything but easy. In 1939, the Second World War broke out and, by December of 1941, the Japanese, who'd aligned with the Germans, invaded Burma. India would be next. The Frontier Rangers was tasked with guarding key installations in the Northeast of India, managing the large flow of refugees, who were pouring in from across the Burmese border, and training civil defence groups to prepare themselves for the coming Japanese invasion.

Lance Naik Aiyar was assigned to the 'Victor Force', a Frontier Rangers' group that operated behind enemy lines, disrupting Japanese communications and supply lines, and launching surprise attacks on the advancing army to slow them down. In one such attack, Lance Naik Aiyar had been badly wounded, shot in his back and legs. He'd survived by dragging himself on his stomach for over a kilometre back to the Frontier Rangers' lines, evading the Japanese forces looking for survivors to shoot at sight. His bravery won him an Indian Distinguished Service Medal and an out-of-turn promotion to naik, but he spent the rest of the war recuperating in a field hospital in Shillong.

Inside the Jeep, the commandant lit another cigarette, and passed the pack and the matchbox to his deputy in the back. The convoy moved slowly, the headlights of the trucks and the lead Jeep switched off. It reminded the commandant of another evening, a couple of years ago, that had irreparably broken him.

A few months after he'd been posted to Lunglei as commandant, Malti and their sixteen-year-old daughter, Radha, had come up to spend a weekend with him at the Lunglei garrison, from Shillong, where they lived. On their first night in the garrison, Commandant Aiyar and his family accepted the police superintendent's invitation to dinner. Unfortunately, they were spotted by a MNF informant leaving the garrison in the commandant's Jeep, with only a single, armed bodyguard to protect them. On the way back to the garrison, a fallen tree blocked the road on the outskirts of Lunglei. While his bodyguard walked across to take a closer look, the commandant stayed back in the Jeep with his wife and daughter, his sixth sense telling him they were in danger. Without waiting for confirmation, he rammed the Jeep into reverse and pushed the pedal to the floor. It was too late. They'd been trapped in a textbook ambush. A guerrilla stepped out from behind the fallen tree, shooting the bodyguard in the head, killing him instantly. Two more guerrillas emerged from behind a rocky overhang, firing indiscriminately, as the Jeep hurtled over an embankment and crashed thirty feet below into a rocky ravine. As he lay semi-conscious in the crushed Jeep at the bottom of the ravine, the commandant saw a man peer at him through the shattered windscreen. The man had shoulder-length hair and wore a green beret with a brass star. The commandant recognized him immediately. He was the one the locals called 'Che', whose 'Wanted' posters were pasted all over Lunglei. Then, on the road above, the commandant heard a vehicle screech to a halt.

'They're dead. Let's go,' he heard Che say as he fell unconscious.

When he regained consciousness, the commandant found himself in the army field hospital in Aizawl. He'd suffered a severe head injury; his right leg had been shattered and three of his ribs fractured by the Jeep's collapsed steering column that had pinned him into his seat. And then there were the superficial injuries – the cuts and gashes that covered his body. The surgeons had spent over twelve hours in the operating theatre, putting him back together again. They said it was a miracle that he'd survived. For Malti and Radha, however, there was to be no miracle. They'd been cremated even as the commandant lay battling for his life in hospital, slipping in and out of a coma. It was months before he could return to active duty. But he wasn't the man he'd been before the attack. He was broken, wracked by guilt, his heart filled with anger. Time had dragged by slowly for him, and there had been no closure, no release for his pent-up grief, no healing.

* * *

At the church in Asakhua, a memorial service for Mengka, one of the village elders, was underway. In his youth, Mengka had been a feared warrior – handsome, built like a bull and brave. But as he grew old, it was his gentle spirit, kindness and deep wisdom that attracted people to him, especially when they needed sage advice or someone who could mediate their disputes. The church, dimly lit by oil lamps, was packed with almost all of Asakhua turning up to pay their last respects to 'Grampa'.

As dusk descended, the cawing, cacophony of crows settling down for the night in the trees around the church filled Martha with dread. Her thoughts returned to Sena, wondering if he was still alive and if she'd ever see him again. When Sena left home, he'd broken all ties with Eoma, Christine and Martha, because he didn't want to endanger their lives. Eoma took Sena's decision to join the guerrillas as a failure of his parenting. He brooded over the loss of his son, becoming increasingly withdrawn and uncommunicative, finding an escape in alcohol. On days when Eoma was too drunk to teach, Christine and Martha filled in for him, but his long absences from school were being noticed and his position was becoming increasingly untenable.

Martha was relieved when the young Mizo pastor asked the congregation in the church to stand for the final prayer. She'd been squeezed into a pew with Christine and two large, elderly ladies for over an hour, and had begun to feel increasingly claustrophobic and uneasy. The service was almost done when the sound of trucks pulling up outside the church caused a commotion, bringing the service to an abrupt end.

The wary congregation hurried out of the church into the dark courtyard. They heard the crackle of a megaphone being turned on and an unseen man barking: 'Lights!' On cue, the entire courtyard burst into an explosion of bright light, startling the villagers, causing them to lift their hands to their faces, to block the harsh beams that criss-crossed them. Parked around the periphery of the courtyard were trucks, their headlights turned on. From behind the trucks, Frontier Rangers' soldiers, their bayoneted rifles held in front of them, stepped forward, encircling the congregation. Then the commandant stepped out of the lone Jeep. He straightened his uniform, adjusted his beret and lifted the megaphone from off the front seat of the Jeep, stepping forward through the circle of soldiers. The static of the megaphone pierced the air once more as he switched it back on. He lifted the megaphone up and spoke into it, slowly: 'I am Commandant V.C. Aiyar of the Frontier Rangers. Your village has given shelter to members of the banned MNF. This is against the law. Therefore, the government of Assam has ordered the immediate evacuation of this village. This evacuation is in your own interest, so that the Frontier Rangers can protect you from the MNF. You will be accommodated at the Lunglei Voluntary Grouping Centre. Anyone resisting this evacuation will be shot. You have thirty minutes to board the trucks voluntarily. Your cooperation will prevent unnecessary bloodshed.'

When the commandant had finished his monologue, murmurs of protest could be heard from the villagers. Then the murmurs grew louder, quickly ratcheting up into loud, panic-stricken screams as the significance of what the commandant had just ordered them to do struck home. Some villagers rushed forward, trying to break through the circle of armed soldiers. The soldiers beat them back ruthlessly with the butts of their rifles.

One of the villagers, a farmer named Nakang, who'd been clubbed to the ground by a soldier, crawled back on his knees and begged: 'Please, my wife and children are at home. I have to get them.' The soldier looked at Nakang pitifully, then he lifted his rifle deliberately and brought its butt down on Nakang's skull, sending him crashing to the ground again, holding his head, whimpering in pain.

Eoma, Christine and Martha had barely stepped out of the church when the uproar began. When he heard the commandant on the megaphone, Eoma quickly pushed his daughters back into the church, looking for a place where he could hide them. He settled on the altar, pushing Christine and Martha under it. Then, Eoma walked towards the exit, determined to put a stop to the mayhem outside. As he walked away, he said a silent prayer, asking Jesus to protect his daughters and to keep them safe.

CHAPTER 5

Sepoy Sujoy Dasgupta was eighteen and had been in the Frontier Rangers just six months when his platoon was assigned to 'regroup' Asakhua. Sujoy had grown up in Calcutta, though his village was on the outskirts of Darjeeling, up in the highlands. Studious and nerdy, he was a misfit in the Frontier Rangers, bullied and ridiculed for his weak physique and his love for books. But he soldiered on bravely, trying to fit in – to be accepted as one of the men. When the action began in the church courtyard, he hung around in the shadows, aghast at the brutality the unarmed villagers were being subjected to.

In the courtyard, some of the villagers had begun to see the hopelessness of their situation and resigned to their fate, allowed themselves to be herded towards the trucks, even as many of the younger men battled on bravely. Frustrated at the repeated attempts to break through their cordon, the soldiers had begun bayonetting villagers who came too close. Soon, a dozen or more men and women lay writhing on the courtyard floor, clutching their stomachs, arms and legs, trying to stem the bleeding from the wounds inflicted by the bayonets.

Sepoy Dasgupta saw an old Mizo man step out of the church and run towards the young priest who lay in a pool of blood on the courtyard floor, even as he continued to be kicked and clubbed viciously by a soldier. Throwing himself in between them and putting his arms around the young priest to protect him, the old man cried out: 'Please, please, he's a man of god, have mercy on him!' The young sepoy watched in horror as the soldier smirked at the old man. Then he turned his rifle around and shoved its bayonet deep into the old man's chest, watching him collapse slowly on top of the injured priest, his life draining away.

Sepoy Dasgupta's subedar yelled out to him in Hindi: 'Hey, Bangla babu! When you've finished jerking off in the dark, go search the church. Shoot anyone you find hiding there.'

Embarrassed at being called out, the sepoy scurried away to do his subedar's bidding.

Sepoy Dasgupta took great pride in being a meticulous man. When he entered the darkened church, he began searching it systematically, starting at the very back, looking between the pews and behind the columns, slowly making his way to the front, his rifle held in front of him, finger on the trigger. Eventually, he lifted the heavy satin cloth that covered the altar and squatted down to look under it. The look of terror in the girl's eyes startled him. He dropped the cloth back down and stood up shakily, uncertain about what to do next. Then he squatted down again and moving the satin cloth out of the way, he peered under the altar. There were two girls cowering under it, clinging to each other. His subedar had ordered him to shoot anyone he found. *But that would be murder*, he thought. Conflicted between his orders and his sense of morality, Sepoy Dasgupta stood up and backed away slowly towards the exit and, when he'd put enough distance between him and the altar, he turned and ran out of the church, pulling the doors shut behind him, hauling their heavy bolts into place, locking it down. Then he yelled out, nervously, to his subedar, 'Church is empty, sir.'

As the trucks began to fill up with the villagers who'd been forced into them, and the dying left to die in the courtyard, the soldiers began spreading out, lugging heavy jerry cans between them. Each hut was liberally sprinkled with petrol even as the villagers looked on in disbelief. Then the commandant barked: 'Burn it down. Burn it all down!'

The huts lit up instantly, their time on earth done. Like pyres at a mass cremation, each with a family watching in horror, mourning their loss. The raging flames consumed not just the structures, but the collective memories and evidence of generations past, of lives lived, an entire village razed to the ground in a flash.

Then the fields were set on fire, destroying the standing crop. And the miller's hut by the stream, where the grain was crushed. And the old shop in the marketplace. The grain store. And the mission homes in which Sammy and Sena's families had lived. Burnt. They were all burnt down. The dark smoke billowed upwards into the night sky, the only sign of the terrible tragedy that had befallen Asakhua. That, and the faint and plaintive cries of men, women and children watching the scene unfold in despair.

Over the crackling of the flames, gunshots rang out, as the soldiers opened fire on villagers trying to flee into the surrounding forests. Many were gunned down, preferring death to a life without liberty. But there were others, broken and hopeless, that trudged towards the trucks that were to take them to the camp where they would be interned. There was nothing left for them in Asakhua.

When the village was burnt down and the villagers forced into the trucks, the commandant turned his attention to the church, a silent witness to the destruction of Asakhua. 'Burn it down.'

Sepoy Dasgupta had been standing on self-assigned guard duty outside the church ever since he'd confirmed that it was empty to his subedar. Now, he saw the subedar and two other soldiers headed his way, lugging jerry cans filled with petrol. He knew what they were about to do. And he was filled with dread.

'You sisterfucker, you think we are your wedding party? Lazy Bengali arsehole, come here and help with these cans,' the subedar, out of breath with all the heavy lifting, thundered at Sepoy Dasgupta.

The subedar's harsh words were like a whip that spurred the sepoy into action. He hurried towards the subedar and grabbed the jerry can he was carrying.

'Sprinkle the petrol all around the church. Don't leave anything dry,' the subedar commanded.

'Yes, sir,' Sepoy Dasgupta replied, as he and the other sepoys rushed to carry out their subedar's instructions.

After they were done, the subedar lit a match and gleefully dropped it on the courtyard floor. A light-blue flame sprung up almost magically, then raced along a thin trail of petrol that had been sprinkled by the sepoys till it reached the edge of the church, where it burst suddenly into a massive inferno.

The soldiers stepped away from the roaring flames in awe of their handiwork. Sepoy Dasgupta stared at the burning church in horror. He should have told his subedar about the girls hiding inside. But he hadn't. And now it was too late. Their deaths were on him. Sepoy Dasgupta broke down, sobbing, hiding his face in his hands from the others, pretending it was the smoke that was causing tears to flow down his face. He staggered towards the trucks, wiping his face with the back of his sleeve. Two of the soldiers pulled him aboard the last truck in the convoy. He clambered into the back and turned to take one last look at the inferno that was the Baptist Church of Asakhua.

As the convoy drove away into the night, the Witch's anguished wails pierced through the billowing smoke. The Witch wailed for the villagers and their suffering. And she wailed for the innocent souls that had been lost that night, when Asakhua was burnt down to the ground.

CHAPTER 6

Sena had found a safe spot to bivouac for the night – a clearing with scattered rocks a little distance away from the trail that was surrounded by tall trees and thick foliage. He quickly got a small fire going and the two of them settled down, resting their sore backs against the rocks.

Sena took out the pack of cigarettes he'd taken off Sammy the night before and lit up two. Passing one to Sammy, he said: 'Tomorrow, we part ways. Serchhip is a couple of hours' walk from here. You'll find many of your army friends there who'll be happy to give you a ride back to Aizawl. Maybe even in handcuffs!'

Sammy ignored the barb. 'Where will you go, Sena?' he asked, puffing on his cigarette.

'You're headed north. I'm going south. That's all you need to know.'

They sat quietly for a while. Then Sammy asked Sena the question he'd been longing to ask ever since they'd met in the interrogation room. 'How is Martha?'

Sena ignored Sammy's question at first, then he lit another cigarette and replied guardedly: 'I don't know. I haven't seen her, Christine or Pa since I left home. After the Mautam, we moved to Aizawl, where we lived with my uncle who runs a motor workshop there. But when I joined the MNF, I broke all ties with them. I didn't want to put them at risk. I guess they're fine. And your family? How are they?'

'Mamma and Pa are back in Mangalore. I haven't met them since the night I left Asakhua. I've been so ashamed and angry. I should never have left Asakhua the way I did. Without clearing my name. Without speaking to Martha. And I guess I blamed them for that. I didn't even go home for Peter's funeral. What was the point?'

'Peter died?'

'Yes. He was killed in the 1965 war. In the battle of Asal Uttar. The Jeep he was in took a direct hit from a Pakistani Patton. Mercifully, he died instantly. Mamma hasn't taken it too well. She's been in depression. I get news of them from Pa's letters.'

'I'm sorry to hear that.'

'It's okay. It's been some time,' Sammy said hurriedly. 'I wrote Martha many letters when I was at the NDA. I never got a reply. Do you know if she got them?'

'If she didn't reply to your letters, she obviously doesn't want to have anything to do with you, Sammy. You should forget about her. In any case, you have nothing in common with her. You never did.'

'You're wrong, Sena. We had a lot in common. Much more than you think. I miss her, man. She meant everything to me. But I guess she must think I abandoned her and hate me for it. But I didn't. I didn't have a choice. Your father said he'd have me thrown into prison for raping her. My mother panicked and forced me to flee Asakhua. I guess she was trying to protect me. But that was a mistake. I should never have left. I should have stayed and fought for her.'

'Yeah, maybe you should have,' Sena said, guardedly.

'I've never understood why you got so mad at me, Sena. And why you never told your father the truth about Martha and me. You knew we loved each other. You knew I didn't rape her. I was your friend, man. I'd have given my life for you. Yet, you destroyed my life. For what? For being in love with your sister?'

'Fuck you, arsehole. You were just using her. If you were sincere, you would have told me how you felt about her. Instead, you were pretending to be my friend, while all along, all you wanted was to fuck her. And when you left her and ran away, I was proven right.'

'No. You weren't right then, and you aren't right now. The truth is, I wanted to tell you how I felt about her. But Martha wouldn't let me. She wanted you to hear it from her first. And you're wrong when you say all I wanted was to fuck her. I loved her, man. How many times do I have to tell you that? When you ran away from home, she became my best friend, my only friend; till you came back. I've never loved anyone after her. Never been with anyone after her.

It was real. And even today, even after all that's happened, I still love her.'

Sammy's honesty caught Sena off guard. Suddenly, all the years of anger, hatred and resentment seemed completely pointless. But Sena's ego was too fragile for him to admit he'd been wrong, or to apologize to Sammy for the violence he'd subjected him to, or for driving a wedge between him and Martha. Nonetheless, for the first time, he acknowledged Sammy's love for his sister. 'Perhaps, when all this is over, you should go and find her. Tell her how you feel. Who knows? It may not be too late.'

'It's been eight years,' Sammy said, bitterly. 'It's already too late.'

At dawn, a red serow and her fawn grazed in the soft morning light at the edge of the clearing where Sena and Sammy lay huddled next to the embers of the fire. A short distance away, Lance Naik Paswan and his sepoys spread out in a wide arc, their automatic rifles held out in front of them as they moved cautiously through the forest. Two of his scouts had tracked the fugitives to the clearing the previous night. While one of them had hidden and waited, observing the fugitives, the other had raced back to inform the lance naik, who wasted no time. Lance Naik Paswan got his men going and, by midnight, they were within striking distance of the fugitives. The lance naik decided they'd attack at first light, and he and his men had settled down for an uncomfortable night in the mosquito-infested forest.

At four in the morning, half an hour before sunrise, the lance naik and his men moved in for the kill. The fugitives were armed and dangerous, and the lance naik knew their best bet to avoid any casualties was to catch them off guard. He ordered his sepoys to fan out and converge towards the clearing from different directions. They'd almost made it undetected when the red serow spotted them and let out a frantic alarm call. The startled animal raced through the clearing, her fawn following close behind. The element of surprise lost, Lance Naik Paswan threw caution to the wind and lumbered forward with as much speed as he could manage.

The serow's call got Sena to his feet in a flash. He ran for cover, ducking behind a large boulder with his pistol drawn. Sammy was slower to react and, before he could get away, one of the sepoys clubbed him to the ground with his rifle. He grabbed Sammy by the collar and dragged him to the far end of the clearing, where Lance Naik Paswan had taken cover, positioned safely behind his men. The scout pointed to the large boulder behind which Sena had hidden himself. On the lance naik's signal, his men surrounded Sena.

The lance naik yelled out in Hindi: 'Come out quietly, chinkie, with your hands over your head, or I'll come there and shove my rifle up your arse.'

Sena considered his options. There was little hope of getting to the safety of the forest, even if he chose to make a break for it. He'd be gunned down the moment he broke cover. If he allowed himself to be recaptured, he might still have a chance to get away – just like he had earlier. His mind made up, he tossed the pistol over the boulder he had hidden himself behind and, with his hands held high over his head, stepped out into the clearing. He had barely made it a few steps when one of the sepoys clubbed him with the butt of his rifle, dropping him down to the ground. Another sepoy quickly mounted him, shoving his knee into the small of his back as he yanked his hands behind him and tied them together. Then he was dragged to the lance naik, just as Sammy had been.

Capturing the fugitives without a single shot being fired was a bit of an anti-climax for Lance Naik Paswan, who'd anticipated a shootout and some casualties on his side – action that would have guaranteed him another bravery citation and possibly another out-of-turn promotion. He toyed with the idea of staging an encounter, but his instructions had been very specific. Headquarters wanted the men alive.

Frustrated by the turn of events, Lance Naik Paswan turned to the two fugitives, who were lined up before him. He pumped up his chest, sucked in his bloated belly and moved closer to Sena. Then, he stopped and pulled back abruptly, his face turning ashen.

Reaching out, he grabbed Sena's throat with both his hands, nearly strangling him. He shrieked: 'Che? You motherfucker! I never thought I'd ever see you again. You don't remember me, do you? In Bungtalang, where you and your men escaped with the guns you dug up? You shot me, you motherfucker. Every time my arse hurts, I think of you. I should put a bullet in your head right now. But my officers want you alive. So, I can't shoot you. But when they start interrogating you at headquarters, you'll wish I had!' Then, slapping Sena hard across his face, he hissed, 'Motherfucking chinkie.'

When Sammy heard the lance naik address Sena as 'Che', he was infuriated. Turning to Sena contemptuously, he said: 'You lied to me. Why can you never speak the truth, man?'

Sena ignored him, staring straight ahead, expressionless.

Angered by Sammy's outburst, the lance naik turned his attention to him. 'Shut up!' he screamed. 'You will only speak when you are spoken to. You open your mouth once more, and I'll strip you naked and parade you all the way back to headquarters. You should be put before a firing squad. Fucking traitor!' He then spat in Sammy's face, his spittle stained red with the paan he'd chewed earlier that morning.

Having established his authority over the prisoners, Lance Naik Paswan turned on his heels and ordered his men to follow him. It would take them all day to get back to their post in Sailam, and the lance naik was in a hurry to get back to the comfort of his tent.

* * *

It was late afternoon when the village of Sailam came into sight. The soldiers were tired and had taken none of the precautions they'd been trained to take as they walked in a single file through the rice fields that surrounded the village. In the centre of the column were Sammy and Sena, their hands bound firmly with rough rope. Leading from the front was Lance Naik Paswan, who, drenched in sweat and dog-tired, was in a foul mood. He had walked more in the past couple of days than he had in many years, and he couldn't wait to get back to his tent, throw off his boots and his soaked, stinking uniform, and knock back a bottle of rum. But first, he'd have to radio headquarters about the prisoners and figure out what they wanted him to do with them. *Damn them all*, he thought to himself.

A group of children came running out from the village when they saw the patrol approach. They danced around the patrol, out of arms reach, pelting the soldiers with pebbles and taunting them with insults in Mizo and broken Hindi. Lance Naik Paswan led the patrol to the large banyan tree on the edge of the village. The soldiers dumped their rucksacks and rifles at the base of the tree, and slumped down on the ground under its shade, as did the prisoners. The three soldiers who'd been left behind on pillbox duty abandoned their positions and reported enthusiastically to the lance naik.

'You motherfuckers,' the lance naik snarled at them, 'I hope you enjoyed your vacation. Now get the fuck out of my sight and go stand guard over the two prisoners we've brought back with us. If they so much as move, shoot them.' The three soldiers saluted the lance naik and hurried away to do as they'd been told.

The village of Sailam was a cluster of twenty traditional Mizo bamboo huts surrounded by rice fields. The villagers treated the soldiers stationed there with contempt and wanted nothing more than for them to leave. Their sympathies and support were solidly with the MNF guerrillas, who they kept informed of the soldiers' activities. In fact, the sudden departure of most of the soldiers on patrol two days ago hadn't gone unnoticed or unreported. Neither had their return with the two prisoners.

Over wireless, the lance naik informed headquarters about the successful capture of the prisoners. He, of course, exaggerated how difficult it had been and conjured up an imaginary gun battle with the 'heavily armed' fugitives before they could be taken into custody. The lance naik's instructions from headquarters were precise: A section of soldiers from headquarters would get to Sailam in about three hours to take charge of the prisoners. Till then, the lance naik was to maintain a state of high alert and ensure that the prisoners were well guarded.

Yeah, like we're all sucking our dicks right now, thought the lance naik, as he acknowledged the instructions and ambled off to check on his men and the prisoners.

The prisoners had been dragged away from under the banyan tree out into the open, where they were made to sit on the ground with their backs to each other. The three soldiers were taking the job their lance naik had assigned to them very seriously. They had their backs to the prisoners while they took up positions facing three different directions, rifles in hand, looking out for any sign of danger. 'Enough farting around,' the lance naik yelled at the soldiers sitting in the shade of the banyan tree, smoking their bidis. 'Spread out and stay alert.'

As his tired men got to their feet slowly, picking up their gear, grumbling quietly amongst themselves at the hard-heartedness of their leader, the lance naik strode off towards one of the nearby huts, outside which an old Mizo man sunned himself on a rickety wooden chair, sipping tea from a cracked cup that was missing its handle.

'Tea, tea, myself and boys want tea,' the lance naik snarled at the old man in broken English.

The old man stared back at him blankly, as if he didn't exist. This infuriated the lance naik, who placed his boot on the chair and tipped it over, sending the old man sprawling to the ground, the cup slipping out of his hands and shattering. Then the lance naik strode past the old man and banged on the door of the hut. At first, there was no response, but when he persisted, the door was opened by a young Mizo girl, the old man's granddaughter, about seventeen, terrified by the sight of the belligerent lance naik on her doorstep.

'What do you want?' she asked him in English.

The lance naik hadn't expected the door to be opened by a young girl and, for a brief moment, he hesitated, unsure of what to do next. Then, he pushed past the girl and entered the hut, which was dimly lit with oil lamps. Inside, all was quiet and it seemed there was no one else at home. Still, the lance naik wasn't taking any chances. He drew his pistol and quickly scanned the hut to make sure he wasn't walking into an ambush.

Meanwhile, the girl had scurried into the kitchen at the back of the hut and cowered in a corner, hoping the lance naik would leave when he was done searching and not come for her. But he did. When he came into the kitchen, he stared hungrily at the girl, saying nothing. Then, he broke the silence, speaking with great tenderness, in the best English he could muster: 'Tea, tea, you make ten cups tea, for me and my boys.'

Unlike her grandfather, the girl understood what the man wanted and she hurried away to make the tea. She grabbed the old, dented kettle from the mud floor and filled it with water. Then she lit the wooden stove and put the kettle to boil, adding the dried tea leaves she'd drawn from the glass jar in which they were stored.

The lance naik watched the girl at work, the hunger in his loins now a raging storm. When he could bear it no more, he placed his pistol on a wooden chair that sat empty in a corner and moved quickly behind her, cupping her small breasts in his hands, pulling her close to him, and running his paan-stained tongue over the side of her neck hungrily.

The terrified girl began to sob quietly, her body trembling. 'No noise, you quiet, okay? Then I no kill, understand?' the lance naik whispered in her ear, even as his fondling became more frenetic.

In the kettle, the water continued to boil. The girl, repulsed by the man, was frozen in fear, her right hand still clenched tightly around the handle of the kettle. The lance naik unbuckled his trousers and let them drop down to his ankles. Then he pushed his underpants down and reached for the girl's free hand, placing it on his hardening manhood, moving it up and down, showing her what he wanted her to do, even as he groped under her puan with his other hand, reaching for her. His eyes half shut, his body shuddering with pleasure, he growled softly into the girl's ear in Hindi: 'Fucking chinkie whore! I haven't had a woman in months. You've come to me at just the right time.' Then, not wanting to waste his approaching orgasm, he grabbed the girl by her throat and slammed her into the wall He held her there with one hand, as he used the other to rip her puan off, exposing her.

Even in the frenzy of the moment, the lance naik registered the first staccato burst of a submachine gun being fired. It caused him to pause awkwardly, as he was preparing to shove his engorged manhood deep into the terrified girl. The second burst, followed by the unmistakable sound of small arms fire and the screaming of men in pain, sent the lance naik into panic. He tore himself away from the girl, pulling his underpants up with one hand as he reached for his pistol with the other. His movements hampered by his trousers still around his ankles, he fell to the floor and crawled to a window with bamboo shutters, taking great pains to stay low. He rested his back against the bamboo wall, desperately pulling his trousers up and buckling his belt. Then, crouching low, he opened one of the shutters slowly, just a crack, and peered outside.

In the village, a fierce gun battle was raging. A group of guerrillas had launched an attack on his men, catching them by surprise. The guerrillas swarmed the main street of the village, taking cover behind the village homes from where they fired on the soldiers. The soldiers returned the fire, but with the lance naik missing, they were leaderless and unable to launch a coordinated counterattack.

The lance naik felt the presence of an intruder in the room, creeping up behind him. Then he smelt her perfume and spun around to face the girl. The searing pain Lance Naik Paswan felt as the boiling water splashed directly on his face caused him to scream in agony. He dropped the pistol as he raised both his hands to his badly burnt face. Then, fear set in. He fumbled around on the floor of the hut, searching for his pistol. When he found it, he pointed the handgun towards where he thought the girl was and released a volley of shots into the darkness.

The lance naik's screams and the shots fired inside the hut hadn't gone unnoticed. The window to the room flew open and a man with a submachine gun appeared at it. The first burst from his weapon slammed into Lance Naik Paswan, killing him instantly. He fell next to the girl, who lay dying on the floor, her body riddled with bullets that the lance naik had fired, her hand still wrapped around the kettle.

CHAPTER 7

The skirmish was over in less than fifteen minutes. When it was done, seven of the Frontier Rangers' soldiers were dead and three had fled, crawling through the rice fields till they got to the safety of the forest. The men that had attacked them were from the Mizo National Volunteers that supported the formally structured MNA. The volunteers were dressed in style – cowboy hats, bell-bottoms, brightly coloured shirts and clodhoppers. That twenty of them had managed to sneak into the village undetected was an achievement. That they'd managed to decimate the well-armed squad, while suffering only two casualties, was nothing short of miraculous.

The bodies of the dead Frontier Rangers' soldiers, including that of Lance Naik Paswan, were dragged under the giant banyan tree and stripped of their watches, rings, wallets and anything else that could be of value. The leader of the volunteer force was taking stock of the captured weapons and ammunition. He was a strapping young man, about thirty, in trendy boot-cut denim jeans, a grey-checked, flannel shirt over which he wore a tightly fitted black leather jacket and an olive-coloured cowboy hat. On his wrist he wore a flashy Seiko Sportsmatic, with an oversized silver metal strap. He had the demeanour of a movie star – cool, confident and arrogant. If it wasn't for the surroundings, and the Sten gun slung over his shoulder, he could easily have passed off as one.

Sammy and Sena had raced to take cover behind a cluster of rocks when the attack began. The leader had just lit himself a Dunhill when they were brought to him at gunpoint. Cigarette hanging loosely from his curled lips, he saluted Sena casually. 'The famous Major Che in my care,' he said, with just the faintest hint of a smirk.

'And you are?' Sena asked.

'Azuala of the Mizo National Volunteers,' he replied. 'We were patrolling the edge of the forest when we received news that you'd been captured and brought to Sailam. We got here as quickly as we could.'

If Sena was grateful, his face didn't show it. Instead, he looked disdainfully at the volunteers as they looted the dead soldiers. Azuala signalled to one of his men, who walked up and quickly cut away the rope with which Sena's hands were bound. With Sena freed, Azuala turned his attention to Sammy in his tattered army uniform, looking dishevelled and tormented. 'Half of Assam is looking for you, Captain. You're a big hero!' he sneered. 'In fact, your army misses you so much, they've put a twenty-five-thousand-rupee reward on your head! You must be very special!' Then, he turned to Sena and asked: 'What do you want us to do with him?'

'He's coming with me. He's my prisoner,' Sena replied firmly.

Azuala stared at Sammy, weighing the pros and cons of taking him with them or getting rid of him.

'I need to get back to my battalion,' Sena snapped, interrupting Azuala's thoughts.

Azuala continued puffing on his cigarette. 'The area will soon be swarming with soldiers, Major. We should get back to our camp and lie low for a while. It's about ten klicks from here, in the jungle. Once we get to camp, I'll give you one of my boys, who knows where the Indian check posts are. He'll escort you to safety.'

'All right,' said Sena, 'let's do it.'

The march to the guerrilla camp took three hours. They walked in a single file along the bunds that separated the paddy fields and then along a narrow path that led deep into the jungle. The mood was upbeat, though the going slow, with each member of the volunteer force weighed down with the weapons, ammunition and trinkets they'd looted from the dead soldiers.

The volunteer camp had been set up in a clearing deep in the jungle. There were ten canvas tents that served as living quarters and a large parachute tent with a few wooden tables and chairs that served as an eating area. The perimeter of the camp was patrolled around the clock by armed volunteers.

Word of the successful ambush of the Frontier Rangers' post in Sailam had already reached camp by the time Azuala and his band of men got back. Azuala was lifted on to the shoulders of one of the volunteers and an impromptu, boisterous parade was held, marching him around the camp, followed by the volunteers cheering him along. The alcohol flowed freely at the campsite that night, and the celebrations carried on into the early hours of the morning.

When they'd got to the campsite, Sena had been escorted to Azuala's tent, where a camp cot and makeshift bedding had been laid out for him. Through the din of the celebrations, Sena slept like he hadn't slept in days – a deep, blissful, healing sleep, devoid of any dreams.

On the other hand, Sammy's night had been anything but restful. He'd been dragged away and pushed into a deep pit in the centre of the camp, which served as a holding cell for prisoners. When he crashed down on to the soft, damp mud floor, Sammy heard something hiss and slither away from him. Terrified, he lay completely still till he sensed the immediate danger had passed. Then, he fumbled in his pockets for the matchbox his captors had overlooked and lit a match, trying to make sense of the space he'd been confined in. The pit was about ten feet deep, and stank of piss and shit. It had been covered with a large rectangular bamboo frame that had been weighed down with rocks, making escape impossible. With the little light offered by the match he'd lit, Sammy saw the snake he'd heard disappear slowly into a hole in the floor. *For how long?* he wondered.

Late that night, Sammy heard the rocks being removed and the bamboo frame being pushed away. He looked up hopefully at the silhouettes standing around the perimeter of the hole. Then he heard their drunken laughter and whoops of delight as a shower of piss cascaded down on him.

As the sun rose, pencil-thin beams of light lit up the pit through the cracks in the bamboo frame. Sammy had crouched in one corner of the pit through most of the night, petrified that the snake would return. He hadn't seen enough of it to judge if it was a venomous cobra or a viper, or the more common keelback whose bite, while poisonous, was rarely lethal for an adult. But, at some point, in the night, sheer fatigue had overcome the fear and he'd slumped down on the ground and slept for a few hours. He woke up to the sound of the bamboo frame being pulled back once again, causing him to struggle to his feet defensively, not sure of what to expect. But it was only breakfast: a roll of chhangban was tossed down to him, which landed in a puddle of piss. Sammy gingerly took the soaked chhangban out of the puddle and placed it on the damp floor to dry. He wasn't hungry, he was thirsty.

It had been hours since he'd drunk any water and his lips were parched. He felt exhausted and dizzy, all signs he recognized of dehydration.

In Azuala's tent, Sena had woken up, refreshed from a good night's sleep. He pushed himself up on his elbows and looked across at Azuala, who lay sprawled across his camp cot, bare bodied, his boots still on, his Sten gun flung carelessly on the floor. The tent reeked of alcohol and tobacco. Disgusted, Sena got off his cot and looked for his clothes that he'd dumped on the floor the night before. The clothes were gone. Instead, lying at the foot of the cot were boxer shorts, a black T-shirt, an olive-and-brown camouflage jacket, with matching trousers, a fresh pair of cotton socks and jungle boots. Sena looked sharp in his new outfit as he stepped out of the tent into the bright sunshine.

But what he saw shocked him.

Everywhere, the camp bore evidence of the debauchery of the previous night, with men and women lying together on blankets that had been used as makeshift bedding. Dozens of emptied bottles of booze lay scattered all over the camp. The remnants of the campfire that still burnt indicated that the party had only just ended.

In the parachute tent, a handful of volunteers who'd called it an early night were up and about, preparing breakfast – pots of *bai* – a stew of wild, edible plants seasoned with local spices, boiled rice – chhangban and kettles filled with tea. Sena strolled around the camp, smoking a cigarette, dismayed by the lack of discipline, the missing perimeter security and the complete breakdown of the chain of command. *If the Frontier Rangers attack now, we'll all be slaughtered*, he thought, his anger mounting. As Sena turned to head back to Azuala's tent, his attention was drawn to the large bamboo frame on the ground. He squatted down and peered through the cracks into the pit below. Then he leapt up and grabbed hold of one end of the rough jute rope that bound the bamboo stalks together into a frame, tugging at it with all his might, till the frame moved, uncovering the pit below and revealing Sammy's limp form, curled up in the centre of the pit, the roll of chhangban still lying uneaten besides him. On Sena's instructions, Sammy was hauled out of the pit and carried into the dining tent, where he was placed on a wooden table. One of the volunteers, who'd been trained to handle medical emergencies, took over. Sammy was alive, but weak and delirious.

By the time Sena returned to his tent, his patience had run thin. Azuala was still passed out. Storming up to him, Sena grabbed hold of Azuala's legs and yanked the snoring man off his cot, sending him crashing to the ground. Startled, Azuala staggered to his feet, the alcohol from the night still coursing through his veins. Before he could make sense of what was happening, Sena had splattered him with a bucket of cold water he'd found lying outside the tent. It caused Azuala to snap back to life. Furious, he lunged at Sena, who side-stepped his charge and tripped him, sending him crashing to the floor once again. Before Azuala could get back on to his feet, Sena was on top of him, one arm around his throat, in a chokehold from which there was no escape.

'You're a fucking disgrace to every Mizo who puts his life on the line for our motherland,' Sena hissed to Azuala. 'I don't know what sort of operation you think you're running here, but you will get your act together right now, or I'll cut your fucking throat and string you up as an example for all the volunteers to see what happens to a debauched, third-rate scumbag like you.' Warning delivered, Sena released the pressure from around Azuala's neck and stood up.

Azuala, seething at the humiliation he'd been subjected to, got to his feet slowly. 'I saved your life, and this is how you repay me?'

Sena took a step forward menacingly. 'You want me to thank you for doing your duty? This isn't a fucking youth camp, you motherfucker. We're fighting a war. Now get dressed and get out there and take charge before I fucking kill you.'

CHAPTER 8

Commandant Aiyar and his deputy boarded the USSR-made MI-4 helicopter for their thirty-minute flight from Lunglei to Aizawl. They'd been summoned to an emergency meeting by Brigadier Kabraji to take stock of the attack on the Frontier Rangers' post in Sailam the previous day.

It was a clear, cloudless day, and the MI-4 quickly climbed to its maximum operational ceiling of 18,000 feet, which would keep it out of range of small-arms fire from the ground. The helicopter flew over thickly wooded, rolling hills, deep valleys with raging rivers and tiny hamlets perched atop ridges on the hillsides. In the distance, the snow-capped peaks of the Himalayas stretched on for as far as the eye could see. But none of this was of any interest to the commandant, who had long grown weary of the scenic beauty of the land. He shut his eyes and let the constant throbbing of the MI-4's engines and the vibrations of its cabin drown out his overpowering sense of hopelessness.

When the MI-4 touched down at the army helipad in Aizawl, a Jeep was waiting to drive the commandant and his deputy to their meeting at army headquarters. When the Indian Air Force bombed Aizawl in March 1966, many areas of the town had been razed to the ground, its residents fleeing into the surrounding hills. But now, just a little over a year later, the town appeared to have bounced back to life. The markets were crowded once again and frenetic reconstruction was underway, with rubble being cleared, and new homes and buildings rising up to replace those destroyed in the bombing.

The headquarters of 61 Mountain Brigade in Aizawl was the nerve centre that controlled and coordinated all anti-insurgency operations in the Mizo Hills. Like the conductor of an orchestra that has many brilliant musicians, but who must play in sync to bring alive a symphony, the man tasked with making sure that the Indian Army, the Frontier Rangers, the local police and the intelligence agencies didn't work at cross purposes was Brigadier Kabraji.

The conference room at the headquarters was well lit and large. It had a rectangular conference table in the centre that could seat about twenty people. There was a large, sturdy oak chair at the head of the table, which was reserved for the brigadier, whether or not he was present at a meeting. For everyone else, there were ordinary, padded, wooden chairs arranged symmetrically on either side of the table. An additional row of chairs ran along the periphery of the room, creating enough capacity for meetings with seating for up to fifty officers. The whitewashed walls of the conference room were decorated with poster-sized, black-and-white blow-ups of men of 61 Mountain Brigade in action in different theatres of war, their wooden frames painted white with a thin sheet of protective glass covering each picture.

An orderly opened the conference room door for the commandant, while his deputy settled down in the waiting area, just outside. The brigadier wasn't in attendance. The meeting was being chaired by his second in command, Colonel Vaibhav Kala, who sat in the centre with Major Niladri Mukherjee, Captain Samuel's reporting officer, on his right. Opposite him sat Colonel Kabir Singh, deputy inspector general of the Frontier Rangers, the commandant's immediate boss. Colonel Kala waved the commandant in, and he slid quickly into the seat that had been kept vacant for him, next to the DIG of the Frontier Rangers.

Colonel Kala wasn't one for idle chit-chat, so he cut to the chase immediately: 'The attack in Sailam yesterday was front page news in the national newspapers this morning, and the politicians in New Delhi have their knickers in a twist. I've been on the phone twice today with the brigadier, and he's furious. He wants a detailed report by 1600 hours today. So, we'd better get started quickly.'

The commandant was the first off the block: 'Is there news of the two prisoners that the Frontier Rangers' men were guarding, sir?'

Major Mukherjee looked up sharply, and there was no mistaking the warning in his tone when he said: 'Captain Samuel is not a prisoner, Commandant. He's a captain in the Indian Army. And I'm his commanding officer.'

The commandant fearlessly picked up the gauntlet Major Mukherjee had flung down. 'Your captain shot one of my men, Major, and escaped with an MNF guerrilla, who we captured in a raid in which he gunned down five soldiers. So, forgive me, but as far as I'm concerned, your captain is one of them.'

Colonel Kala was disturbed by this sudden skirmish, and he moved quickly to rein in both parties: 'What's this all about? Mukherjee, you told me the captain had been abducted by the MNF.'

'Yes, I believe that to be true, sir. I know the captain well. He's a good soldier – brave, sensible and sincere. I have no doubt at all that if he's missing, it's because he was abducted.' He added, 'Incredibly, the commandant has placed a bounty of twenty-five thousand rupees on his head, sir. There are men hunting for an Indian Army officer all over the Mizo Hills, quite literally to make a killing! I want to know who in the Frontier Rangers authorized this?'

Colonel Kala turned sharply to the DIG. His voice on edge, he asked: 'Is this true, Kabir?'

The DIG was caught off-guard, but he recovered quickly enough to adroitly deflect the colonel's question towards his subordinate. He said, 'I hope not! Commandant?'

The commandant's face betrayed no trace of fear, or that he was lying, when he replied: 'Of course not, sir. It's just a rumour doing the rounds.'

Colonel Kala probed further. 'The charges you've made against the captain are very serious, Commandant. Can you prove any of this?'

'Yes, sir. In fact, I have my men verifying reports of previous links between them.'

This was the first time Major Mukherjee had heard that there might be proof of a link between Captain Samuel and the escaped prisoner, and his voice betrayed his uncertainty when he addressed the colonel, sounding a note of caution. 'I don't think we should jump to conclusions about Captain Samuel without concrete proof, sir. He comes from a distinguished army family of war heroes. And he's had an excellent record so far.'

But the commandant knew he had the advantage, and he didn't let up. 'What Major Mukherjee needs to tell us, sir, is why this captain was handpicked by him and sent to us? It's a huge security gaffe, sir,' he said, ignoring Major Mukherjee and addressing the colonel, who shuffled uncomfortably in his seat.

Major Mukherjee was clearly on the defensive and unprepared for the commandant's direct attack. He replied: 'I sent Captain Samuel to interrogate the prisoner because he spoke the local language. That's all. There's nothing more to it.'

'You think there's a link between the attack on the Frontier Rangers' post and the guerrilla they'd apprehended?' Colonel Kala asked the commandant.

'I think there definitely is, sir. According to our informants, he's quite senior in the MNF and close to Laldenga. The attack could have been to secure his release, sir. And that of Captain Samuel.'

'Are you saying Captain Samuel is working for the MNF, Commandant?' the colonel barked.

'All the evidence seems to suggest so, sir,' the commandant replied, nonchalantly.

The room was silent while Colonel Kala took his time lighting up his pipe, carefully considering all the information he'd been presented with. Then, his mind made up, he said: 'Okay, Kabir, I want your Frontier Rangers' boys to figure out what's going on. And try and get us back Captain Samuel and the prisoner alive.'

'Yes, sir,' the DIG replied.

'Unfortunately, I've now got to go give the brigadier the bad news. And I'm not looking forward to that conversation. This meeting is over. Thanks for coming across,' the colonel said, curtly.

The men stood up and saluted the colonel, as they headed out of the conference room. 'Mukherjee, you stay,' the colonel ordered.

'So, there's a bounty on your boy's head, eh, Mukherjee?' the colonel asked, when the room had cleared, puffing away on his pipe. 'That's a new low, even for the Frontier

Rangers. Find out what this is really about, Mukherjee. Be discreet. And report back to me. Got it?'

'Yes, sir,' Major Mukherjee replied, standing up and saluting the colonel smartly, before exiting the room.

* * *

DIG Kabir Singh was a man of few words, and he usually chose those words carefully. But now, he was livid. When he and the commandant had exited the building that housed the conference room and were out of earshot of the sentries guarding it, he swung around to face the commandant.

'You fucking moron! How dare you spring this shit on me without any warning? Why haven't you kept me in the loop on the investigation you're running on the captain? You think you run the Frontier Rangers? Vinay, I'm sick of your insubordination and your attitude. Who the hell do you think you are?' His sudden outburst startled the commandant.

The commandant moved quickly to de-escalate. 'I'm sorry, sir,' he said. 'I thought we'd have time before the meeting to brief you on the latest developments. But the flight was delayed due to bad weather and, by the time we got here, the meeting had already begun. I'm sorry that we were late and that we didn't brief you in advance.'

'This isn't the first time this is happening, Vinay. We're all aware of the personal tragedy you've had to deal with. And believe me, I feel for you. But your behaviour is increasingly erratic, insolent and insubordinate, and I have no option but to report it. You're just a cog in a large wheel; it's time you stop behaving as if you're the fucking wheel,' the DIG snapped.

'Yes, sir. I'm sorry, sir,' the commandant replied, sounding sincere and contrite, even though all he really felt was contempt for his boss.

'You will keep me posted about every aspect of the operation to get back the escaped prisoner and the captain. You won't even piss without my permission. Am I clear about this, Commandant?'

'Yes, sir, absolutely, sir,' the commandant replied, with only the faintest hint of a smile playing out around the edges of his lips. It wasn't lost on his boss, who turned around and stormed off towards his waiting vehicle.

Left alone with his deputy, the commandant took out his packet of Charminar and lit himself one, passing the pack to his deputy. 'Fuck him!' the commandant spat out viciously. 'We've got a job to do, let's go do it.'

Deputy Commandant Saikia took a long drag on his cigarette, then he said: 'While you were in the meeting, I managed to connect with one of our informers, Commandant. He's got a concrete lead, but he's heard about the reward and refused to tell me anything more on the phone. He wants to meet in person. He's in Serchhip. It's a three-hour drive. We should go see him.'

'What are we waiting for? Let's go,' the commandant said, striding purposefully towards the Jeep that was waiting for them, his deputy scrambling to keep up.

CHAPTER 9

The day at the volunteer camp in the jungle passed uneventfully, with the attack by the Frontier Rangers that Sena had been worried about not materializing. Azuala had stayed out of Sena's way after their ugly confrontation earlier that morning. But, late in the afternoon, he sent word to Sena through one of his volunteers, Fakawma, a young, awkward lad in his teens, that guerrillas from Sena's Vanapa Battalion would rendezvous with him at the Replang Bridge at ten that night to escort him to safety. The bridge was a two-hour drive from the camp, but it could take them much longer if Indian patrols were spotted in the area. Azuala wanted Sena to be ready to leave at sundown.

'How is the captain?' asked Sena.

'He's fine,' Fakawma replied. 'He's even eaten some lunch.'

'Good,' said Sena. 'Get him in a fresh set of clothes; he's coming with me.'

Fakawma saluted Sena sloppily and sauntered off to carry out his instructions.

At dusk, an old, battered Willy's Jeep was rolled out from under a camouflage cover and jump-started. Sammy, dressed in khaki fatigues, his hands bound behind his back with a rough rope, was hauled into the back of the Jeep, wedged in between Fakawma and another heavily armed man.

With a quart of rum inside him, Azuala was back to his jovial self. 'Should we go, Major Che? I'm sorry you won't be staying with us longer; we were just getting to know each other better,' he chortled.

Sena glared at Azuala, fighting the urge to slam a fist into Azuala's face and drop him to the ground. But he knew that wouldn't serve any purpose. He needed to get back to his battalion. Teaching Azuala manners and discipline would have to wait for another time. So he said nothing. He merely nodded and followed Azuala out of the tent, walking briskly towards the waiting Jeep. With Azuala driving and Sena riding shotgun up front, the Jeep pulled away slowly and soon disappeared into the jungle.

It was a dark, moonless night. With the headlights of the Jeep turned off, the drive was painfully slow. The disused track they drove on wound deep into the jungle, eventually rising steeply to join a narrow, untarred road that led to Replang Bridge. Parts of the bridge had been washed away in a flood years earlier, and the road now ran through the rivulet that flowed below the damaged bridge.

About a hundred metres beyond the bridge was a large, open field – about twenty acres in all – surrounded by the jungle on three sides, with the road forming the boundary in the front. The field had once housed a Frontier Rangers' camp, but it had been abandoned after the adjoining village was 'regrouped'.

Azuala parked the Jeep at the edge of the jungle at one end of the field and turned off the engine. The only sound was the overpowering chirping of crickets and the gurgling of the rivulet close by. About an hour later, from the other end of the field, they saw a flash of light. A pause, then three quick flashes. The signal! 'They're here!' Azuala whispered, flashing the headlights of the Jeep in the same pattern as he'd just observed.

Sena got down, looking warily across the field towards where he'd seen the flashes of light. He could make out the outline of another Jeep in the distance, but little else. Azuala ambled up to Sena and saluting him smartly, he said: 'Well, Major Che, I guess this is where we say goodbye. You're in safe hands now. Fakawma will escort the captain to make sure he doesn't try anything stupid.'

Sena nodded curtly at Azuala. 'Let's go,' was all he said, as he began walking slowly across the field, with Sammy following, his hands still tied, the butt of Fakawma's rifle shoved firmly into his back.

Sena, Sammy and Fakawma were halfway across the field when they spotted a man walking slowly towards them. Sena stopped and peered into the darkness at the approaching silhouette.

'Who is that?' Sena spun around towards Fakawma.

Fakawma had stepped away from Sammy. His rifle was raised, but it wasn't pointing at Sammy any more but at Sena. 'Keep walking, Major,' Fakawma said quietly, his finger on the trigger. Sena glared at him, his face filled with anger and contempt.

Focused on the approaching figure, Sammy had missed the exchange between Sena and Fakawma. Then, he exclaimed, 'Paul!'

The man stopped when he heard Sammy's exclamation. It was Subedar Major Paul, though not in uniform. His left hand was heavily bandaged, his right hand firmly gripping a pistol that was pointed at Sena, a duffel bag slung over his shoulder.

Fakawma piped in: 'No sudden movements or I'll blow your head off, Major. Now, drop your pistol on the ground.'

Sammy was aghast by the sudden turn of events. 'What's going on?' he asked, perplexed.

'We've been sold to the Frontier Rangers by this traitor and his leader,' Sena spat out viciously.

'Your pistol, Major. I won't ask again,' Fakawma said, his voice cold and dispassionate.

Sena reached behind slowly and took out Sammy's pistol, which he'd tucked under the waistband of his trousers, and let it drop to the ground.

'Kick it to me,' Fakawma ordered.

Sena kicked the pistol firmly towards Fakawma, who reached down and picked it up, pocketing it. Then he looked towards Paul and barked: 'Give me the money!'

Paul pulled the duffel bag off his shoulder and flung it towards Fakawma, who moved quickly to take possession of it. With his rifle still pointed at Sena, he began moving slowly away from him. 'Goodbye, Major,' he smirked. 'Enjoy!'

And with that, he turned and ran.

With Fakawma gone, Paul gave Sena and Sammy his undivided attention. 'Gentlemen, we meet again! Don't try anything stupid. I have been ordered to shoot you both if I have the slightest doubt. And I'm already in great doubt.'

Sena and Sammy moved forward slowly in a single file, with Paul following close behind, his pistol pointed at Sammy. Sena didn't know who was in the waiting Jeep, but he knew that if he didn't take his chances right there and then, he was a dead man. So, he did what he'd been trained to do.

Dropping down and twisting around, he hurled his body at Sammy, sending him crashing into Paul, catching him by surprise. Instinctively, Paul's finger pulled at the trigger it was wrapped around. The pistol went off with a loud bang, the bullet whizzing harmlessly into the dark night. In a flash, Sena was on Paul, clambering on top of him, grabbing the hand holding the pistol, even as he smashed his fist into Paul's injured shoulder, causing him to scream in agony. 'Let go of the pistol or I'll tear your arm out!' Sena cried, as he slammed his fist into Paul's shoulder again and again.

Unable to bear the pain, Paul finally loosened his grip and flung his pistol into the darkness, away from Sena.

The shot had alerted the men waiting at both ends of the field. Caution was thrown to the wind as the headlights of both Jeeps came on, illuminating the field. Then the firing began, targeting the silhouettes wrestling on the ground, with no concern for the safety of either combatant. Rolling away from Paul, Sena ran, crouching low, towards the cover offered by the jungle, bullets thudding into the ground all around him.

Desperate to get out of the crossfire, Sammy followed Sena, mimicking his movements, keeping low, handicapped by the fact that his hands were still bound behind his back.

With the threat from Sena gone, Paul, who was in great pain and not thinking clearly, crawled around in the mud on his hands and knees, searching desperately for the pistol that he'd flung away. When he found it, he stood up and, pointing his weapon in the direction he'd seen Sena escape, opened fire. It was a mistake. He looked surprised and disappointed when a hail of bullets, fired from both ends of the field, slammed into him, killing him instantly.

Sena had run, zig-zagging, towards the jungle when he came across an old irrigation canal that cut across the field. The canal was three feet deep and offered excellent cover. Sena leapt into it to buy himself some time. He knew he didn't have long. The two Jeeps had converged to the centre of the field. Soon they'd start searching for him. Then Sammy leapt into the canal beside him, looking crazed and out of breath.

'Why are you following me?' Sena growled.

'Oh, shut up! Do you have a plan?' Sammy whispered.

'We've got to make a run for the jungle. We won't last long here.'

'But there's no cover. We'll be shot for sure,' Sammy replied uncertainly.

'We're going to be out in the open for about a minute,' Sena said. 'Keep your head down and don't run in a straight line. Got it?'

'You better untie me first,' Sammy said, twisting around to offer Sena his hands. Sena yanked at the knots impatiently, loosening them enough for Sammy to be able to free his hands himself. Then he crawled out of the ditch and made a run for the jungle, weaving left and right, followed closely by Sammy. As they ran, they heard a voice yell out an alert.

The two Jeeps spun around and raced across the field, rapidly gaining ground on the fleeing men. Sena and Sammy would not have made it to the safety of the jungle had the lead Jeep not crashed into the irrigation ditch, forcing the driver of the second Jeep to slam the brakes, bringing the chase to an anticlimactic end.

CHAPTER 10

The hounds were relentless. They'd taken on an almost demonic obsession with the scent they were tracking, baying with excitement every time they smelt it. It was the flagging stamina of their handlers that held them back – the constant straining at their leashes tiring them. Left to themselves, the hounds would have run the fugitives down in under an hour.

Above, on the ridge, Sena and Sammy could hear their pursuers get closer. The river offered them the best chance of escape. But to get to it meant wading through the gushing mountain brook that flowed down the hill to the river, as the foliage along its banks was too thick to push through. Sena leapt into the brook, with Sammy following close behind. The moss-covered rocks in the bed of the brook made the going painfully slow, especially for Sammy. Sena was moving much faster, stopping every now and then, turning back to check on Sammy. 'We've got to keep moving,' he said. 'We're almost there. I can hear the river now.'

Sammy tried to pick up the pace. He shouldn't have. His left foot slid out from under him, throwing him off balance and sending him crashing down on to the jagged rocks in the bed of the stream, his body twisting desperately to break his fall. He landed heavily on his right shoulder and felt it slip right out of its socket. The pain that followed was more intense than anything he had ever experienced before, causing him to forget that they were running for their lives and scream out in agony.

Sena was on Sammy in a flash. Cupping his mouth and dragging him out of the brook and into a small clearing by its side, he growled, 'Don't scream! You'll get us killed. Do you understand?' Sammy nodded, his face contorted in agony, trying not to vocalize the excruciating pain he felt. Sena was feeling around Sammy's injured shoulder with his fingers. 'It's not broken! It's dislocated,' he said. 'I'm going to have to put it back.'

Sammy wasn't sure what he meant. And he didn't care. All he wanted was for the pain to stop. 'How will you do that?' he groaned.

'Just relax,' Sena said. 'I've got this.' Sammy grimaced as Sena laid him down on his back, in the clearing. Then, he grabbed a thin, dried wooden branch and forced it into Sammy's mouth. 'Chew on this. And relax the muscles in your shoulder, okay? That's the most important thing.'

'I'm trying to.' Sammy groaned loudly.

'Well, try harder,' Sena snapped.

Moving behind him, Sena gripped Sammy's right hand firmly by his wrist. Then he began moving Sammy's hand back, slowly, to the nape of his neck. Sammy grimaced in pain, biting down hard on the piece of wood in his mouth.

A few hundred metres away, the baying hounds had picked up Sammy and Sena's scent once again. Their pursuers had found the brook and, like Sammy and Sena, they were coming straight down it. Ten minutes, maybe fifteen … Not more.

'On the count of three, two …' And then Sammy felt one, intense, blinding moment of pain, as Sena tugged his hand down towards his left shoulder blade. A popping sound and Sammy's world went dark.

'You okay, man?' Sammy heard Sena, before he saw his blurry face inches away, peering down at him, looking worried. But the pain was gone. Totally gone. Like it had never existed. And his shoulder had slipped right back into its socket!

Sammy let out a deep breath and picked himself up slowly. 'That was incredible, man. I feel no pain! How did you do that?'

Sena didn't explain. There wasn't time for that. 'We need to go. We need to go now!' he said, urgently.

Sena set off again. Sammy tried his best to keep pace with him. It was tougher now. The slope had become steeper and the water flowed faster. Somewhere below them, they could hear the raging river. Above, they could hear the excited voices of their pursuers, shouting out to each other. The hounds had finally been released. Freed of their leashes, the fugitives' scent firmly imprinted in their memory, they raced forward, eager to hunt down their prey.

Just when it seemed that the jungle would never release Sammy and Sena from its clutches, they found themselves ejected out into the open, on to a rocky overhang that jutted out over a steep cliff face over which the brook cascaded, its waters dropping down into the river.

Sena moved cautiously to the edge of the overhang, crouching low, his hands outstretched like an expert tight-rope artiste, balanced on a rope high up in the sky. Sammy lay down on his belly and crawled slowly after him.

From the edge of the overhang, Sammy and Sena could see that the water flowing off the sheer cliff face had created a pool at the base, eroding away the rocks around it. The pool had a radius of fifteen or twenty feet, no more.

'We've got to jump,' Sena said, matter-of-factly.

Sammy looked horrified. 'Are you fucking crazy, Sena? It's suicide. Let's go back into the jungle. There has to be a path down to the river.'

'We don't have time for that, Sammy. Those bastards will show us no mercy. We can't let them get their hands on us.' Sena walked backwards, slowly and deliberately, making room for himself.

'Stop!' Sammy called out weakly.

Sena made a furtive sign of the cross, then took off without an iota of self-doubt, his arms pumping back and forth like a champion sprinter, his knees lifting high, accelerating, hitting peak speed before he reached the edge of the abyss and threw himself over it, his arms flailing wildly, as he hurtled down towards the pool below.

Sammy crawled hurriedly to the edge of the overhang, afraid of what he might see. The pool below was strangely tranquil. Then, Sammy saw Sena break to the surface and swim strongly to the edge of the pool. He hauled himself over the rocks and flopped down on his belly, panting, on a small, sandy patch of beach, just beyond the rocks. Sammy saw Sena turn and look at him. He waved frantically, urging Sammy to jump.

Somewhere above him, in the jungle, Sammy could hear the baying hounds get closer. *Soon they'll be here on this rock, gnawing at me,* he thought. *Perhaps jumping off the cliff to a certain death is a better option.* Sammy's thoughts were interrupted by the first bullets fired by their pursuers crashing into the rocky overhang all around him, sending a spurt of adrenaline racing through his body. Their pursuers had him in their sights and were shooting down at him from an elevation. Sammy knew it was now or never. His mind made up, he walked backwards from the edge of the cliff face, like he'd seen Sena do. When he had no more room, he made a wild dash, leaping off the rock face, his eyes shut tight, a terrible grimace on his face, his fists clenched, certain he was about to die.

As he fell through the air, Sammy felt his spirit free itself of its body. An overpowering feeling of love washed over him, as he surrendered himself unquestioningly and unequivocally to his fate. It was just as his father had told him it would be. All those he loved and cared for were there for him, drawing him away, deeper and deeper into the darkness, even as each of their faces grew brighter, allowing him to see them so very clearly, filling his heart with joy. Martha was there, smiling at him, reaching out for him, drawing him into her, and his father, so proud of the man he'd become, and there floating towards him, his birth mother, beautiful and radiant, touching his face tenderly. Then, he felt Sena's presence and everything changed; the faces of those he loved disappeared and he was alone once again – cold and scared. Some unseen hand hurled a bamboo spear at him, causing him to twist and turn in panic, to try and escape, to get out of its way, but it tracked him unrelentingly; and then the rats, hundreds and hundreds of rats, gnawing at his body, feasting on his flesh, his eyes bulging as if they'd explode, blood pouring out of his nose, gasping, desperate to breathe and then, suddenly, complete darkness.

Eighty feet is a long way to fall even for an experienced cliff diver. To survive that fall, Sammy needed a miracle, nothing less. That morning, there were at least three. The first: missing the jagged rocks and landing feet first in the deepest part of the pool. The second: not having his spine irreparably damaged when his head was wrenched backwards by the force of the impact, when he slammed into the water at over a hundred kilometres an hour. The third: Having a strong swimmer like Sena looking out for him, who dived into the pool after Sammy had failed to surface even twenty seconds after impact, finding his lifeless form floating at the bottom of that dark pool, dragging him back up to its surface and resuscitating him.

When Sammy regained consciousness, spluttering and gasping for air, he found himself lying on the sand behind a clump of bushes, out of sight of the cliff, a worried Sena peering down at him. He breathed in deeply and slowly, the increased flow of oxygen burning his throat and his chest. Other than a few cuts and bruises, he had no major injuries. His body hurt terribly though, thanks to the beating it had taken the past few days. He wished for nothing more than to lie there in the warm, comforting sand, not moving, not running, just lying absolutely still.

But Sena had other plans. 'Sammy, we need to get going. Azuala and his men will be down here soon; we've got to go.'

Sammy knew Sena was right, but if he could only rest, just a little more, he'd find the stamina to keep running. But it wasn't to be. Sena reached down and, grabbing hold of Sammy's hand, yanked him to his feet. Sammy felt his world spin as the blood rushed to his head. He swayed unsteadily, like someone who'd had too much to drink. When the spinning stopped, he opened his eyes. Taking a deep breath, he set off determinedly, following

Sena, who was already pushing his way through the undergrowth.

* * *

After the disastrous exchange at Replang Bridge, Azuala knew that if word of his betrayal leaked out, the MNF would show him no mercy. His only chance was to hunt Sena and Sammy down before they could get to safety. Luckily, the area they'd escaped into was surrounded by thick jungles and it would take them at least a day to get to the nearest village. That gave him enough time to find them. But he couldn't do it on his own. So, he called for Izak, a local tracker who Azuala often used on his hunts, and his bloodhounds.

They'd set off at the crack of dawn – Azuala, Fakawma, Izak and three other heavily armed men from Azuala's gang – moving quickly through the jungle. The baying hounds picked up the scent of the men they were tracking in the first hour itself and raced ahead, forcing their way through the thick foliage Within a couple of hours, they had the fugitives in their sights, but as they moved in for the kill, their suicidal leap off the cliff had left Azuala and his gang stumped.

As they peered over the cliff's edge, Fakawma was the first to offer his opinion. 'Nobody could have survived a jump from this height. We can head back.'

Azuala turned on him angrily. 'Shut up, Fuka. We're going to keep searching till we find them or their bodies.

If Major Che gets away to tell his story, we're dead men. The MNF will cut off our balls and feed us piece by piece to the dogs.'

Izak was circumspect. 'The dogs always find what they're looking for. It's only a matter of time,' he said to no one in particular.

'We need to get down and search at the bottom of the cliff. If they didn't survive the jump, their bodies will be splattered on the rocks. There must be a path leading down. Let's find it,' Azuala ordered as he headed back into the jungle, his men following him sullenly. The hounds, silenced by the sudden disappearance of the scent they'd been tracking, were back on their leashes.

An hour later, Azuala was down at the edge of the pool, peering into its dark-green waters, while his men and the hounds searched around its periphery, looking for the bodies of the two men.

In the sand, at the edge of the pool, they spotted a faint hint of footprints and the signs of something heavy being dragged. Izak followed the tracks that led to a clump of bushes, behind which there had clearly been a lot of recent activity. He called out to Azuala, who arrived quickly by his side, followed by the others. Izak silently pointed out the footprints leading away from the clearing and into the thick jungle. Azuala knew then that the fugitives had survived. His face betraying no emotion, he nodded at Izak, who walked over to the hounds that had picked up the scent of their prey once again and were furiously tugging at their leashes. Izak released the hounds. The hunt was on once again!

* * *

After an hour of pushing their way through the thick undergrowth, Sammy and Sena stumbled upon a worn-out path that had led them down to the fast-flowing Tlawng River. The path ran just above the river, parallel to it, with gentle undulations that made their going much easier. Surviving the mad leap of faith from off the high cliff had filled Sammy with a renewed sense of confidence and the belief that they'd escape their pursuers and get to safety. *It has to be,* he thought, *it's why we survived the jump.* That belief fuelled a second wind, a burst of endorphins, in him that allowed him to match Sena step for step, keeping pace with him, as they moved quickly down the path.

Three hours into their march, Sena suddenly ducked behind a stack of freshly cut bamboo stalks that lay on the side of the path. A startled Sammy did likewise. Then they heard voices close at hand. Inching out from behind the bamboo, Sammy and Sena moved cautiously forward. Up ahead, the path dropped suddenly down to the river's edge. From a vantage point, the two men surveyed the scene below.

Four women, each carrying a bamboo basket filled with bundles of pruned tree branches and driftwood, were by the riverside. To each basket was attached a flat, frayed cloth strap that was used to support the load on the women's foreheads. Just then, in the distance, the two men heard the dreaded baying of the hounds and knew then that their pursuers were once more on their trail and closing in on them quickly. They had little time to lose, but they couldn't risk being spotted by the women. So, they waited!

The women were pulling on a rope that ran across the narrow river. One end of the rope was tied to a rickety bamboo raft that lay loosely secured on the opposite bank. The raft had two metal hoops hammered into its frame at each end, through which two ropes were tied. One end of each rope was lassoed around the trunk of a large tree on each riverbank, with enough play in the ropes to allow anyone on either bank to pull the raft across to them. Once on board the raft, they'd simply pull themselves across the river using the other rope. Sammy and Sena watched as the women hauled themselves across the river on the raft, before securing it on the other side and setting off in a single file to their village.

Sena knew that the odds were stacked against them and it was only a matter of time before the hounds ran them down. Their only chance was to put as much distance as they could between them and their pursuers as quickly as they could. The raft gave them an opportunity to do just that.

When the women disappeared from view, Sena leapt to his feet. Racing down to the riverbank, he grabbed the rope attached to the raft and began pulling it back across the river. Sammy lent him a hand, assuming Sena's plan was to cross over to the other bank, just like the women had. But when they'd pulled the raft over, and he'd clambered on board, he saw Sena race back up the track and return with a long bamboo stem, about ten feet long, that he threw on to the raft. Then, he untied the knots that secured the ropes to the metal hoops, freeing the raft, allowing the current to grab hold of it and send it spinning into the centre of the river. Sena stood upright at the back, trying to guide the raft with the long bamboo stem, even as Sammy lay spreadeagled, his hands grabbing the sides of the raft, watching terror-stricken as the raft picked up speed and raced down the river.

CHAPTER 11

The commandant and his deputy sat across from each other in the former's office at the Frontier Rangers' garrison in Lunglei, smoking in silence. The events of the previous night, and the death of Subedar Major Paul, though yet unreported, had the potential to destroy both their careers. They knew they had some difficult decisions to make and that they needed to agree on how to proceed. Like two experienced poker players sizing each other up, their expressions didn't give away what they were thinking, even as they waited for the other to make the first move.

The deputy blinked first. 'We can't cover up Paul's death for long. He obviously hasn't reported for duty this morning. Questions will soon be asked about his whereabouts. What do you want to do about him?'

That his deputy hadn't used any of the usual prefixes – 'sir' or 'commandant' – when he addressed him, wasn't lost on his superior. 'Sir! What do you want to do about him, sir?' he shot back, his beady eyes locking in on his deputy.

The deputy wasn't impressed. 'I'm sorry, sir! I meant no disrespect, sir!' he responded smoothly, staring down the commandant, not the slightest hint of regret on his face.

The commandant shifted uncomfortably in his chair, breaking his deputy's gaze. Then, he said: 'Have Paul's body dumped in Lunglei town. Make it look like he was picked up by the MNF and killed. That should buy us some breathing space while we figure out how we're going to get the captain and Che back.'

The deputy was silent for a moment, expressionless, processing the commandant's instructions and evaluating the risks associated with its implementation. Then conceding that it was probably the best option, he said: 'Yes, I think the sooner we get that done, the better. I'll take care of it.'

'What are we doing about the captain and Che?' the commandant asked. 'If the captain escapes and talks about last night's operation and our role in it, we're finished. We have to get to him before the army does.'

'My informant tells me that Azuala and his men are in pursuit of them. They're using hounds and should be able to track them down. I've also alerted all our units in the area and our informant network. I'm sure we'll have news before long. They won't get away,' the deputy said confidently.

'I can't believe we handed that scumbag Azuala fifty-thousand rupees from the stash we got off Che. We got nothing in return, and we lost Paul. The entire operation was clumsy. I should never have let you talk me into it.'

'The transporter from Rangoon will be in Lunglei in three days with the gold bars. Once we flip the money, we're safe. It'll be difficult to trace and easier to store. We need to stay focused till then,' the deputy replied. Then, as an afterthought, he added, 'sir', with only the slightest hint of a smirk on his face.

CHAPTER 12

When Azuala and his men arrived at the river's edge, they found a thick bamboo rope, one end of which was secured around a large tree on the riverbank, floating carelessly in the water. Azuala correctly deduced that Che and the captain had stolen the bamboo raft the villagers used to cross the river. His men and the hounds were tired, and Azuala knew he couldn't keep pushing them. But to allow Che to escape would be to sign his own death warrant.

Turning to his men, Azuala said: 'It appears Che has taken to the river. It's a suicidal thing to do. The Tlawng River is too powerful, and there are too many large rapids that cannot be run on this stretch of the river for anyone to try and navigate it. They'll drown when they hit the first rapid. But we can't afford to take any chances. We're going to have to keep pursuing them till we find them or their bodies. You all know what is at stake if they escape to tell their tale. We can't afford to take that chance.'

'We've been walking for over ten hours now. We can't keep going. We need to rest,' Fakawma mumbled defiantly, looking down at his feet.

Azuala stared back at him coldly, tempted to impose his will on his insubordinate underling just to show him he was the boss. But if he pushed the men too hard, there was a chance they'd rebel. So, instead of being inflexible and harsh, he took on a more conciliatory tone. 'Yes, you're right, Fuka. We need a break. But just two more hours, okay? Then we find a nice beach by the river and camp for the night.'

* * *

Up ahead on the river, the raft entered a deep gorge with sheer granite rock faces on either side. The current became stronger and the volume of the river, now constricted by the gorge, increased dramatically. An alert Sena stood at the back of the raft, his feet spread out wide, crouching low, using the bamboo pole to push the raft away from the large rocks that would appear every now and then in the river. Sammy had gotten over his initial fear and had settled down in the centre of the raft, his feet folded under him. *There's little chance Azuala and his gang will be able to catch up with us now, that too on foot,* he thought. *Sena's gamble has paid off. We're going to be fine.*

As the afternoon gave way to evening and the shadows grew longer, the temperature began to drop. A cool breeze blew, causing the two men to shiver. Sena knew they had to get off the river before it grew dark and bivouac for the night. Around a bend, he spotted the perfect campsite – a sheltered cove with a stretch of sandy beach. He guided the raft towards it. When they got there, they pulled the raft up over the waterline and anchored it down with rocks.

Stripped down to his waist, a spear fashioned from driftwood, Sena was soon back in the water, spearing fish for their dinner. After many failed attempts, he finally managed to spear an adult ngahvang, a Burmese kingfish, which the two men devoured raw, picking away at the flesh with their fingers. They slept well that night, basking in their freedom, safe for the moment from the men who were hunting them.

* * *

At dawn, Azuala and his men set off from their campsite at the mouth of the gorge, keeping to a narrow path that led up to the plateau on the cliff face. Azuala figured that even if Che and the captain were still alive, they wouldn't have been able to navigate the gorge on a bamboo raft, and that they'd eventually need to ditch it and trek their way out of the gorge. And that's when he and his men would have their best chance of ambushing them.

* * *

An hour later, the early morning sun, blocked by the steep cliffs in the gorge, lit up the beach on which Sammy and Sena had spent the night. Sena was up first, quickly scanning the river and the cliffs that surrounded them for any signs of danger. He nudged Sammy awake with his foot.

While Sammy lazed on the beach in no apparent hurry to get moving, Sena evaluated their options. They could either take their chances on the river with the raft, or try and climb the cliff to make their way out of the gorge. The climb was steep, but not impossible. On his own, he'd have opted to climb. But with Sammy in tow, he wasn't confident they'd make it out of the gorge. *The river is probably our best option*, he thought to himself.

Twenty minutes later, Sena pushed the raft out on to the river. The first hour was uneventful, though they were badly swamped in some of the larger rapids. They hung on desperately, trying to prevent the raft from flipping over. Sena did an incredible job of reading the river and guiding them through the many cunning traps and dangers that lurked below its surface. But in the second hour, their luck ran out.

The change in the tone of the river was subtle, a slight shift in its audible frequency that most untrained observers would have missed. But Sena's survival instincts, honed over the years as a hunter and a guerrilla on the run, were sharper than most. He didn't just hear the river's tone change, he felt her very nature transform through the haptic feedback he got from the bamboo pole.

A sharp bend in the river blocked Sena from seeing the danger that lay ahead. Around the bend, the river dipped suddenly, creating powerful cross-currents, boils and whirlpools, with large boulders and jagged rocks strewn in the water. As they approached the bend, the current grew stronger, dragging them towards a massive boulder that jutted out of the river. Sena tried desperately to guide the raft to safety, but the current was just too strong and he knew he was no longer in control. They had to get off the raft if they were to have any hope of surviving.

'Jump! We have to jump!' Sena screamed, leaping off the raft, twisting his body to reposition himself on his back, pointing his feet downstream to reduce the risk of smashing his skull on the boulders and jagged rocks in the river, shifting his weight to the left and to the right like a bobsled driver, desperately trying to steer himself towards the riverbank.

The suddenness of Sena's action caught Sammy by surprise. But he reacted quickly and leapt into the river, trying to float on his back like he'd seen Sena do. Not a moment too soon! The raft, caught in the raging current, smashed into the boulder, flipping over like a rag doll before it disappeared into a whirlpool hidden behind the boulder.

CHAPTER 13

A kilometre downstream of where the raft had capsized, four Lushai tribesmen, carrying bamboo ropes, sharp bamboo sticks and baskets, were walking cautiously along a rocky path that ran just above the Tlawng River. They were looking up at the towering, granite cliffs that rose to the sky, searching for honeycombs. They'd had no luck that morning, and were tired and on the verge of giving up, when Lalchema, the leader of the group, spotted a cluster about forty feet up on the cliff. Excited by his discovery, he drew the attention of the group to his find.

The tribesmen got to work quickly. One of them scaled the cliff, a bamboo rope ladder slung over his shoulder, looking for an anchor on the cliff face for the ladder the others would use to climb up to the honeycombs. The tribesmen below foraged for dry branches, twigs and straw to build a large fire at the base of the cliff.

When the smoke from the fire had driven the bees out from the honeycombs, Lalchema carefully wrapped a thick cotton cloth around his face. With a sharp, long bamboo pole in one hand and a bamboo basket attached to a rope in the other, he climbed up the flimsy ladder. Once he got to the hives, he used the bamboo pole to expertly slice through them and drop them into the basket. When the basket was full, he lowered it slowly to the waiting tribesmen below.

Within an hour, the cliff face had been wiped clean of the hives. Lalchema began his slow descent, his limbs badly swollen in places where the bees had stung him. Halfway down, a lifeless form on the beach below caught his attention. He called out to the tribesmen: 'There's a body on the beach!'

The tribesmen moved quickly down the steep path to the river. In the sand, lying face down, was the body of a man in tattered khaki fatigues. One of the tribesmen rolled the man over and put his face close to his nostrils. 'He's alive,' he said to the others.

While two of the tribesmen tried to revive the man by gently patting him on his face and moving his head from side to side, Lalchema's attention turned to the tracks in the sand that led to a cluster of rocks. Intrigued, he set off stealthily, following the tracks, the sharp bamboo pole he'd used to slice honeycombs now held firmly in front of him like a spear. Peering cautiously over the rocks, ready to defend himself if attacked, he was surprised to find another man, in an olive military camouflage jacket and matching trousers, soaked to the bone, propped up against the rocks, his face slumped down on his chest. He used the bamboo pole to gently prod the man to check if he was alive. The man staggered to his feet, looking around furtively, evaluating the risk posed by the sudden appearance of the tribesman.

Lalchema called out to him in Mizo: 'Don't be afraid, I will not harm you.'

'Where is my friend? Did you find him?' Sena asked, slumping down in the sand again.

'Yes, by the river. He's lucky to be alive,' Lalchema said, squatting in the sand beside Sena, his body language indicating he meant no harm.

'Take me to him,' Sena said, slowly getting back on to his feet. Lalchema led Sena to where Sammy was.

'Sena!' Sammy called out hoarsely, relieved to see him.

'You okay, Sammy?'

'Yeah. That was scary though. I thought it was game over for us!'

Eager to get moving as soon as they could, Sena turned to Lalchema. 'How far is your village? My friend and I need a place to stay. Just for tonight.'

'It will take us till afternoon to reach our village,' Lalchema replied. 'You may accompany us if you wish.'

Sena was quick to accept the invitation. 'Thank you for your kindness,' he said. 'We will accompany you.'

With Lalchema in the lead and the honeycombs distributed amongst the tribesmen, they set off for their village, walking briskly, Sena and Sammy bringing up the rear.

* * *

Azuala and his gang had descended down to the Tlawng River. Azuala heard the roar of the river change as it dropped in altitude. He turned to Izak. 'The Mwanga rapids are up ahead. They can't be navigated on a raft. If Che and the captain have survived and got this far, they'll have to get off the raft before the rapids. When they do, the hounds should be able to pick up their scent again.'

* * *

Four hours after they'd set off from the beach, the tribesmen's village, Sabha, came into sight. The village was a permanent cluster of about thirty bamboo stilt huts, built on the crest of a hill. The villagers were mostly fisherfolk or canoe-builders, for whom their village near the Tlawng River was ideal. When the group led by Lalchema neared the village, children playing on the riverbank ran up to greet them with whoops of joy! The two strangers, particularly Sammy, attracted a lot of attention.

Although the position of village chief, or lal, had been formally abolished by the government in 1955, former chieftains were still highly respected and informally continued to rule their villages. It was no different in Sabha. Lalchema, followed by a crowd of curious villagers, led the two strangers to the largest hut that stood in the centre of the village, which belonged to the lal. They stood outside till the lal, alerted by the commotion outside, stepped on to the veranda of her hut.

The lal was a squat woman with a wizened old face and a no-nonsense demeanour about her. Her name was Pibuki and she was the only child of a fierce warrior chief who'd ruled over Sabha for twenty-seven years. Pibuki had become the lal after her father's passing in 1935, long before Independence. But the title hadn't come to her easily. She first had to prove herself as a warrior and a leader, before the villagers would accept her writ. Which she did, by leading raids on British tea plantations in the plains below, bringing back prisoners who were forced to work as free labour in the village. Over time, Pibuki's courage and wisdom had won her the respect of her tribe and made her their undisputed leader.

'Who are these strangers?' she asked in Mizo after she'd spent more than a minute looking them over.

'Honoured lal, we found them lying beside the river,' Lalchema answered.

'Why did you bring them here? They look like trouble,' she growled.

Sena stepped in quickly to reassure her. 'We won't be any trouble, revered lal. We need a place to rest for tonight and some food. We will leave in the morning,' he said earnestly.

But the lal wasn't done with her interrogation. 'What were you doing on the river?'

'We were fishing,' Sena replied. 'Our boat capsized, and we nearly drowned. Your brave warriors found us on the beach and brought us here at our request.'

The lal looked unconvinced, but she didn't quiz Sena any further. 'There are many Indian patrols in the area. I don't want any trouble. Is that understood?' she asked Sena pointedly.

'Yes, certainly, revered lal, we will be no trouble at all,' he replied quickly. 'We thank you for your kindness. You will have no cause for worry.'

Turning to Lalchema, the lal ordered: 'Put them in the zawlbuk and give them some food. I want them gone in the morning.'

Lalchema bowed reverentially. 'Yes, certainly, honoured lal. It shall be as you say.'

The *zawlbuk*, or bachelor's dormitory, was the largest building in the village and built close to the lal's hut. It was made of timber and bamboo, and had a thatched roof. Inside, in the centre, was a fireplace with firewood stacked nearby. Around its perimeter ran a low platform on which the inhabitants of the zawlbuk put down their mats and bedding to sleep.

From ancient times, the zawlbuk was integral to life in Mizo villages. It was where unmarried males in the village over the age of fifteen lived and trained in wrestling, hunting, warfare and village government. It was where boys became men and inculcated the spirit of *Tlawmngaihna*, selfless service for the benefit of the community. The zawlbuk also served the purpose of giving the village chief a standing army of trained men who could be called upon to defend the village at short notice. But the arrival of Christian missionaries in the Mizo Hills had sounded the death knell of the zawlbuk. The missionaries placed great emphasis on textual knowledge. Without being able to read, how could the tribes they were trying to proselytize study the Bible? Soon, missionary schools sprung up across the hills, where young boys and girls were taught English and immersed in a Western style of education. In time, parents stopped sending their sons to the zawlbuk, preferring missionary schools instead. By the mid-1930s, the zawlbuk was dead as an institution. Where the structures still stood, they served as guest houses for travellers and storage units. In Sabha, too, the zawlbuk had been converted into a guest house, which was where Sammy and Sena were escorted by Lalchema, who lit a fire in the hearth and rolled out bamboo mats for them.

* * *

On the banks of the Tlawng River, Azuala and his gang made their way down to a narrow river beach, where the hounds were baying in excitement, having once again picked up the scent of the fugitives.

'Several men have been here recently. Look at all the footprints!' Azuala exclaimed.

Izak dropped down on his haunches and studied the footprints carefully. 'There were six men in all,' he said. 'Two wearing boots. The others were barefoot.'

'The men in boots have to be Che and the captain,' Azuala said. 'That's why the hounds are going crazy.'

'But what about the barefoot men?' Fakawma asked, sounding confused. 'Che and the captain were alone.'

'They must belong to men from a nearby village. It's the only possible explanation,' Azuala replied.

'The closest village is Sabha,' Izak said. 'It's a three-hour walk.'

* * *

At the Frontier Rangers' garrison in Lunglei, Commandant Aiyar and two other officers were peering over a set of topographical maps, reviewing ground operations to hunt down Captain Samuel and Che. None of the patrols had anything to report. There had been no sightings or clues after the botched-up operation at Replang Bridge two nights ago. It was as if the two men had vanished off the face of the earth.

For the commandant, time was running out. There were rumours of an inquiry into the operation that had bagged Che and his subsequent escape. What also didn't help was the complete breakdown in communication with DIG Kabir Singh, his boss, who'd made it clear he thought the commandant was insolent and insubordinate.

As the meeting was wrapping up, Deputy Commandant Saikia burst into the room. 'We have a sighting, sir!' he gushed.

'Where?'

'An informant spotted two strangers marching with a group of tribesmen south of the village of Sabha this morning, sir. He reported it to one of our patrols about an hour ago. They just radioed in the information and are awaiting instructions.'

'Show me where,' the commandant ordered, his attention returning to the topographical map.

Saikia quickly located the Tlawng River on the map and traced its path with his finger down to Sabha. 'There are no other villages in the area, sir. They can't possibly be headed anywhere else.'

The commandant took a moment to process the information, then barked out a set of instructions. 'Saikia, get Alpha Section moving immediately. We're going to need urgent helicopter support. There's a helipad about ten klicks from the village. We'll put down there and get to the village on foot. We don't want to attract too much attention and scare them away. Got it?'

'Yes, sir. I'm on it, sir,' said his deputy, saluting the commandant smartly.

The men were dismissed. With his officers gone, the commandant lit up a cigarette, looking pensive. He'd ordered an operation, but there were too many unknowns he was up against. The information wasn't confirmed, yet he was committing troops with no advance planning or intel. Also, once his deputy put in the request for a helicopter, news would reach 61 Mountain Brigade headquarters in Aizawl, and they'd start asking questions. There was also the issue of informing his boss, who'd explicitly told him to keep him in the loop on any ops he planned to nab Captain Samuel and Che. But he knew if he asked for permission, it would be denied. He also knew that if the information they'd received was accurate and they didn't act quickly, the two men would vanish into the wilderness again, and they may never get another chance to hunt them down.

CHAPTER 14

It was late afternoon, and Sabha was a hive of activity. The fishermen who'd set off at dawn had returned with the day's catch, as had the women who had wandered deep into the forest to forage for mushrooms and roots, and collect firewood. Wooden fires had been lit in each home to prepare the evening meal and smoke billowed up into the clear blue sky.

In the courtyard of the zawlbuk, a dozen young wrestlers practised their *Inbuan* moves within a mud ring of about fifteen feet in diameter. Each wrestler was bare-chested, with a catch-hold belt worn over a loincloth. The wrestlers were practicing in pairs, each trying to lift his opponent off the ground. The crowd that had gathered around the ring shouted out encouragement and advice to the combatants.

Sammy and Sena sat on the steps of the zawlbuk, puffing on cigarettes, watching the wrestlers practise. Hminga, a well-built young man with a puffed-up chest, approached them. 'Do you know how to wrestle?' he asked.

Sammy was quick to respond. 'Not me. But my friend here used to be the village champion when we were growing up!'

Caught off guard, Sena glared at Sammy. 'That was a long time ago.'

But Hminga wasn't to be fobbed off so easily. He yelled out to the other wrestlers in jest: 'We have a champion wrestler here!'

Now, all the wrestlers' curiosity was piqued. One of them called out to Sena: 'Come on, old man. Let's see what you've got.' His challenge was received with much hooting and clapping, drawing the entire village to the mud ring. Egged on by the tribesmen, Sena stood up and took off his shirt. He slipped out of his trousers and stripped down to his shorts. Someone threw him a loincloth and a belt. Hminga stepped forward to challenge the newcomer.

In the Inbuan ring, Sena's first moments were embarrassing. It had been years since he'd wrestled and he was rusty. Hminga lifted him effortlessly off his feet again and again. The villagers cheered on their local hero. After a few rounds, Sena finally started coming into his own, matching Hminga move for move. Some in the crowd even began cheering for him. Frustrated by his opponent, Hminga punched Sena in the head, sending him sprawling to the ground. Pindrop silence followed. Sena, angered by Hminga's unsporting attack, picked himself up, his fists raised.

But the lal, who'd stood by watching the men wrestle, now stepped into the ring to break up the fight before it turned ugly. She admonished Hminga: 'Is this how you treat an honoured guest? What you did was unacceptable. You must apologize at once.'

Hminga walked up to Sena sullenly and bowed to him. Sena hesitated at first, then he returned the bow. The match was over. Sena put his clothes back on. But before the crowd could disperse, a gun went off!

* * *

Azuala and his gang had been on the march all afternoon, following the hounds at a brisk pace. The men were tired and hungry, and at breaking point. As they came around a bend in the track, they could see the smoke from the fires of Sabha. The loud cheering of the villagers carried across to them.

'Sounds like they're celebrating,' Fakawma muttered.

'The laughter before the tears,' Izak responded cryptically.

'Tie up the dogs here, Izak, and stay with them. Keep them quiet. I don't want them alerting Che and the captain to our presence. If a single dog barks, you're a dead man,' Azuala growled. 'The rest of you, come with me.'

Azuala and his men spread out and slipped quietly into the village, unnoticed by the villagers who were preoccupied with the bout underway at the wrestling ring. As he got closer to the ring, Azuala saw that it was Che wrestling another man. The man punched Che in the head, causing an old woman to step into the ring and bring the bout to a halt. As Che wore his clothes and the crowd began to disburse, Azuala fired his pistol in the air and pushed his way to the front of the stunned villagers. He walked towards Che with his gun drawn. 'Game over, Major Che, it's time to go,' he chortled.

Meanwhile, Fakawma had sneaked up on the captain, who'd been standing on the stairs of the zawlbuk watching the wrestling bout. Now, he pushed him forward at gunpoint to the centre of the wrestling ring next to Sena.

The other members of Azuala's gang took up positions around the ring, their guns pointing at the villagers.

'You thought you had got rid me of me, eh, Major? But I missed you so much, I had to come looking for you,' Azuala grinned at Sena.

'I thought you'd learnt your lesson after our last meeting. But you clearly didn't learn a thing, you traitor!' Sena shot back.

Furious, Azuala took a step towards Sena, his gun pointed at Sena's face. Then the lal stepped in between the two men, facing Azuala. 'We have no quarrel with you,' she said. 'I am the lal of this village, and these men are our honoured guests. No harm may come to them while they are under my protection.'

Azuala was momentarily thrown by this unexpected intervention. He reacted with aggression, shoving his pistol against the lal's head. 'If you wish to die for these men, I'm happy to grant your wish.'

The tribesmen were aghast at the disrespect shown to their lal. Hminga and another young wrestler stepped forward. But the lal lifted her hand, asking them to back down. 'Your actions are disrespectful,' she said firmly. 'You must stop before there is bloodshed.' In the distance, Izak's hounds had begun to howl.

Azuala knew he was running out of time. Though armed, they were outnumbered by the villagers and, if the situation got ugly, they could easily be overpowered. He lowered his pistol and took a step back to try and defuse the situation.

'I meant no disrespect, honoured lal,' he said. 'But these men are my prisoners. They are traitors and cowards who escaped by deceit. I am taking them back to be brought to justice for their crimes.'

Sena cut Azuala short. 'This man is a liar. He betrayed us to the Frontier Rangers, but we managed to escape. He wants us dead to cover up his crime. He's been hunting us with dogs for two days now.'

Azuala's patience was running thin. He wasn't going to get sucked into explaining himself to an unarmed old woman who'd dared to stand up to him. He signalled to Fakawma, who pushed the butt of his gun into the small of Sammy's back. 'Enough talking,' Fakawma growled. 'Let's go!'

Sena knew, if challenged, Azuala's men wouldn't hesitate to open fire on the unarmed villagers. Not wanting to put the villager's lives at risk, he began walking forward slowly. 'Fine,' he said to Azuala, 'we'll come with you.' He and Sammy walked ahead, with Azuala and his gang trailing them, their guns trained on them.

Just then, a loudspeaker crackled and a booming voice blared: 'Villagers of Sabha, this is Commandant Aiyar of the Frontier Rangers. We have surrounded your village. You have ten minutes to hand over the two criminals you have sheltered or else we will be forced to open fire!'

An advance party of scouts from the battle-hardened Alpha Section had sliced the throats of Izak and his baying hounds when they'd chanced upon them on the outskirts of Sabha. When the scouts had reported that the coast was clear, Commandant Aiyar had ordered a cordon to be set around the village. He had issued explicit orders to shoot anyone trying to break their cordon. As he put down the loudspeaker after delivering his ultimatum, the commandant could see that his words had spread panic amongst the villagers, sending many of them scampering away into their homes.

'The Frontier Rangers are here!' Fakawma cried out in fear. 'We're just five of us. God knows how many of them. We have no chance. We should surrender!'

Azuala reacted brutally to Fakawma's suggestion, grabbing him by the collar and slapping him across his face. 'You fucking coward. One more word out of you and I'll put a bullet in your head.'

The rest of Azuala's gang got the message. There would be no surrender. They scrambled to take cover, forgetting about Che and the captain.

The lal, who was struggling to make sense of everything, turned on Sammy and Sena. 'I should never have let you into my village. I knew you were trouble the moment I set my eyes on you. Who are you? And what have you done? Why are so many people hunting you?'

Sammy bowed respectfully to the lal. In scratchy Mizo, he said: 'We're not criminals. I'm a captain in the Indian Army.' Then pointing to Sena, he added: 'He's Che, from the MNA. The Frontier Rangers wanted to murder him. I saved him.'

'It is true, honoured lal. I'm a major in the MNA. My friend speaks the truth. It is as he says,' said Sena, his gaze locked firmly on the lal.

The lal glared at the two of them, torn between her moral duty to protect her guests and putting her tribe at risk. Finally, turning to the tribesmen, she said: 'These men are our honoured guests. In our culture, it is our duty to protect our guests even at the cost of our own lives. Warriors of Sabha, arm yourselves and prepare to defend our homes. These are my orders.'

After the lal had spoken, there was a flurry of activity. The warriors of the tribe raced to prepare themselves for battle. She then turned to Sammy and Sena. 'You two will not leave the zawlbuk till I command you to.'

'Let me fight by your side, honoured lal,' Sena said, bowing reverentially to the old woman.

'No!' she replied firmly. 'You and your friend will withdraw to the zawlbuk. My warriors and I will protect our village.'

'It will be as you command, honoured lal,' Sena replied.

Ten minutes later, the lal, now ceremonially dressed, with about forty warriors carrying bows and arrows, axes, lances, swords, and old shotguns, took up positions around the village. The women, children and the elderly were ordered to stay inside their homes. As commanded by the lal, Sammy and Sena had withdrawn to the zawlbuk, where they clambered up into a loft with a window that gave them a bird's-eye view of the action unfolding below.

Then the commandant's voice boomed over the loudspeaker once again. 'People of Sabha, we have waited long enough. This is your final warning.'

The commandant had barely finished speaking when an arrow shot by one of the tribesmen zinged past him. He instinctively dropped to the ground and scrambled to take cover behind a boulder – his move greeted by derisive laughter from the tribesmen. Furious, the commandant screamed: 'Attack!'

The soldiers moved forward, their guns drawn. The village archers who'd taken up positions at vantage points around the village, waited patiently for the soldiers to get into range and for the lal's signal. When it came, they released a shower of arrows, with sharp metal arrowheads, at the soldiers, taking one of them down.

The retaliation was swift. The soldiers opened fire with their automatic weapons, spraying the village with bullets from all directions. Screams erupted as the entire village was enveloped in chaos. The bullets fired by the soldiers ripped through the thin bamboo walls of the huts. In panic, some women raced out of their huts, carrying their young, looking to flee the village to safety. But their escape routes had been cut off by the soldiers, and they were gunned down mercilessly. Outraged by the attack on their unarmed women and children, the tribesmen fought back courageously, even though the soldiers armed with modern automatic weapons clearly had the advantage.

Azuala and his gang had at first stayed hidden, watching the unfolding battle. But, as the soldiers drew closer, they'd thrown in their lot with the tribesmen. The sudden burst of automatic fire targeting them took the soldiers by surprise. They dropped to the ground, taking cover, their advance temporarily halted.

Not everyone in Azuala's gang had the heart for a fight, though. When the soldiers opened fire, Fakawma had ducked into the zawlbuk looking for a safe place to hide, unaware that Sammy and Sena were in the loft above him. Sena watched him crawl behind a large metal drum filled with water. Dropping stealthily down to the floor, Sena crept to where Fakawma was hiding. Reaching into the darkness, he grabbed hold of his throat with one hand, while, with the other, he twisted the pistol out of Fakawma's hand. Then, with his hand still around Fakawma's neck, he slipped the other around his belt and, lifting the bewildered man effortlessly off the floor, he shoved him headfirst into the drum, holding him underwater till he stopped struggling and his body went limp.

The lal led her warriors from the front, shouting out instructions to them and wielding her traditional bow with great skill. But it was an unequal battle, and she knew they couldn't last long. Sabha had been built on the crest of a hill and the large boulders strewn around it now served as cover for the soldiers as they moved forward steadily towards the village. They were now close enough to select their targets, which they did with deadly accuracy. The warriors of Sabha, brave as they were, were being picked off one by one.

Unable any longer to sit out the battle raging all around them, for which they held themselves responsible, Sammy and Sena slipped out of the zawlbuk. Sena was armed with Fakawma's pistol. Sammy, an iron rod he'd found lying on the floor. Once outside, they went their separate ways, each with his own agenda: Sammy to try and stop the mindless bloodshed the Frontier Rangers' soldiers had unleashed on the tribesmen, Sena to settle scores with Azuala.

Azuala and his gang had been firing indiscriminately at the soldiers, but they hadn't come prepared for an intense firefight and were soon running low on ammunition. With two members of his gang already killed by the soldiers and Fakawma missing, Azuala knew they were fighting a losing battle. Deserting the two surviving members of his gang, he quietly scurried away looking for a place to hide, when he and Sena entered opposite ends of a large open courtyard in between a cluster of huts. Sena had his gun drawn on him, and Azuala knew he'd shoot him down easily if he tried to make a run for it.

'You fucking traitor, it's because of people like you that our cause falters,' Sena snarled at Azuala.

Trapped in the open with nowhere to run, the wily Azuala dropped his pistol to the ground and raised his hands up in the air. 'The famous Che, the great guerrilla hero, will shoot an unarmed Mizo, will he?' he asked craftily.

Sena, who could easily have gunned Azuala down, took the bait. He dropped his pistol and, fists raised, moved forward menacingly. 'I'm going to rip you apart with my bare hands.'

As Sena stormed towards him, Azuala dropped to the ground, reaching for his pistol. Sena realized he'd been tricked, but it was too late. As he threw himself at Azuala, Azuala fired, the bullet slamming into his abdomen. Though badly wounded, Sena managed to lock his arms around Azuala's neck in a flash, dragging him down and twisting his body, wrapping his legs around his torso, even as Azuala thrashed around trying to break Sena's stranglehold. But it was hopeless. Azuala was dead in less than a minute. Sena, blood dripping from the gaping bullet wound, dragged himself back to the zawlbuk.

The village of Sabha, now overrun by the soldiers, had turned into a deadly battleground. At a distance, the ancient weapons of the Lushai warriors were no match for the automatic weapons of the soldiers. But the equation changed when the soldiers entered the village. The tribesmen knew their village and its layout, and they pressed home that advantage, hiding themselves and launching close-quarter surprise attacks that rendered the soldier's automatic weapons useless.

Sammy, who'd stepped out of the safety of the zawlbuk, armed only with an iron rod, in the hope of somehow being able to bring the bloodshed to an end, now found himself caught in the crossfire between the two sides. Taking cover, he surveyed the deadly battleground. Sammy knew it was only Commandant Aiyar who could call off the attack and so he searched desperately for him in the chaos of the battle.

Even though the commandant was in the thick of the action, fighting alongside his men, his single-minded focus on finding Che was rewarded when he spotted him crawl into the zawlbuk. Pistol in hand, the commandant set off in pursuit.

'Hey chinkie, chinkie, I know you're in here. Stop hiding like a rat and come out,' the commandant called out softly into the darkness, as he stepped into the zawlbuk and shut the door behind him, his pistol drawn. The hall was pitch dark and the commandant stood quietly beside the door, giving his eyes time to adjust.

The moment he'd heard the door open, Sena had rolled under the sleeping platform to remain out of the intruder's sight. Now, the commandant and he began a dangerous game of cat and mouse, as the commandant searched the zawlbuk for Sena. 'Chinkie, chinkie, come out now. I can smell your fear, you little piece of shit. Come out and be a man instead of hiding like a coward.'

Sena was huddled in a corner under the sleeping platform, considering his options. He was unarmed and the loss of blood had weakened him. There wasn't much he could do to defend himself. But he wasn't going to be shot down like a dog. *I'm going to kill this motherfucker,* Sena thought, as he rolled out from under the platform and crawled stealthily towards the commandant, who had his back turned to him.

The commandant was caught by surprise when Sena grabbed his legs, pulling him down to the floor. Before he could react, Sena was on top of him, slamming his fist into the back of his head repeatedly, stunning him. Then Sena got up slowly to his feet and stomped on the commandant's hand, causing him to scream in pain, forcing him to release his grip on his pistol. Picking up the weapon, Sena pointed it at the commandant. But Sena was already weak with the loss of blood, and the effort involved in disarming the commandant had pushed him over the edge. Just as the commandant thought he was done for, Sena fell to his knees and collapsed in a heap on the floor.

The commandant staggered back onto his feet, confused by the sudden turn of events. He stared at Sena, lying unconscious on the floor. Then, all the pent-up anger and rage he'd kept bottled up poured out. He began viciously kicking the limp figure on the floor in his back and his head, again and again. 'You piece of shit! You murdered my wife and my daughter. You destroyed my life. Now you'll die. But I'm not going to make it easy on you. I'm going to personally skin you alive and take my time doing it,' he snarled.

Obsessed with inflicting as much damage as he could on Sena, the commandant failed to notice Sammy enter the zawlbuk. The world went dark for him when Sammy brought the iron rod he was carrying crashing down on his head, splitting his scalp wide open.

'You okay, Sena?' Sammy asked, running his hands over his fallen friend in the darkness.

Sena stirred weakly. He groaned: 'Yeah, I'm okay. Did you kill him?'

'No, not yet. But I'm going to,' Sammy said decisively, grabbing the commandant by the collar and dragging him out of the zawlbuk and to the centre of the wrestling ring. He screamed out at the top of his voice: 'Stop! Stop shooting! Or your commandant dies. Drop your weapons and come out, or I'm going to kill him. I swear!'

The soldiers of the Alpha Section were thrown by this unexpected turn of events. Seeing their leader fallen, with Captain Samuel holding a gun on him, the soldiers decided that the life of their leader was worth more than the meaningless battle with no clear objective that they'd been sucked into. One by one, they dropped their guns and, with their hands raised in surrender, they stepped forward, moving slowly towards the wrestling ring. The battle was over.

The lal and her surviving warriors moved quickly to grab the weapons of the soldiers who'd surrendered and restrained them, tying their arms behind their backs with bamboo ropes. They then turned their attention to the injured and the dead. Seeing the bodies of the villagers of Sabha piled up, Sammy's anger and guilt boiled over. As the commandant stirred to life and tried to rise to his feet, Sammy slammed the butt of his pistol on his head, causing him to crash back to the ground, whimpering in pain. 'Where do you think you're going?' Sammy screamed, his hands trembling as he tightened his finger around the trigger.

Sena, who'd crawled out of the zawlbuk, leaving a trail of blood behind him, shouted out to Sammy, hoarsely: 'Stop! Don't do it, Sammy!'

'Pull the trigger, you fucking coward,' the commandant snarled at Sammy.

'Don't do it, Sammy,' Sena pleaded.

'Why not?' Sammy yelled. 'Look at him. He's a disgrace to the uniform. And he's a murderer. Why should I not kill him?'

'Because it's not who you are.'

Sammy looked at the commandant, who smirked at him despite the blood flowing freely down his face. Then, he flung the pistol away in disgust and staggered towards Sena, who'd collapsed to the ground. The tribesmen grabbed the commandant and dragged him off to where the surviving soldiers had been herded together.

When Sammy got to Sena, he realized something was terribly wrong. There was a patch of blood where Sena lay and a trail of blood could be seen all the way to the door of the zawlbuk. Sammy dropped to his knees and turned Sena over gently, cradling his head in his arms. He gasped in disbelief when he saw the huge crimson patch on Sena's abdomen. His voice quavering, he whispered: 'Oh god! Sena you've been shot. Why didn't you tell me, man?'

Sena groaned softly, his eyes barely fluttering open.

'Hang in there, man,' Sammy pleaded. 'The soldiers must have a medical kit. I'm going to get it and bind you up. You're going to be okay. Just hang in there.'

Sena, his life ebbing out of him, grabbed Sammy's arm firmly. 'Stay!' he whispered. 'I'm done, man. I'm done running. I'm done fighting. It's over for me.'

And once more, Sammy begged: 'Please, Jesus, save him! I'll do anything you want. Anything. Just save him!'

Sena smiled back weakly at him. 'I'm sorry for what I did to you Sammy, forgive me.'

And with that, he was gone.

CHAPTER 15

Well-guarded and restricted to civilians, Fort William – built of brick and mortar in the shape of an irregular octagon – is spread over 170 acres on the eastern banks of the Hooghly River in Calcutta. Named after England's King William III, it was built in 1696 by the East India Company. In 1758, after the Battle of Plassey, the fort was rebuilt by Sir Robert Clive. One of the dungeons in the old fort, a poorly ventilated room measuring fourteen feet by eighteen feet, is infamously known as the 'Black Hole of Calcutta', where 120 British soldiers and civilians, imprisoned by the Nawab of Bengal, Siraj ud-Daulah, died of suffocation. In 1963, Fort William was turned into the headquarters of the Indian Army's Eastern Command.

In October 1967, four months after the Frontier Rangers' attack on Sabha, a high-powered Army Committee, appointed by the general officer in charge of the Eastern Command, Lieutenant General Sam Manekshaw, was in session in one of the massive conference rooms inside the fort – the room's solid oak doors guarded by the military police.

The committee was chaired by Brigadier Julius Packiam, with Colonel Ashish Swaroop and Colonel Gaurav Soral, from Eastern Command headquarters, as its other members. The members of the committee sat on large, imposing padded chairs, behind a substantial oak table. In one corner of the room, a secretary sat hunched behind an old Remington typewriter, typing a verbatim record of the meeting. Commandant Aiyar and Captain Samuel, stood at ease, facing the committee.

Brigadier Packiam got the proceedings underway with his opening remarks. 'Gentlemen, after a detailed investigation in which we interviewed more than sixty witnesses and recorded both your testimonies, this committee has arrived at a unanimous recommendation. This is not a court-martial, and our recommendation is not binding on you, unless you agree to subject yourselves to our recommendation.' Signalling to the secretary, who stopped typing, he said: 'Off the record, no one in the army or the government in Delhi wants the embarrassment of what happened in Sabha to become public knowledge. The press would skewer us, and the separatists all over the Northeast would celebrate the public relations disaster we've handed them on a platter.'

The brigadier paused to collect his thoughts. 'For the record, do you agree to abide by this committee's recommendations?'

'Yes, sir, I do,' said Commandant Aiyar, gruffly.

'Yes, sir,' said Captain Samuel, softly.

'Good,' said the brigadier. Leaning forward, his elbows on the oak table, he said, 'Off the record, Commandant, not only did you authorize the murder of an unarmed prisoner, you also offered a bounty on a serving army officer. Your unauthorized raid on Sabha cost the lives of twelve people, four of them your own boys, besides injuring many others, including civilians. You, Commandant, are an embarrassment to your uniform and a disgrace.' The commandant held the brigadier's gaze without a trace of emotion. The brigadier wasn't done. 'Commandant, if you were an army man, I would have seen to it that you were court-martialled and made an example of. But you are not an army man. When you leave this room, you will put in your papers. Your request for premature retirement from the Frontier Rangers has already been accepted.'

Looking towards the secretary, he dictated: 'On the record, this committee thanks Commandant Aiyar for his dedicated service. His request for premature retirement with full benefits has been received. This committee recommends that it be approved with immediate effect.' As an afterthought, he added, 'Is there anything you'd like to say for the record, Commandant? If there isn't, you're excused from further proceedings of this committee.'

'Yes, sir, there is,' the commandant said. Caught off guard, Brigadier Packiam pushed himself back in his chair, his fingers interlocked, a frown appearing on his face. But

Commandant Aiyar wasn't going to be intimidated or silenced.

'Sir, I'm a decorated officer of the Frontier Rangers. I've worked my way up the ranks and served my country loyally and with complete dedication for over thirty years. My service and dedication cost me the lives of my family and left me broken and scarred, physically and mentally. As a reward, everything I believed in, everything I ever loved, has been taken away from me. I'm left with nothing. I may not be an army man, Brigadier, but thousands of men like me in the Frontier Rangers and other paramilitary forces, we do the dirty work that army men such as you don't want to do. We may not be army men, but we are patriots who put our lives on the line each day for our country, facing the wrath of our own countrymen for policies made by fools sitting in Delhi.' The commandant's voice choked with emotion. Getting hold of himself, he continued: 'I do not regret my actions. I did what I had to do to hunt down a dangerous escaped prisoner, who'd murdered many of our men in uniform and my family. A prisoner, may I add, an army man helped escape. You may want to think about that before you pass judgement on me. That's all I have to say. And, if you will, I would now like to be excused.'

An uncomfortable silence followed, broken only by the clickety-clack of the typewriter as the secretary banged away her record of the meeting.

'You are excused, Commandant,' the brigadier said tersely.

Commandant Aiyar saluted smartly and, turning on his heels, exited the room, refusing to acknowledge Captain Samuel's presence. The brigadier, disturbed by the commandant's closing remarks, looked pensive, his elbows resting on his chair, his chin on his interlocked fingers. Snapping back into the moment, he turned to the secretary. 'Nothing of what the commandant said needs to go on the record.'

Leaning forward again, he turned his attention to the captain. 'Captain Samuel, off the record, what you did was incredibly brave. To put your life at risk for your beliefs is admirable. You have all the qualities of an officer and I'm proud of you, son.' The brigadier's tone was gentle and kind, his face softening momentarily. 'However, for the record, by not bringing to the attention of Commandant Aiyar that the prisoner, aka Major Che, was your childhood friend, you compromised the security of personnel involved in counter-insurgency operations in Assam, putting their lives at risk. Under the circumstances, this committee has no option but to recommend your immediate discharge from the Army without any benefits. Captain, is there anything you'd like to say for the record?'

'No, sir,' said Captain Samuel, 'I have nothing to say.'

'Very well then, you are excused. These proceedings are brought to an end and this committee is now disbanded,' Brigadier Packiam said firmly.

When Sammy walked out of the gates of Fort William, he felt lighter and happier than he'd felt in years. A massive cloud that had hung over him and had left him feeling disillusioned, confused, bitter and angry, all at once, had finally lifted.

'How did it go?' Reverend Joachim Rego, who was waiting outside Fort William, asked Sammy.

'Fine, just fine, Pa,' Sammy replied. 'I'm done with the army and the army is done with me.' He smiled wryly at his father.

'Come home, son. Your mother and I want you back home with us. Let's get away from this madness. Come home,' the reverend pleaded, holding Sammy's face in his hands and kissing him gently on his forehead.

'There's something I have to do first, Pa,' Sammy replied. 'It's what I should have done a long time ago. I just hope it's not too late.'

CHAPTER 16

Sammy looked dishevelled and worn out when he stepped off the bus in Aizawl after a two-day, 1500-kilometre bus journey from Calcutta. His army uniform had made way for blue jeans and a blue flannel shirt over which he wore a black polyester jacket. With his rucksack, he looked like a tourist who'd strayed off-track and had been picked up by the army and dragged to its headquarters for questioning. But Sammy was at the headquarters of 61 Mountain Brigade in Aizawl of his own volition.

The headquarters were strangely calm, unlike what one would expect at the nerve centre of the army's campaign against the Mizo guerrillas. Officers in uniform ambled about without a sense of urgency, while the sentries faked their alertness, their thoughts running free of the pillboxes they'd been confined to.

'It's good to see you again, Sammy,' Major Mukherjee said warmly, getting up from behind his desk and offering Sammy his hand, when he was shown into his office.

'Thank you, sir,' Sammy replied. 'I'm grateful you agreed to see me.'

'I'm sorry about what happened. The army has lost a good officer. Sad that it had to end this way,' the major said, ushering Sammy into one of the chairs in front of his desk.

'I've made peace with it, Major. Perhaps it's for the best,' Sammy replied uncomfortably. 'You received my request, sir?'

'Yes, indeed I did. I had to get the brigadier's sign-off, Sammy. Non-local civilians aren't welcome in the Mizo Hills at the moment.'

'Yes, sir. I'm aware of that. But this is important to me, sir,' Sammy said earnestly.

'You've got three days Sammy, no more,' the major said, pushing an envelope across his desk. 'It's not much, but it's the best that I could do.'

'Thank you, Major. I'm truly grateful.'

* * *

In the days before the troubles began, the Shangri-La Hotel in Aizawl was a thriving upmarket establishment, patronized by traders from Calcutta and Shillong with money to spare. Although rebuilt after being razed to the ground during the bombing, it had lost its sheen, its former clientele no longer willing to risk travelling to Aizawl for business. But Sammy didn't care. All he needed was a place to dump his rucksack and a bed for the night, both of which the decrepit Shangri-La offered him.

That night, lying on a creaky bed with unwashed linen and a lumpy pillow, Sammy took out the old, faded photograph of Sena, Martha and him, that had been clicked at the dance in Asakhua, on New Year's Eve, 1959. Now, it was the only physical evidence he had that he'd once known Sena and Martha.

When they'd been on the run, Sena had told Sammy that he and his family had moved to Aizawl after the Mautam, where he'd worked at his uncle's garage before joining the MNF. It was a long shot, but it was worth a chance. The next morning, Sammy set out, determined to check every garage in Aizawl for Sena's uncle who could, maybe, help him find Martha.

It was late afternoon by the time he arrived at the Gideon Motor Workshop on the outskirts of town. The workshop was no more than a small metal shack off the Aizawl–Silchar road, with old tyres and discarded metal parts stacked outside. The ground all around the shack was black with oil and sludge, evidence of the many cars, trucks and buses that had been fixed at the workshop over the years.

A heavily dented black Hindustan Motors Landmaster with Calcutta number plates was getting its fuel pipe fixed. The mechanic's feet – with cracked soles and long uncut toenails – peeked out from under the car. An apprentice, a thin, hungry-looking boy in tattered, oil-stained clothes, sat on his haunches, passing the mechanic tools from an old, rusted toolbox whenever he was ordered to. A short, corpulent man, his lips stained red with paan, prowled around, looking under the car every now and then, checking on the mechanic's progress. Sammy surmised he was the owner of the car.

Hot and tired, his spirits sagging, Sammy sat down on a grease-stained metal chair outside and waited. Half an hour later, when the old mechanic was done fixing the Landmaster and had haggled his fee in broken Bengali with the owner, he turned his attention to Sammy. 'You have a car you want me to fix?' he asked curiously.

'No, I don't,' Sammy replied. 'I'm looking for somebody and maybe you can help me.' He pulled out the old photograph of Sena, Martha and him from his front shirt pocket.

The old man looked at him quizzically. Then he retreated into his garage and returned with his eyeglasses, the lenses smudged with his greasy fingerprints. Putting them on, he peered at the photograph. Then he asked Sammy nervously: 'Who are you and what do you want?'

'I'm an old friend of Sena's,' Sammy said hurriedly.

'If you're his friend, you should know he's dead,' the old man shot back, handing the photograph back to Sammy.

'I know he's dead. I was with him when he died.'

The old man stared hard at Sammy. 'I don't want any trouble,' he said.

'Look, grandpa, I'm not here to cause trouble. I'm looking for Martha.'

'What do you want with her?'

'We were very close friends when we lived in Asakhua; like family,' Sammy said, reaching out and holding the old man's hand to reassure him.

'You're from Asakhua?' the old man asked incredulously.

'Yes, grandpa. My father was the pastor of the Baptist church. Sena, Martha and I, we went to school together.'

The old man pulled up another chair and ordered his young apprentice to bring them tea. The boy returned with two small enamel cups with tiny handles that served no purpose, carrying them on a rusted hubcap. Sammy and the old man sat in silence for a while, sipping their tea in the hot afternoon sun, watching army trucks and goods carriers pass by on the highway. Then the old man broke the silence: 'After Sena joined the MNF, my brother was angry and upset. He blamed himself for bringing Sena and the girls to Aizawl. Besides, over here, he had no work, no job. He felt he was a burden on me. After Sena left, he moved back to Asakhua with the girls.'

'Are they still in Asakhua?'

The old man smiled wryly, setting his teacup down on the ground. 'Asakhua no longer exists.'

Sammy was startled. 'What do you mean?' he asked.

'The Vais found out that Sena was from Asakhua,' the old man said slowly. 'About four months ago, a hundred or more Frontier Rangers soldiers showed up at the village and burnt it down – all the homes, the fields, the church, everything. They left nothing behind. The villagers were marched off to the regrouping camp near Lunglei at gunpoint.'

'Is that where Eoma and the girls are now?' Sammy asked desperately.

Tears welled up in the old man's eyes. He took a moment to compose himself. His voice cracking, he said: 'Eoma died that night, bayoneted by a soldier. He died a brave and honourable death, as he'd have liked to. When I got the news, I went to the camp at Lunglei to search for the girls. They hadn't made it there. No one has seen them again after the night Asakhua was burnt to the ground.' The old man reached out for Sammy's hand and squeezed it gently. 'Many died that night. They were gunned down by the soldiers when they tried to escape, their bodies buried in unmarked graves. I fear Christine and Martha met the same fate.'

Sammy felt his world collapse around him. After Sena's death, Sammy had been determined to find Martha. But now, confronted with the possibility that she may have been killed, he felt an overpowering sense of despair – his dream of reconciling with her fading away into nothingness, replaced instead with an overwhelming sense of guilt when he realized that by telling Commandant Aiyar that Sena was from Asakhua, he was responsible not just for Martha's death, but also for the deaths of Eoma, Christine and God knows how many others in the village.

Sammy slumped forward in his chair, holding his head in his hands, his elbows resting on his thighs, once again broken and defeated, his dreams crushed. He began to weep. 'I did this. It's all my fault, I killed them all,' he sobbed incoherently. The bewildered old man leant forward in his chair and patted Sammy gently on his head, comforting him.

Before he left, Sammy ripped a page out of his diary and jotted down his name and his father's phone number on it. He handed the page to the old man. 'Grandpa, if you ever hear from Martha or Christine or have any news about them, can you please call me on this number and let me know?'

The old man pocketed the paper and nodded. 'Where will you go?'

'I'm going to Asakhua,' Sammy said. 'I need to see for myself.'

At dawn the next day, Sammy was at the Aizawl bus stop, waiting to board the only bus of the day to Lunglei. The journey would take eight hours, maybe more if there was trouble. Besides, the bus would be stopped and searched at every one of the ten army checkpoints they'd pass along the way. How long each of those searches would take was difficult to say. The bus was packed as usual that morning, with villagers carrying goods that they'd bought in Aizawl's bazaars back to their villages. Most of the passengers seemed to know each other, and they collectively viewed the stranger, Sammy, with suspicion. The driver made good time, hurling the old weather-beaten bus around the hairpin bends with great confidence.

With only a handful of passengers onboard, the bus rolled up at a deserted stop up in the mountains, with rolling meadows all around, over which hung a light winter mist. In the distance was a heart-shaped lake with pearly blue waters and a little village on its banks.

In the village, a young woman was hanging freshly washed clothes on a clothesline, outside a bamboo hut, built on stilts. She spotted the stranger in the distance. Still holding the clothes basket, she stepped forward, away from the clothes hanging on the clothesline, fluttering in the wind. Then she slowly put down the basket, her face lighting up in excitement. She dusted her skirt and grabbed one of the shirts drying on the clothesline to wipe her face clean of the sweat on it. Then she threw the shirt on the ground and raced through the meadows. When the woman was about ten feet away from the stranger, she stopped running.

'Martha!' Sammy exclaimed, dropping his duffel bag to the ground.

'You came back to me!' Martha said, tears welling up in her eyes.

'Did you ever think I wouldn't?' Sammy asked, walking up to her, cupping her face gently in his hands.

'I prayed for you every day that we've been apart.' She slipped into his arms.

'It's what kept me alive, Martha.'

'How long are you here for?' she asked.

'Forever!' Sammy replied.

* * *

The bus screeched to a halt a few kilometres before Lunglei, where the footpath to Asakhua met the highway, bringing Sammy's dream to a jarring end, dragging him back into the numbing reality of his existence. 'Isn't this where you wanted to get off?' the conductor yelled out to him.

Sammy scrambled off the bus, watched by the curious passengers and the conductor. As the bus pulled away, he slung his rucksack over his shoulder and set off down the path. An hour later, when he got to what used to be Asakhua, he saw that the old man in Aizawl had been right. There was nothing left of the village. Like the Witch had prophesied in the spring of 1959, on Sammy's seventeenth birthday, the hellfire had rained down on Asakhua. All that was left were the burnt ruins of homes that the jungle had already begun to reclaim. The once carefully tended rice and potato fields were overgrown with shrubs and thorny bushes. The roof of the church had fallen in when it was set on fire, though its solid, stone walls still stood intact, if charred black. The massive wooden cross that had been fixed atop the church had survived the fire as well, but it had fallen to the ground and had been eaten away by white ants, with colonies of fungi thriving in the decaying wood.

In the adjoining cemetery, there was evidence of fresh graves. Sammy searched amongst them, till he found Eoma and Sena's graves, next to each other, rough wooden crosses, marking where they'd been buried, with their names, dates of birth and the dates on which each died engraved on them.

That entire afternoon, Sammy wandered aimlessly through the ruins of Asakhua. Every nook and corner held a memory that was precious to him, but other than his memories, there was nothing left. Just deafening silence, set against the sounds of the jungle and the stream trickling down into the village tank.

As the sun began to sink in the horizon, the shadows lengthened and the cacophony of the crows returning to roost in the trees that surrounded the ruins of Asakhua became unbearable. Sammy knew it was time for him to leave. He sat on the rocks at the edge of the tank, skipping pebbles across its surface – like he'd done with Martha when they were children. He knew in his heart that his search for her had drawn to an end. He'd come to Asakhua in the faint hope that he'd find a sign, some proof that Martha was still alive, someone who'd tell him that she'd got away and was safe. Anything to give him hope. But there was nothing. The grotesque evidence of the terrible violence Asakhua had been subjected to left Sammy feeling crushed and hopeless. 'I'm sorry, Martha,' he whispered into the growing darkness. 'I should never have run away. I should have stayed and fought for you. I made a terrible mistake. Wherever you are, I hope you're okay and at peace.'

Then he dropped the amulet Martha had given him on his seventeenth birthday into the water and watched as it sank slowly out of sight. 'Goodbye, my love,' he whispered. 'I'll always love you.'

LAMENTATION

On 30 June 1986, after twenty years of fighting, the guns of war finally fell silent in the Mizo Hills. The resilient and wily Pu Laldenga had outmanoeuvred and outlasted all his rivals, and affixed his signature on a peace accord with the Indian government. The Mizos would finally get their independent state, Mizoram, but within the Union of India, not as the independent nation that Pu Laldenga had promised.

In return, the guerrillas would lay down their arms and register themselves in camps set up all over Mizoram, with a general amnesty against prosecution guaranteed to them by the accord. Simultaneously, the ban on the MNF was lifted, allowing the organization to return to the political mainstream and participate in elections to the state legislature. The MNF would go on to sweep the elections. Pu Laldenga would become the chief minister of the new state of Mizoram, although he would soon find himself out of office, voted out by his own people.

The road to peace had been a long and difficult one, paved with the sacrifices of thousands of Mizo men, women and children. Through the 1960s, modelled on harsh colonial British counter-insurgency measures, the Indian government authorized village grouping schemes, in which over 87 per cent of the Mizo population living in 500 villages were shifted, at gunpoint, to internment camps along major highways. In one of the darkest chapters in independent India's history, many villages like Asakhua were burnt down, never to rise again. Communities that had lived together for hundreds of years were broken up, with no regard for their social or economic well-being. The atrocities that those who were interned in the camps were subjected to only drove them further into the arms of the MNF and against the Indian state.

The 1970s had seen a massive escalation in violence, with assassinations and killings by the MNF becoming commonplace, as did the draconian, retaliatory crackdowns by the Indian security forces. With the liberation of Bangladesh in 1971, Pu Laldenga and his guerrillas were forced to abandon their camps in that newly independent country and flee to the mountains of Arakan in Burma. At the end of 1971, Pu Laldenga arrived in Islamabad, Pakistan, from where he continued to lead the MNF, which had also found a new supporter in China.

Over the years, challenges had emerged to Pu Laldenga's authority, with new leaders emerging in the vacuum left behind by his absence, the most prominent being

Brigadier T. Sailo, who'd built a formidable reputation as a straight-talking war hero with little patience for traditional Mizo politics. But Pu Laldenga had kept his lines of communication with the Indian government open even in exile. The Indians had correctly surmised that despite being thousands of kilometres away from the action, he still commanded the respect and loyalty of the heavily armed guerrillas and, unless they agreed to give up their arms, no lasting peace was possible. Only Pu Laldenga could ensure that.

Returning from the ruins of Asakhua, Sammy had, at first, moved in with his parents, in the family home they'd built in Mangalore, where he bided his time, trying his hand at different jobs. Sammy continued to wait, unable to get Martha out of his head, consumed by the terrible guilt that grew from his belief that he was responsible for her death. For many years, Sammy waited for a call from the old mechanic in Aizawl. But none came. Finally, giving in to his parents' persistent pressure, Sammy married. But the marriage had little chance of surviving the ideal of Martha burnt firmly into Sammy's heart and, in two years, he was divorced.

Sammy caught a break in 1975 as the defence correspondent for the newly launched *The India Day* in Delhi. Sammy took to the job like a natural. It was a young team, full of energy and bursting with ideas. The magazine was edited by Laila Somiah, a feisty investigative journalist who protected her reporters from the publisher's greed for money and his insatiable hunger for power. There was no story too crazy or too risky to chase, and no politician or industrialist too big to pull down.

Sammy had been at the magazine for eleven years, rising through the ranks to become assistant editor, when the phone on his desk rang one morning in July 1986. It was his editor.

'Sammy, I'm assigning you the Mizoram Accord story,' Laila said.

'Why me?' Sammy protested. 'It isn't my beat.'

'I have no one else to assign this to at the moment. Besides, you're from the area, aren't you?'

'I am. But I haven't been to the Mizo Hills in twenty years, and I've lost touch with the people I used to know on the ground.'

'It doesn't matter,' Laila snapped, impatiently. 'I want you on a flight out the first thing tomorrow morning. There's a big reception for the surrendering guerrillas later this week in Aizawl. I need you there.'

Early the next morning, Sammy was on an Indian Airlines, Boeing 737-200 to Calcutta where he switched planes – to a Hawker Siddeley HS 748, a turboprop, for the hour-long flight to Guwahati, in Assam. The last leg of his journey was a 500-kilometre, fourteen-hour Jeep-taxi ride to Aizawl, stopping for the night in Silchar.

A fortnight before Sammy got to Aizawl, Parva, a tiny cluster of villages in the southern-most tip of the Mizo Hills, bordering Bangladesh, over sixty kilometres from the nearest roadhead, began attracting journalists from all around the world as hundreds of Mizo guerrillas trekked back into Indian territory, from their camps across the border, guaranteed protection from prosecution by the Mizoram Accord. The guerrillas were accompanied by their families, who had lived in exile for more than twenty long years, and they carried with them all their worldly possessions, trudging for days through the slush-covered and leech-infested jungle tracks, to freedom and a new beginning as law-abiding citizens of India.

In Parva, each of the returning guerrillas and their families were photographed and registered, and their guns, ammunition and explosives collected by the local authorities. After two weeks in the temporary camps set up in Parva, the guerrillas began the 400-kilometre journey to Aizawl, in a huge convoy of trucks and buses that had been made available for them at the roadhead. Some of the trucks carried the coffins of those who had died in exile, whose remains had been exhumed and were being brought back for burial in their homeland.

The guerrillas took their time getting to Aizawl, stopping at villages en route where welcome functions were held in their honour and lavish feasts prepared. The villages were decked in black-and-white flags – black for the dead and white for peace.

In Aizawl, the returning guerrillas were given a welcome befitting a victorious army returning from battle. Thousands of Mizo men, women and children lined the streets, and were perched on rooftops and balconies, shouting slogans and singing songs of freedom as the procession of guerrillas accompanied by their families wound its way through the town towards the main market, where a platform, made on a row of flatbed trucks, had been set up. But the coffins that were carried in procession tempered the festive mood and the cheers turned to wails as the Mizos mourned their dead, who'd sacrificed everything for their freedom.

Sammy had been moving through the crowd all morning, clicking photographs and pulling aside guerrillas for quick, short interviews, when he saw a face from his past that caused him to turn ashen. Sammy pushed through the surging crowd, towards a guerrilla wearing a green camouflage jacket, high-fiving strangers with his free hand, while, in the other, he clutched a bottle of rum, from which he took big swigs every now and then. When Sammy finally caught up with the guerrilla, he grabbed his arm and yanked him around, to face him. The guerrilla swung around angrily, his fist raised. Then, recognition dawned and he broke into a huge grin.

'Sammy!' he yelled over the roar of the crowd, grabbing Sammy by his shoulders. 'How are you, man? I never thought I'd see you again!'

'I'm fine,' Sammy yelled back. 'Can we talk?'

'Sure, after all this is over. There's a bar in the market called "Old John". I can see you there at about 5 p.m.'

'Will do!' Sammy mouthed, as the surging crowd separated them and carried the guerrilla away with it.

At 5 p.m., Sammy was seated at a table at the Old John – a dingy local bar, with a few wooden tables, frequented mostly by the town's alcoholics. The owner had noted that Sammy wasn't a regular, and he personally cleared a table at the back of the bar for him. Sammy ordered a quart of rum and two glasses. Then he poured himself a stiff one and waited.

Half an hour later, Rempuia sauntered into the bar. He had changed out of the guerrilla fatigues he was dressed in earlier that day. Now, he wore a plain, white shirt, over a pair of Levi's jeans and cowboy boots. His long hair was combed neatly back and held firmly in place by a thick smattering of hair cream. He looked nothing like the muscular bully, his tormentor-in-chief, from their childhood. Rempuia threw his arms around him, embracing him warmly. 'Sammy! We meet again. It's so good to see you. How are you?'

'I've been fine, just fine,' Sammy said, thrown by Rempuia's unexpected warmth and affection.

'How long has it been? More than twenty-five years?' Rempuia asked, pulling up a chair and sitting down at the table.

'Yeah, time's flown, hasn't it?' Sammy asked, settling down and pouring Rempuia a drink.

Their uncomfortable past set aside, the two men chatted like old friends, remembering their shared youth, their village and asking after each other's parents. But they never spoke about Sena or Martha, or the events leading up to their deaths. It was like they were ghosts from their past, never to be spoken about lest their memory poison the present.

Rempuia asked, 'When were you last in Aizawl, Sammy?'

'In October of 1967, a few months after Martha and Christine were murdered,' Sammy said.

Rempuia looked up sharply. 'Martha and Christine were murdered?' he asked.

'The Frontier Rangers burnt Asakhua to the ground when they regrouped the village. Many of the villagers were killed that night, shot in cold blood. Martha and Christine were amongst them,' Sammy said, his voice choking, tears welling up in his eyes.

Rempuia looked at Sammy in stunned silence. Then he leant forward in his chair and, putting his hand on Sammy's shoulder, he said gently: 'I have something to tell you, Sammy.'

* * *

The waiting room of the Presbyterian Hospital in Durtlang, on a hill overlooking Aizawl, was empty that evening. The hospital was quiet – most of its staff was on leave; they were in the town, celebrating the return of the guerrillas. Sammy sat alone on a wooden bench that was placed beside a large bay window, which offered an unfettered view of Aizawl in the distance, as the sky turned crimson.

The silence was broken when a chubby boy, about five years old, in tiny denim jeans, sneakers, a red-checked flannel shirt, an oversized cowboy hat, with two toy pistols holstered in his leather belt, which had a large metal buckle, barged into the room. His eyes had the epicanthic fold that gave the indigenous people of the Mizo Hills their distinctive almond-shaped eyes. Sammy immediately saw the striking resemblance he bore to Sena when he was a boy.

The cowboy bounced up to Sammy and hoisted himself up on the wooden bench beside him. 'Who are you?' he asked nonchalantly.

'I'm Sammy.' He smiled down at the boy.

'Do you know any cowboys?'

'No. I don't believe I do,' Sammy replied earnestly.

Then a nurse entered the waiting room. 'Come with me,' she said to Sammy, even as she reached down and ruffled the cowboy's head affectionately.

Sammy followed the nurse out of the waiting room and down a dimly lit corridor. The boy trailed them, his guns drawn, ready to ward off an attack from make-believe baddies out to get him. At the end of the corridor, the nurse held the door to a private room open for Sammy, and he stepped inside. The nurse grabbed the cowboy as he tried to follow Sammy into the room and, hoisting him up into the air, she said: 'You stay here with me, Mr Cowboy. You're under arrest. And I've got some chocolates for you!'

The room was well lit, small, but spotlessly clean, with a large wooden window, besides which was a metal bed. A white cotton bedspread covered the cotton-filled mattress and a thin pillow rested atop. An ancient ceiling fan, freshly painted white, turned slowly, creaking with every laboured revolution it made. In one corner of the room was a small couch, upholstered in a cheerful pink fabric. Standing beside the bed, in a white hospital gown, her short hair neatly combed back and held in place with a pink hairband, like she'd never gone away, like she and Sammy had never been apart, not for a single minute, of twenty-seven long years, was Martha.

'Sammy!' Martha exclaimed.

Sammy, a terrible knot in his stomach, his breathing ragged, stood in the doorway, frozen, as Martha walked quickly across the room towards him, with no hesitation or caution in her step. When she got to Sammy, she threw her arms around him embracing him tightly, sinking her head into his chest, weeping bitter tears.

Sammy held her close, kissing the top of her head again and again. He whispered: 'I missed you, Martha, I missed you very much.'

'I missed you too,' she said. Then, holding his face gently in her hands and looking deep into his troubled soul, she asked: 'How are you, Sammy?'

Sammy laughed at the innocence of Martha's question, as he pulled her close again, letting her scent wash over him.

When they'd pulled away from each other, Martha held Sammy's hand and she led him to the couch. When they'd settled down on it, Sammy took a closer look at Martha. She looked frail but the happiness on her face wasn't fake. 'After I left the army, I came looking for you, Martha. I searched everywhere,' Sammy said, softly. 'I even tracked down your uncle, your father's brother, the mechanic. He told me that you and Christine had died, the night the soldiers burnt Asakhua to the ground. I didn't believe it at first. So, I went to Asakhua to look for you. But there was nothing there. It's all gone, Martha. There's no Asakhua. It's like it never existed."

'I know,' Martha said, her face reflecting the anguish in her heart. 'Pa hid Christine and me in the church when the soldiers came. Then he went out to try and stop them, but they murdered him,' she said, her voice breaking. 'We managed to escape from the church through the service entrance at the back, before they burnt it down. The Witch took Christine and me in, and kept us hidden for weeks, before the MNF found us and got us to the safety of a camp in Chittagong and later the Arakans. That's where we've been for the past twenty years. Living in exile. Till the peace accord made it safe for us to return home.'

Sammy wanted to tell Martha all that had happened to him since they'd last met, on his seventeenth birthday, but he knew there'd be time for that later. So, he said nothing. The room was silent, but for the sound of the old creaking fan, as its blades turned on their fixed path, blowing gusts of air over them.

Bored with the two adults, who, deep in conversation had failed to spot him entering the room and had ignored him completely, the cowboy butted in impatiently. 'Where's Nu?' he asked.

'She'll be here soon, Simon,' Martha said, trying to grab the boy, who twisted out of her reach and fled the room.

Sammy looked bewildered. 'He's not your son?' he asked Martha, hesitantly.

'He's Christine and Rempuia's son, my nephew, you idiot!' Martha chortled. 'Can you imagine Rempuia and me, married? It would be a complete disaster!'

'You're not married?'

'I was. It didn't work out,' Martha said wistfully, looking away.

As they sat there on the couch, nothing more said, time at a standstill, Sammy prayed. He prayed for the first time since that terrible evening in Sabha, when he'd begged his God for Sena's life and had been left bitterly disappointed. Now he prayed silently, in thanksgiving, with love and gratitude in his heart:

For keeping Martha safe.
For bringing her back to him.
For giving their love another chance.

* * *

Martha died on a Sunday, in early December. The cancer had spread too extensively by the time she'd been admitted to the hospital in Aizawl for the doctors to be able to do anything meaningful to save her. Sammy was there with her, by her side, holding her hand, when the end came.

At the funeral service, the pastor read an old Celtic prayer that Martha had loved:

May the road rise to meet you.
May the wind be always at your back.
May the sunshine warm upon your face.
May the rains fall upon your fields.
And until we meet again,
May God hold you in the hollow of His hand.

Martha was buried in the cemetery, in the compound of the burnt-down church, in Asakhua, at dusk, next to Eoma and Sena. It was what she had wanted. On her finger, she wore the gold wedding ring that Sammy had slipped on while they lay beside each other, on the hospital bed, a few nights before she passed, when Sammy had told her he would love her forever and that he'd never leave her. She'd smiled then, squeezing his arm gently, tears welling up in her eyes, too weak to tell him how much she loved him. In those last days, they'd made their peace with their destiny, grateful for the little time they'd been given together.

Sammy, who'd been stoic through the funeral ceremony, only broke when Martha's coffin was being lowered into the ground and the cawing cacophony of the crows roosting for the night, in the trees around the cemetery, reached a crescendo. Then, overwhelmed by a terrible feeling of dread and an unfathomable emptiness that crushed him and brought him to his knees sobbing uncontrollably, he began to wail. A shrill, high-pitched, anguished wail that rose from the ruins of Asakhua, rising above the giant bamboo stalks and soaring up into the heavens above.

ACKNOWLEDGEMENTS

My interest in the stories of the people of the Northeast of India developed over numerous visits and journeys, made with my mother, Margaret Alva, who was the Congress Party's go-to person for the region in the 70s and 80s. It's from her that I received my first 'master classes' in the history and politics of the Northeast. It's only fitting then, that she was the first person I shared an early draft of this novel with. Her enthusiastic support gave me the confidence to keep labouring on!

Some of my earliest memories, growing up in New Delhi, are of politicians and leaders from all over the Northeast visiting our home for a meal, a drink or just to say 'hello' to my parents, who would always welcome them warmly. Amongst them were former guerrillas who had fascinating stories to tell of their days 'underground'. I was struck by their *joie de vivre*, their infectious energy and their wonderful sense of humour. But even as a young boy, I could see that there was a deep sense of sorrow for those they had lost and anger at the injustices and humiliation they had been subjected to. These memories, emotions and experiences have helped shape the characters in this novel.

I'm grateful to my father, Niranjan Alva, who had an insatiable appetite for books. It was from him that I developed not only an enduring interest in reading and writing but also the desire to always tread off-the-beaten-path. One of his unfulfilled dreams was to have authored a book. I think he would have enjoyed reading this one.

I'm grateful to Pria, my friend and fellow adventurer, my harshest critic, my most loyal fan and the love of my life, whose rock-solid support, belief and encouragement gave me the courage not only to write but also to stay the course. And my children, Rian and Laila, who are always supportive of every new 'crazy' idea their father is working on!

I'm grateful to Shashi Tharoor and Sanjoy Roy for their invaluable feedback, support and encouragement.

I'm grateful to Rahul Gandhi for the opportunity and space he gave me to sharpen my writing skills, over the five years I worked with him, developing his social media presence across platforms and expanding his mass media reach. It rekindled my love for writing and sent me down a path that led to this novel.

I'm grateful to Amish Raj Mulmi, Julius Packiam, Nivedith Alva, Tavish Pinto, Premila Nazareth Satyanand, Sugandha Garg and Manmat Singh Deo, for labouring through the early drafts of this novel and for their feedback.

And also to Susan Ralte and Apuii Tochhawng for their inputs on the Mizo language terms used in this novel.

I'm grateful to my agent, Kanishka Gupta, whose belief in this book and his unabashed pursuit of publishers (to get the manuscript into their hands), resulted in numerous offers, helping validate the potential this novel has.

I'd like to thank the wonderful team at HarperCollins, especially my editor Rashmi Menon, for her critical feedback and support; Jyotsna Raman, for her copy suggestions and fixes; and Poulomi Chatterjee, who has been an enormous source of strength and encouragement.

I pay homage to the hundreds of soldiers, from the Indian Army, the Assam Rifles and other paramilitary forces, and the local police, who were martyred during the two-decade-long insurgency in the Mizo Hills, fighting to protect the territorial integrity of India.

I wish to acknowledge and honour the hundreds of Mizo men, women and children who perished when the *Mautam* struck the Mizo Hills in 1959-60 and in the violent insurgency that followed.

I acknowledge the struggles and sacrifices of over 70,000 innocent Mizos, citizens of India, who were herded into camps at gunpoint, when the villages they lived in were forcibly 'regrouped' in the early years of the insurgency by the Indian Government, with no consideration for their liberty or human rights.

I pay homage to the civilian victims of the bombing of Aizawl by the Indian Air Force, an unfortunate, dark chapter in the history of India, that we cannot and must not forget.

I recognize and acknowledge the courage of thousands of Mizo youth, men and women, who became guerrillas and put their lives on the line for a cause they believed in. The Mizoram of today is built on their sacrifices.

And finally, I would like to acknowledge and celebrate the tenacity, courage and fortitude of the great Mizo people, who bounced back from two decades of violence and devastation, to build a modern Mizoram, that is today one of India's most developed and progressive states, an oasis of peace and prosperity that makes every Indian proud.

ABOUT THE AUTHOR

Nikhil J. Alva is an award-winning producer, director and writer. His work has been screened on major broadcast networks and platforms all over the world.

Nikhil earned a BA (Hons) in Mathematics from St. Stephen's College and later an MBA from the London Business School. He is a serial entrepreneur, a climate -change warrior, a communications and social media maven, a national shooting champion, a pianist and an avid golfer. He's a rebel without a pause, a chronic supporter of underdog causes, and loves the challenge of trudging off the beaten path.

This is his first novel.

HarperCollins *Publishers* India

At HarperCollins India, we believe in telling the best stories and finding the widest readership for our books in every format possible. We started publishing in 1992; a great deal has changed since then, but what has remained constant is the passion with which our authors write their books, the love with which readers receive them, and the sheer joy and excitement that we as publishers feel in being a part of the publishing process.

Over the years, we've had the pleasure of publishing some of the finest writing from the subcontinent and around the world, including several award-winning titles and some of the biggest bestsellers in India's publishing history. But nothing has meant more to us than the fact that millions of people have read the books we published, and that somewhere, a book of ours might have made a difference.

As we look to the future, we go back to that one word—a word which has been a driving force for us all these years.

Read.

Harper Collins

HARPER PERENNIAL

HARPER BUSINESS

HARPER BLACK

हार्पर हिन्दी

HarperCollins *Children's Books*

HARPER DESIGN

HARPER VANTAGE

Harper Sport